Praise for Leonard Tourney's Matthew and Joan Stock mysteries

"Vividly evocative of the era and marvelously readable."
—*People*

"Mr. Tourney seems to have a good understanding of his scenery, and his dialogue has a nice unmannered period feel. He gives us just enough of sixteenth-century culture to establish the appropriate tone."
—*The New Yorker*

"Tourney writes so well that we are drawn into another world."
—*The Pittsburgh Press*

"A student of the time, Tourney paints a vivid picture of Elizabethan England, one full of the detail of daily life and custom"
—*The Anniston Star*

Also by Leonard Tourney
Published by Ballantine Books:

THE PLAYERS' BOY IS DEAD
LOW TREASON
FAMILIAR SPIRITS
THE BARTHOLOMEW FAIR MURDERS
OLD SAXON BLOOD
KNAVES TEMPLAR

WITNESS
OF
BONES

Leonard Tourney

BALLANTINE BOOKS • NEW YORK

Library of Congress Catalog Card Number: 92-24914

ISBN 0-345-38319-2

This edition published by arrangement with St. Martin's Press, Inc.

Manufactured in the United States of America

First Ballantine Books Edition: September 1993

For Jolene
Fairest of cousins, best of friends

Some graves will be opened before they
be quite closed.

Sir Thomas Browne,
Hydriotaphia

1

*I*T was a city churchyard, draped in yews and fat with the dead. The day's rain still clung to the monuments, and in the darkness of the March night such little faith as the men had quivered before the cold stones.

One of the men was a sailor without a berth. He had a blind eye, patched; the other eye glared with pupil so enlarged that hardly any white showed. The sailor's name was Simkins. He had agreed to this unsavory task because he was desperate. It was either this or starve—a difficult choice for any man to make. But he was no shirker. One had to give him that. He shoveled the skull up from the moist, hummocky earth and flung it against a neighboring gravestone with no more pity nor horror than if it was a stone or an old boot. The skull made a hollow crack when it struck and buried itself in the ivy beneath which in the darkness neither Simkins nor his companion, Motherwell, could see it.

Leaning upon his pickax, Motherwell, a barrel-chested man of fifty or more with a face ruined by smallpox and a habitual grimmace, snorted with amusement. "I warrant that'll knock some sense into his coxcomb, whoever he was. Dig to the left. He whom we seek is hardly a year planted. The wood will not yet be rotted."

Motherwell looked at the sailor, a lean-bodied man with sharp features. Simkins said nothing in response. He kept digging, informed earlier that the coffin would be found a good three to four feet down in a section of the churchyard that was so thick with the dead of the last plague that the earth could hardly be penetrated but it divided asunder some wretch's bones.

Motherwell wondered what sort of man it was who would take a handful of silver to dig up a body by moonlight and not ask wherefore it was done nor what poor soul was to have his mortal remains so molested. He had found Simkins loitering near the church, had determined he was a man of the sea, in London today, next week in hell—so far, so good. No danger from him hanging around to speak too loosely of how he made easy money for an hour's work while the rest of London slept.

Yet Simkins had seemed to know the work was not mere grave robbing or body snatching. He had demanded no share in the spoils. He had only asked at what peal of St. Crispin's bells was he wanted and how soon they were to finish and if he was to be paid upon finishing or later. He said he had been a ship's officer. He wanted a ship more than anything in the world. As it happened, Motherwell knew someone who knew someone who was a shipmaster. That had been part of the bargain. The silver and the name of someone who'd get him back to sea again.

"When the work's done you shall have your money as promised," Motherwell said. "And the name of one to help you to a berth."

Simkins complained he had nothing wherewith to dig.

"I'll provide, never fear," said Motherwell. "Bring but a sober mind and a willing back and keep the project to yourself."

Now the two men took turns digging. One dug and the other watched, squatting. A quarter moon was the only light. Motherwell stared into the darkness bravely. He wasn't afraid of the night or of the dead. Of those who rested in the churchyard, he had buried many—and dug them up again after a decent interval to place their bones in the charnel house. Lay the stiffs to bed and yank 'em forth again, such was his creed. Make room for new occupants. There was just so much space in God's acre. Headstones could curse all they might those who disturbed their bones, but one had to be practical. There was just so much land, and a great many of the dead. More of them were being born every day. Motherwell laughed to himself at the very idea, persuaded it was his own.

His bladder full to bursting, Motherwell went off to make water against a tree, came back, squatted some more and watched, envious of his companion's unflagging physical strength.

After a few minutes, Simkin's shovel scraped against wood.

"That will be it," Motherwell said. "Careful now, there's to be no damage to the coffin. Here, man, get yourself down into the hole and uncover the earth away by hand."

Motherwell noticed the man seemed hesitant. He gave the order again.

"You said I was but to dig," said Simkins.

"So I did. But you may dig with your hands as well as with a shovel."

Simkins grunted. It was so dark Motherwell could barely make out his companion's face, but he remembered it from daylight—a thin, desperate countenance and the glaring eye of an unemployed man. No one, certainly, that Motherwell would want as an enemy, but Simkins's hesitancy annoyed him. What, did this one-eyed son of the sea think he was too good to touch a dead man?

After a few minutes in the grave, Simkins said, "It's cleared of earth. What'll you have now?"

"Why, we shall wait. Anon comes a certain gentleman to give us our final instructions and our due."

Motherwell sat down beside the open grave and leaned his back against the tombstone the skull had struck. In the cold and dark he wished he had a bowl of hot caudle or sweet wine to comfort his innards, or perhaps juicy Liz, the hot whore of Bankside, to wrap around him in a warm blanket of female flesh. He heard Paul's authoritative chime. One o'clock. He cursed Stearforth for being late. Did the young puke think the sexton of St. Crispin's had all the night to loll about the churchyard?

Motherwell heard footsteps and looked up to see a man's form emerge from the trees.

"Master Stearforth?" Motherwell said in a hushed voice.

"Sexton?"

"Good morrow to your worship."

The man Motherwell had called Stearforth came over and looked down into the grave. He was a solidly built, youngish man, with a heavy brow, prominent nose, full lips, and neatly trimmed beard. "I came near to breaking my neck back there stumbling over a vine. Have you come to the coffin?"

"We have."

"You're sure it's the right one?"

"Did I not watch while the man was buried and see to the placement of the stone? We shall have a look at his face presently."

" 'Twill do no good, if you're mistaken. I never saw the man, myself."

"I'faith, I did and will certify him to be even who he should be."

"If you can see in the dark."

"Trust me, sir. My eyes are not so old they cannot make out a proper face," Motherwell said although privately he knew his eyes were not what they used to be when like a hawk he could spot his quarry, some buxomy tart, at a hundred paces.

Motherwell scrambled into the grave and with the shovel's blade as a pry, he began to unfasten the coffin lid. The wooden pegs gave readily and when the lid was removed he stuck his face down into the coffin to take a good look at the corpse before the stench of decay overpowered him.

"Blessed Jesu, his corpse is as rotten as his life was saintly," Stearforth said above him.

Motherwell looked up to see the young man pull a handkerchief from his sleeve and cover his nose and mouth. The sailor, also in the grave, seemed indifferent to the smell. Perhaps, Motherwell thought, sailors could not afford delicate noses, with the bilges of ships no better than floating privies.

"I warrant the man was not so saintly but a little sin could make his corpse noisome," Motherwell said. "All saints are but hypocrites, whited sepulchers, if you ask me." Motherwell stared at the corpse. All was shrouded in a winding sheet save for the white face.

"Have no fear, sir," Motherwell said to Stearforth. "*Ecce Homo*, as the priests say. Or what he was when quick."

"You have no fear of this place, this deed then?" Stearforth asked.

The sexton laughed and stood up in the grave so that ground level was at his belly. "I care not for life nor death nor God or whatever else men imagine in their hearts to be but never was nor will."

"That's a strange philosophy for a sexton," Stearforth said.

"Marry, sir, it's the only philosophy for a sexton, for what is our work but to ring bells and dig graves? I have buried my shovel's blade often enough in moldering corpses to believe in naught but the worm, sir. I have never once come upon a soul, only the worm that feeds upon the body. And so I am become a devout believer in the worm and would fain worship at his altar if one had the courage to erect a church to his honor."

"Is the good Master Graham aware of his sexton's blasphemies?" Stearforth asked.

Motherwell laughed again, although it was a laugh without merriment in it—a hard, cynical laugh. "Master Graham is a devilish hypocrite. I care not a groat what he thinks or why. A great fool he is, hardly aware of himself, much less does he care that I ring the bells and bend my back planting the dead, as this fellow here."

"Which fellow we must now transplant," Stearforth said. "The question is where. The river, perhaps."

"A good league," said Motherwell, shaking his head. "Besides, the body may be found unless we put lead in his pockets. Even then the tide—"

"Right, of course, sexton."

"Now, sir, I have a thought."

"Yes."

"Where it will never be found—and if found taken no notice of."

Motherwell told Stearforth his plan. Stearforth agreed it was a good one.

"First, we must look to the coffin," Motherwell said.

"How so?"

Motherwell climbed out of the grave. He picked up the lid where it lay by the grave and propped it against a headstone. He gave it a few swift kicks.

"Good," said Stearforth when the lid was smashed. "It will look as though our friend below escaped by his own strength. Now to the body."

Stearforth nodded to Simkins who all this while had stood watching the two other men. "Here, fellow, lend the good sexton a hand with the corpse. He'll tell you what to do with it."

Simkins wanted to know about his money, and about the ship he had been promised.

"Never fear, fellow," Stearforth said with easy assurance. "Return here when the body is disposed of and for your labors and your silence you shall have your deserts."

An hour later, the moon having drifted behind clouds and the churchyard an even murkier confusion of dripping shadows, Motherwell and the sailor came back and found Stearforth awaiting them.

"It is done?"

"It is, sir," Motherwell said.

Stearforth handed the sexton of St. Crispin's a small leather purse. "Let neither of you speak of this—or even think of it," he said.

"Speak of what, sir?" asked Motherwell, grinning. "If I am asked, I slept all the night and can find ten men and not a few women who will swear it is so. As for this fellow, he'll be gone to sea, have his mind on wind and sail, isn't that right?"

Simkins said it was so and looked eagerly at the purse in Motherwell's hand. Noticing the man's expression, Motherwell opened the purse and took out his money. "Here," he said.

The sailor took the money. Stearforth told him where to come the next day about the ship. "Yes," he said. "I'm good friends with a shipmaster. He's looking for an experienced man."

"You have done well, sexton," Stearforth said after Simkins was gone. "I may have more business to send your way."

"Grave-digging by moonlight?"

"Perhaps something along different lines."

"I aim to please in everything, sir. If your money is good, then my work will be likewise, for he who is paid well for his labor has no cause to regret it after, save of course it is a hanging offense. I trust what I have helped you to this night will not come to that?"

"Perish the thought," said Stearforth, suddenly light-hearted. "You shall see presently what it shall come to and, given your philosophy, you will no doubt take as much delight in the jest as I."

"Oh, I have ever loved a good jest, Master Stearforth. I wish you a very good night, or what's left of it," Motherwell said.

"The same to you, honest sexton," said Stearforth.

2

MATTHEW STOCK paused to catch his breath at the top of the hill and survey the farmstead hunkered down in the bottom as though it were ashamed of its poverty. A wisp of smoke came up from a hole in the thatch. In the uncertain light of dawn, Matthew could make out the farmer moving around in the muddy enclosure next to a small shed. Matthew smelled pig dung and chicken dung and the more wholesome scent of sodden earth and thatch.

He walked down into the bottom and was almost to the farmer's house before he hailed its owner. The farmer turned quickly and looked in Matthew's direction.

"Fair day, Goodman Brewster."

"Less fair than yesterday," replied the farmer, scowling as though Matthew were somehow responsible for the weather, which had been wretched for a week, with no sun and almost constant rain.

Giles Brewster was a tall, rawboned man with shaggy dark hair and a jaw bestubbled with a growth of beard. The sleeves of his loose-fitting shirt were rolled up to reveal sinewy forearms. He stared at Matthew suspiciously, obviously wondering what the town constable wanted, torn between curiosity and annoyance at having his work interrupted. Matthew knew Brewster well. There was a wife too, somewhere, a pitiful slight creature half her husband's height and so fearful of him that she would rarely speak in his presence. There were Brewster children, grown, however, moved off someplace, embittered at the father. Matthew could understand why.

"What trouble brings you, Matthew?"

Matthew walked to the edge of the pen but Brewster didn't move. He stood fixed and defensive, as though he already had an inkling of what the trouble was. A resonant snort came from within the shed and its occupant appeared, waddling out, snout in the air, a huge animal that took up a position behind his owner like an obedient dog.

"It's about your boar," Matthew said. "There's been a complaint."

Brewster said nothing.

"The parson says the boar has been seen three times in the churchyard. He did damage to some of the monuments. He rooted up one of the graves."

Brewster wanted to know whose grave it was, as though that made some difference in the gravity of the offense.

"Cyrus Terrill's, John Terrill's grandfather who died upon Michaelmas. The body was half eaten. Found by some children. John is vexed. The parents of the children also. It's a great disgrace."

"Is it?" said Brewster, suddenly calm. "Well, Master Stock, I would fain know who has seen my boar and how it can be claimed to be mine rather than some other's."

Matthew recited the names of witnesses. There had been other complaints too. The boar had made himself free of the town's midden heap. Had strewn garbage hither and yon. Had frightened this widow and that goodwife and not a few stout men out of their wits. Matthew looked at the boar. How much must an animal of that size weigh?

Brewster glanced down beside him at the boar, as though inquiring as to whether any of these testimonies were true. Then he looked up at Matthew again. "It must have been some other beast. It was not mine."

"The witnesses swore it was. The boar was huge, mottled like unto yours."

Brewster stood his ground. "It wasn't mine."

"But how can you be so sure?"

"The pen is fenced, as you can plainly see, Constable."

"The pen is fenced now," Matthew said. "But I see that you have made fresh repairs. See, where the paling is new."

"I swear it was no creature of mine," Brewster said more vehemently. "And he who says otherwise is a liar. I will call him so to his very face."

Matthew took a deep breath and looked up at the sky. It was gray, but a few birds flew aloft. Brewster had been right about the weather. It was not a fine day and yet too fine for rancor over an undisciplined animal. With a man like Brewster, conflict was difficult to avoid. The issue was a sensitive one. The boar was obviously dearer to Brewster than was his wife and with such intimacy Matthew was loath to meddle, despite his lawful authority to do so. He imagined the farmer laying hands on him in anger. If it came to that it would be an uneven match. Brewster was much taller than Matthew and muscled where Matthew was soft. Matthew might have called out the watch, brought a half dozen men to support his cause, but that would only have made confrontation more certain.

"Well," Matthew said slowly. "In a way I'm sorry to hear you say what you do."

"How's that, Constable?"

"It puts my labors to naught."

Brewster's hard face showed no sign of regret. "Your coming all this way from town, you mean?"

"No, the agreement I had with John Terrill."

There was another pause during which Brewster glanced down at the animal again. He looked up and said: "You made an agreement? Regarding my boar—I mean the boar in question."

Matthew nodded.

"And what would that agreement have been? I ask, you

understand, only out of curiosity as to how matters such as these might be settled—"

"Amicably?"

"Yes."

"Why, I told him that if you—or whoever owned the beast—would see fit to pay for the reburial—"

"Of John Terrill's grandfather?"

"The same."

"Then—?"

"And promise to keep his boar penned that he would cause no complaint, press no suit. It's a fair compromise, if you ask me, considering the offense to the man's dignity and the fact that the offender has more than once been at mischief in the town and caused other damage there. I suppose otherwise Terrill will sue—and he will surely prevail, so grievous a complaint he has, and win more than the cost of the reburial."

Brewster considered this, stroking his beard. Above, more birds had gathered; Brewster looked up at them for a moment, then back at Matthew.

"How much would it cost to rebury the old man?"

"Oh, a shilling or two. The sexton works for next to nothing."

Brewster looked prepared to haggle; then sighed heavily. It was a sigh of resignation. Matthew knew he had won.

"You have Terrill's word he won't sue?" Brewster repeated.

"By a dozen oaths, each more binding than the one before."

"Oaths are cheap," growled Brewster. "A man may buy them by the dozen."

"Terrill's as straight as a stick. His word's his bond."

"I cannot deny that," Brewster said.

"Well, then?"

"In such a case, it might be easier for me to help Terrill to the sum required. Out of friendship rather than constraint, you understand."

"I understand perfectly," Matthew said, suppressing a grin.

"Not that I'm admitting it was my beast who rooted graves, Constable. But to be at peace with my neighbors and stand free of the law."

"A wise decision, Giles," Matthew said.

Matthew waited in the yard while Brewster went into the farmhouse to fetch the money, the boar at his heels until he came to the door and Brewster's sharp command that he stay brought the animal to a halt. Matthew was breathing easier now, grateful that he could enjoy the day without worrying that his constableship might lead to a cracked skull. He was a short, plump man of about forty, dark and plain faced and with a mild disposition that seemed, at times, ill suited to his office. Yet he had demonstrated more than once in his tenure a compensating intelligence, and his resolute honesty and dogged pursuit of truth were proverbial in the town.

Brewster returned in no time and handed Matthew three shillings. Matthew said that the sum would suffice and that he would see it got to Terrill.

"Will you eat with us, Constable?" asked Brewster, as stony faced as ever.

Remembering that Brewster's wife was a tolerable cook, Matthew accepted the invitation. He had eaten before leaving home, but the walk from town had sapped his strength. He was hungry again. Besides, he was in a better mood now. It had been a good morning's work he had done, not the trouble he had expected.

In his shop on High Street—for Matthew was clothier before he was constable and presently was both—he found his assistant Peter Bench cutting a bolt of cloth for John Terrill's wife. Which gave Matthew the opportunity of assuring that good woman that in the matter of Brewster's boar justice had been done.

"Justice indeed," returned the wife, "when a dead body is regarded so lightly."

Yet for her scowling, Matthew noticed she took the shillings.

Matthew asked Peter where his own wife could be found. Peter pointed the way to the adjoining kitchen. Like most dwellings on High Street, Matthew's house was shop on the lower floor and living quarters on the upper, a very sensible arrangement to his way of thinking.

Joan Stock was the same age as her husband. She had a winsome, oval-shaped face, dark eyes and complexion, firm mouth and chin. A woman to be reckoned with, her neighbors said, who generally liked her and often sought her counsel. In the kitchen Matthew found her engaged in conversation with a man in clerical garb who spoke in the clipped speech of a Londoner, not the slower drawl of Essex. The stranger rose from where he was sitting and gave Matthew a polite nod when introduced.

"Matthew, this is Master Stephen Graham of St. Crispin's Church, Eastcheap. Master Graham, this is my husband, Matthew Stock."

The cleric extended his hand and smiled encouragingly. Matthew asked him if he had come all the way to Chelmsford to buy cloth.

"More solemn business, I am afraid, Master Stock. It is not your cloth I seek, but your skill."

"Master Graham tells a strange story," Joan said, sitting at the long trencher table which after the open hearth was the most conspicuous feature of the room. "Perhaps, sir," she continued, addressing Graham, "you could tell my husband your tale from the beginning."

Matthew sat down at the table. Graham leaned forward, his heavy brow accentuating his rather intent eyes.

"Perhaps you have heard of Christopher Poole?"

"A Jesuit priest," Matthew answered. "Taken in London last year and charged with treason."

"This is the same," Graham said. He had seemed somewhat stiff before, but now appeared relaxed and friendly. He smiled often at Joan and as often at Matthew. "He fasted until he died. Refused to eat the jailer's bread. Desired to be a martyr to his faith—and had his wish. But not before receiving a vision as he called it that within twelve months of his burial he would see God in the flesh."

"Resurrect?" said Matthew.

Graham nodded, frowning. "Last week the event occurred."

Matthew was astonished; before he could speak, Graham went on. "I should say that the prophesied event was made to *appear* to have occurred. Someone entered the churchyard, dug up the grave, and made off with the body. By the next day, half of London had heard the rumor that the priest's prophesy had been fulfilled. The more ignorant sort claimed to have seen him, eating and drinking, walking about the streets, still in his graveclothes, but his complexion as pink as a child's."

"A seeming miracle," Matthew said.

"*Seeming* is the most proper word for it, Master Stock. But of course the whole incident is a palpable fraud, devised doubtless by Papists wishing to propagate the faith and undermine the kingdom."

"You say, Master Graham, that many have taken Poole's resurrection as gospel truth?" Joan asked.

"Last Sunday, there was a greater congregation than St. Crispin's has seen in two hundred years since it was built. And such a show of crossings and prayer beads and other Papist paraphernalia that you would have thought Queen Mary lived again to thrust Papist dogma down our throats."

Master Graham spoke with great conviction. He frowned, suggesting that Papistry was the worst thing of all, worse than thieves and robbers and murderers.

"I think I perceive your dilemma, sir," Matthew said. "A man of the church can hardly wish for a small congregation, and yet—"

"Quite so, Master Stock."

"But I don't understand what I can do—"

"You can come to London. Come to London and discover who stole Poole's body. Confirm their purpose." Graham leaned forward intently. His heavy brows hooded his eyes so they seemed to have no color. "I trust you will find the culprit was some Papist fanatic, eager to advance his lewd faith and sow seeds of discord in our otherwise happy commonwealth."

Matthew exchanged looks with Joan, who had been following Graham's words with as much interest as Matthew. He could read her mind, couldn't he? Hadn't twenty years of marriage made it possible? Another trip to London? When they had only returned at Christmas?

"I am afraid I cannot at this time," Matthew said. "My shop, my duties as constable here—and my family. Why, our grandson is a virtual stranger, so rarely are we home."

As Joan showed by her expression her agreement with this response, the cleric looked deeply grieved. "Oh, Sir Robert will be most disappointed then."

"Sir Robert?" Matthew asked, looking up quickly at the name of the man who had in times past been both Matthew's good friend and his patron.

Graham smiled broadly and continued. "It's part of the story I did not tell you. Christopher Poole was the cousin of Lady Elyot, who is a great friend of Sir Robert's. It was through her influence that Poole was buried in St. Crispin's churchyard and the theft of the body has caused suspicion to fall upon her, although she claims to have no Papist sympathies. It's for this reason that Sir Robert is especially eager to have your assistance. It was he who commended you. He said that if any man in England could ferret out the truth, that man was Matthew Stock of Chelmsford."

Graham flashed another ingratiating smile; he had good teeth and seemed aware of it.

Matthew said, "Would you excuse my wife and me for a moment, sir, while we converse on this matter?"

"Most certainly," said Graham.

Wife followed husband into the passage that separated kitchen from shop.

"Speak your mind, Joan," Matthew said.

"Sir Robert's commendation is weighty. What do you think, husband?"

15

"I have no desire to go to London."

"Nor I."

"No interest in Papist plots."

"Nor I."

"We are of one mind then," he said.

"And yet Sir Robert's commendation—"

"Ought to be considered."

"Can we confirm what this parson says?" she asked.

"He's a man of God. Do you think he's lying?" He was astonished that she could suspect such a thing.

"His godliness rings false," she said, folding her plump brown arms across her chest in that way she had when she was resolved not to be persuaded to the contrary. "I don't know why. There's too much honey on his tongue. You should have heard his flattery before you came in. Full of compliments he was for my kitchen, for this well-worn gown, for my dark eyes. I tell you he smells more of the court than the cloister."

"Indeed," said Matthew, who had found the man's appearance and conduct unexceptional and did not know how much to credit Joan's suspicions.

"Can we confirm his story?"

"We could send a message to Sir Robert," Matthew suggested. "But would we have time to send and receive? The case stands at a difficult point. I am fixed upon a dilemma's horns. If Graham speaks truly, my loyalty to Sir Robert bids me go. If there's some deceit in the tale, should I not search it out? How can I say nay in either case?"

"Well, do as you see fit, husband," Joan said after a short pause. "Let your conscience guide. I'll be your companion to London as always. Who knows but that the matter will be settled in a few days, the mischief revealed, and Poole's body where it belongs again."

Since they were agreed, then, they returned to the kitchen where they found the rector of St. Crispin's standing with his face to the window that looked out on High Street. As the Stocks entered he turned slowly and the ingratiating smile spread slowly across his face as though he already knew what Matthew's answer should be.

"What, to London again? Why it's not been three months since your last visit."

Matthew gave no reasons to his assistant. Nor did Peter, accustomed to the Stocks' coming and going in service greater than their own business, ask for any. Peter went to make ready Matthew's gear for the journey.

"A strange thing has happened," Joan said as Matthew sat down to supper. Matthew looked up from his plate.

"What strange thing?"

"My good knife. The one with the carved haft and the initial *S* engraved theron. I was using it just this afternoon. I can't find it now, although I've searched the whole kitchen twice over."

Matthew resumed eating. "Ask Betty if she has seen it," he suggested between mouthfuls.

"She says she has not."

"Oh, I think it will turn up. Things lost always do. Let's not make more mysteries than we already have," Matthew said in his commonsensical way.

3

BACK in London, Humphrey Stearforth felt happier than
he had felt in months. Like hungry trout, the clothier and
his wife had opened their mouths wide and swallowed the
story whole. It all went to show how gullible country folk
were. You could tell them any tale and they'd believe it.
Any tale at all.

He stopped at an inn in Milk Street to quench his thirst
and toast his own ingenuity, having taken care first to
change into his own clothes. That part of the impersonation
had not been so agreeable to him, the garb being drab and
conferring no credit upon what he considered a well-turned
thigh and broad, manly breast. It had given him an uneasy
feeling, truth be told, but it was over now. He had imitated
Stephen Graham to the last detail and Stearforth's only regret was that he had lacked an appreciative audience for his
performance.

He spent a good hour in the inn until heady with wine he
mounted his horse to go to the house of him whose generosity now paid for Stearforth's good satin suit and gave
promise of advancement according to his deserts.

The house itself was a goodly one, maintained by the
personage in question as a part of his family inheritance. It

was well furnished with servants, most of whom had now become accustomed to Stearforth's comings and goings and while unsure of his rank in the hierarchy of their master's affairs, they were nonetheless confident that he had one and they treated him with a satisfactory deference that Stearforth trusted in the fullness of time would swell to reverence.

But when he arrived outside the great man's study, he was vexed to find that he had to wait his turn. Several gentlemen he did not recognize preceded him—each with some compelling suit, Stearforth supposed by their anxious faces. Stearforth nodded to each and sat down on a stool, his report hanging heavy on his mind.

It was another hour before he was ushered in. Invited to sit, Stearforth poured his story forth to the gentleman before him without waiting for a command to do so.

"You're certain then that Stock will come to London?"

"He said as much, Your Grace. If he keeps his word, he should be at St. Crispin's by late today, or by tomorrow at the latest."

"Well and good, Stearforth. I presume you accomplished this end by invoking the mighty name of the queen's little pigmy?"

Stearforth responded to this diminishing characterization of Robert Cecil with a sneer. "Indeed, Your Grace. At first Stock begged leave to stay at home. He said he had been back in Chelmsford only three months since his last sojourn in the city. He didn't say what business detained him then."

"Nor would he," said Stearforth's employer. The large man clothed in a velvet dressing gown with a great jewel upon his finger and lace at his wrists stared thoughtfully at the bookcase beyond him as though he were searching for some title. Stearforth looked on in silence, waiting for his employer's next question or command. He was full of envy of the man before him. Subtly arrogant, swollen with pride and rich food, soft spoken because those around would take trouble to strain to hear—this was indeed how Stearforth himself aspired to live, what he aspired to be.

Surrounded by obsequious servants tiptoeing through the great house like ghosts, a handsomely furnished study beseiged by suitors, not common folk but people of name and means, begging favors, offering bribes, extending invitations and proposing alliances. Yes, this was the world of which Humphrey Stearforth was an eager apprentice, and as he regarded the great man before him, his envy surrendered to a deeply felt gratitude. For it was this person who would pull him up from poverty and scorn. It had happened to other men of meaner birth than his own. Service was infinite in its possibilities; one could lick boots—or advise a prince. Even Cecil, arguably the most powerful man in the realm despite his diminutive stature, alluded to himself as Her Majesty's obedient servant.

"I thought Cecil's name would do the trick," said the employer after a few moments. "Now we are ready for the next step."

Stearforth leaned forward expectantly.

"Go to the church and await the Stocks' arrival. It is likely they will lie at the Blue Boar, for the Chelmsford merchants are wont to stay there while in London."

"And what should I do, sir, when he appears?"

"That depends how eager you are to advance, Stearforth."

"I am passing eager, Your Grace."

"Yes, I can see you are."

The great man in the velvet robe paused and seemed to study Stearforth's face as though he were searching out the character behind the visage.

"I trust you are a good Christian, Stearforth?"

"As I hope for heaven, sir," Stearforth replied, not because the statement was true but because he believed it was what he was expected to say.

"In which case you comply with the Ten Commandments given by God to Moses upon Sinai and reaffirmed by Our Lord himself."

"Yes, Your Grace."

"Good, Stearforth. I should not wish it otherwise. But let me put to you a case."

"A case, sir?"

The employer smiled thinly and Stearforth found himself smiling back. His heart stepped up its beating and he felt himself beginning to sweat beneath his shirt. He knew he was about to be manipulated but somehow too that this manipulation would be ultimately to his advantage.

"The case I put to you is this. What say, there is a man—an ordained clergyman—who by his preachments vexes the Holy Word, seduces others to follow his heresies, and, in brief, makes himself the means by which a whole generation may be spiritually deluded?"

"Why, I am no theologian, sir, but he would surely be in a damnable position."

His employer nodded. "You know, I take it, the scripture that says it is better for one man to suffer than a whole nation dwindle in unbelief?"

Stearforth dimly recollected the passage, although he could not tell whether it was being quoted correctly or not. "Yes, sir, I know the scripture."

"Christ himself said it."

"Yes, Your Grace."

"And therefore its authority is beyond question."

"Although I thought the passage referred to Our Lord's own sacrifice."

"Well, yes, that's true," conceded the employer without allowing the confident smile to vanish from his heavy face. "And yet you do not deny that it has the force of a general rule. Reason supports it."

"The good of one must give way to the greater good," Stearforth said.

"Ah yes, I see your Oxford education has not been wasted, Stearforth. But let me move from generals to particulars."

Stearforth waited; the movement promised was interrupted by the great man rising from his chair and walking around to where Stearforth sat so the servant was forced to look up to the master looming above him.

"The rector of St. Crispin's is just such a one whose works impede the greater good. You are close enough to me to know where my religious sympathies truly lie."

"I think I am, Your Grace."

"In short, I have no patience with either Rome or Geneva."

"Both Papist and Puritan are detestable. I'm of the same mind."

"Then we are of one mind. Certain persons at court whose names I won't mention have advanced Graham's name as the next Bishop of London."

"Indeed, sir."

"It is not generally known. But it must not happen. There is a better candidate, a much better candidate. One who deserves the position by long and futile suit, both to Cecil and earlier to Essex."

"I am not sure how Matthew Stock fits into all this."

"That you will presently see, Stearforth, but let me come to the crux of things. Graham must not obtain a bishopric, and particularly *that* bishopric. He is an obstacle to my purposes. Should I hear that he met his end by . . . some misadventure, or perhaps even calculated homicide, I should, of course, be outwardly grieved and pray for his soul, but lose no sleep knowing the danger he represented is gone. Do you understand me?"

Stearforth was not altogether sure he did. Was he being asked to murder Graham, the man he had imitated only hours earlier, or only countenance it? Was his employer speaking hypothetically or literally? He knew he was treading on unfirm ground. He felt a constriction in the throat.

"What do you say, Stearforth?"

Stearforth's eyes met his employer's. There was a moment of silence during which Stearforth hesitated, and then realizing that hesitation was worse than a wrong answer, he said what he believed he was expected to say.

"I live to do your bidding, sir."

"And you are satisfied that the means is justified by the end?"

"Most sincerely."

"Graham may be one of the most dangerous men in England. But his present death may do as much good for true religion as his life does now harm it."

Stearforth said he was entirely in agreement; he was prepared to say anything to please his new master.

"Excellent, Stearforth. Then let me see, you brought me what I asked for?"

"I did."

"Let's see."

Stearforth took the knife from inside his cloak. "It is an unusual design; there is an initial *S* upon the haft."

"Very good. The weapon, Stock's presence, and the implausible story circumstances shall force him to relate will make him a most credible murderer. You have done well, Stearforth. You exceed my expectation of you by several leagues. Now Cecil and his minion are where I would have them. Stock shall himself be entangled in such a web that the spider will eat out his heart before he is half aware of his peril."

"You have a great hatred for the queen's principal secretary, sir."

"A profound hatred—it's a story I'll tell you when we are better acquainted."

"I trust that will be soon."

"If you serve me in this it shall be. Remember, make no move against Graham until Stock is in the vicinity of the church. Let him have no alibis to save him."

"It shall be as you wish, Your Grace."

The great man made a motion indicating that the interview had ended. Stearforth rose slowly, hoping that his master would not be so forgetful as to overlook his promised payment.

"Oh, Stearforth."

"Your Grace?"

"You'll find something for you in the coffer on yonder

table. When I hear of Graham's death and Stock's arrest the sum will be trebled."

Stearforth opened the coffer and scooped up the leather purse. He did not look inside although his curiosity about the amount was almost beyond his enduring. He turned slowly and bowed at the waist to his patron, who in turn nodded to him.

In the street Stearforth thought more about what he had just undertaken to perform in God's name. Although he was not a particularly religious man, he was not without qualms at the thought of murdering one of the Lord's annointed, even if Graham was a ranting Puritan. If his employer's judgment of the man as one of the most dangerous in England was excessive in Stearforth's mind, the excess was his employer's business, not his own. Yet he would gladly find a way to carry out his assignment without bloodying his own hands. As a middleman in the murder his complicity would be less. Or so Stearforth reasoned as he mounted his horse and began to ride through the streets toward Eastcheap, where St. Crispin's was.

But as he drew near the church the solution to his moral qualms became more and more evident. Did he not know just the man for the deed, one who had already proven himself in the present enterprise and proclaimed himself without love for Stephen Graham? Why should not a gravedigger by trade expand his vocation to include the extinguishing as well as the undertaking of the deceased? Motherwell was a moneygrubber, just like Stearforth, even if somewhat lower in the social order.

Stearforth felt the heft of his master's purse as he rode. It gave him a satisfied feeling and he laughed outright. What if anyone seeing him thought him mad? His problem was solved. Having Motherwell as an accomplice would lighten the purse only slightly—and lighten Stearforth's conscience considerably.

* * *

On the second day of the week Master Stephen Graham (he would not let his congregation call him "father," which savored overmuch of damnable Papistry) administered the blessed sacrament to a handful of his parishioners at a noon service. At least that is how it had been until all the fuss about Christopher Poole. Now the church of St. Crispin's Eastcheap—an old edifice greatly in need of refurbishing—had become one of the most popular gathering places in London, the resort of the idle curious and the truly pious who expected where one miracle had occurred more would follow.

At the moment, however, Graham had the church to himself. It was nearly eleven—a whole hour before the worshipers would be admitted through the heavy oak doors. They had always stood open during the day. Since the Poole affair, they had been shut and barred. The church had become a fortress against Roman fanaticism. The weight of his responsibility to true religion hung heavy upon him. He was sure that was why he had been sick at his sister's house. The heaviness of his burden. But God had strengthened him against Satan. Stephen Graham was not well yet, but daily he improved.

He thought of his sermon, written out and in his pocket. It was another version of his favorite, a stinging indictment of Papist superstition. It had been his theme since Poole's body had been snatched and the whole silly tale of a prophesy fulfilled had fired the imagination of the ignorant. Against the alleged miracle, he spoke fearlessly in the pulpit, regardless of the fact that for the past week he had received three letters from Papist sympathizers threatening his life. Let them do what they would, Graham thought as he inspected the altar to make sure everything was in order for the service. He suspected the letters were really pranks. Everywhere Papist superstition was condemned. Why should he be singled out for special treatment when the archbishop himself had decried the so-called miracle of St. Crispin's only a few days earlier?

Graham's thoughts were now interrupted by footsteps in

the rear of the nave. He looked around to see Motherwell approaching and recoiled a little. He had inherited Motherwell from his predecessor and because of the man's long tenure as sexton and grave-digger did not feel free to replace him. But there was something about Motherwell that Graham did not like and he suspected the feeling was mutual. Their relations were coldly formal.

"What is it, Motherwell?"

"It's Great Harry, sir. He's cracked."

"You don't say. How bad is it?"

"Bad enough. If he be rung he will be as tuneless as an iron pot," Motherwell said.

Graham shook his head and told Motherwell to lead the way to the belfry. He would have to inspect the bell himself sooner or later and it might as well be now.

The stairs to the bell tower were in the rear of the nave. The stairs were narrow so Graham followed the sexton up. They came to the top of the tower where the bells hung. There were three bells, Great Harry being the largest. Graham walked over to have a look at the bell. "I see no crack, Motherwell. Where is it?"

"Why it is right at your neck."

Graham felt Motherwell's strong arm around his chest and something hard and cold pressed against his throat. He started to cry out but the pressure of what he now was sure was a blade rendered him speechless.

Motherwell dragged him over to the window. "Say nothing, sir priest, or the words will be your amen to this life. Now we are going to watch for a while and you will keep silent or so help me God this blade will cut your head off."

Graham's heart thundered in his ears. His mouth went as dry as bone. He was only partly aware of the instructions he was being given. He had known Motherwell to be a man of dubious piety but had not suspected him to be a robber—or perhaps even a murderer. Graham looked down into the street, the knife still at his throat. He felt a trickle of warm urine run down his leg, his eyes began to tear, he couldn't seem to breathe so tight was Motherwell's grip. He tried to think of a prayer, but found himself so terrified that his mind could not sustain a thought.

It seemed like a very long time that he was held hostage in the belfry, so long that Graham began to wonder if somehow Motherwell had decided to forgo his murderous design. Then he heard a chuckle behind him and Graham looked down to see in the street below a short stout man making his way across the street to the door of the parsonage.

The vision was still in his mind when he felt a searing pain at his throat, and a great rush of air expelled from his lungs and would not seem to stop.

4

*O*N the first day of that week the Stocks traveled by horse and cart, having left before dawn and achieved the thirty-some miles with no broken wheels or lamed horse to delay them, and coming within sight of steeple and tower, by mid-morning the following day they found themselves in such a confusion of coaches, carts, wagons, and foot traffic that they could have made better time to their usual stopping place, the Blue Boar Inn without Aldgate, if they had simply walked.

Conducted to their chamber by a courteous host who knew them well from other visits, Joan announced that she was too bone weary from the journey to view any churches. She sent Matthew off alone to enjoy the antiquities of St. Crispin's and sniff out any clues as to the identity or purpose of the body snatchers.

So having seen to the needs of horse, cart, and wife, Matthew went off alone, feeling uncomfortable as he always did outside the so much more manageable environs of his native place with its sweet flowing Chelmer, familiar faces, and rural peace. London was not so, even though the more temperate season began to assert itself in first buds of green. In a month or two the city would become a veritable garden; rains would wash the skies heavy with wood smoke and coal smoke and freshen the air of noxious smells. But there would be no respite from the press of humanity there; the streets would not widen to accommodate the throngs, nor would the rancorous cry of beast, man, and his mechanical contrivances give way to quiet.

It was a good mile walk to the area of London known as Eastcheap, for all the merchants who sold their wares there. Matthew had to ask directions to the church of St. Crispin's.

"I warrant you've come to see Poole's empty grave," remarked the tall, filthy-handed blacksmith whom Matthew had asked the way.

Matthew said that he had.

The blacksmith nodded sagely and stepped to the side of his forge. The event was a great miracle, he said. One had to believe that even if he himself was no Papist, as he assured Matthew he was not. "Does not the Holy Writ speak of a general resurrection of the dead? And must it not commence somewhere? I'faith, then, why not at our own St. Crispin's as well as some grander churchyard?"

"Have you seen this Poole walk the streets since his death?" Matthew asked.

"No, sir, not I, but others have. My wife, for one, and two of her friends, and Samuel Davies the barber who lives in the next street."

"All these, I trust, knew the man while he was alive?"

The blacksmith considered the question. "I cannot speak for the others, but my wife says that she once saw the man when he was more a youth and had not yet gone to France to fall into the clutches of the Jesuits. She swears the man she saw in the street was the spit and image of the young man—or as he might appear were he somewhat older, as he was when he starved himself for his false religion's sake."

Matthew thanked the man for his information and proceeded in the direction he had pointed. Within minutes he spotted the bell tower of a church and asking another less amiable passerby which church it was, was told it was St.

Crispin's Church "and a stronghold of heresy and deviltry too."

The speaker was a prosperous-seeming merchant of about Matthew's age. He eyed Matthew suspiciously. "I can tell by your speech you are a stranger here," the merchant said. "Come to see the churchyard?"

"The parson of the church, rather, Master Graham."

"He's a relative of yours?"

"Distant kin," said Matthew, thinking an innocent fiction might arouse less suspicion.

The merchant warned Matthew that the excitement at the church had brought a flock of pickpurses to feed upon pious pilgrims and that he had better look to his possessions and then moved off.

Matthew drew nearer the church and saw that all along the iron fence that surrounded the adjoining churchyard were the pilgrims the merchant had spoken of. By their garments they were of every station in life. They were a quiet orderly group, watched over by three or four leather-vested constable's men who stood guard by the gate to the yard, forbidding entrance to the curious. To the right of the churchyard was the church of St. Crispin's itself, a tall edifice of stone constructed in the older style with a plain front and porch, a pitched copper roof, and a bell tower at one side with a flat roof and a brace of lancet windows where the bells were.

Matthew looked up at the tower and for a moment thought he saw someone standing in the window, looking down but then he could see nothing and thought it might have been no more than a shadow. Next to the church was a modest house he surmised was where the parson lived. He spotted a side door with a little bell hanging on a post.

He walked across to the other side of the narrow street and rang the bell. Almost immediately a little window in the door opened and Matthew heard a voice ask who he was and what he wanted.

"I've come to see the rector—at his request," Matthew

thought to add, supposing admission to the church would not be easy under the circumstances.

"What is your name?" asked the voice.

"Matthew Stock of Chelmsford."

"I've never heard of you. Master Graham said nothing of an appointment. Go away."

"But I have come to London at his request. He came to my house in Chelmsford and asked me to come."

There was a pause within. The little door window was opened only slightly and it was impossible for Matthew to see with whom he spoke. It was not Graham's voice, however, and he assumed it to be that of a lesser church official, say a sexton or curate.

The voice repeated its command.

"I will go, if you wish it," Matthew said. "But both Master Graham and Sir Robert Cecil will surely be angered to find I have been treated so rudely."

Matthew turned to go.

"Wait," said the voice. "Who did you say you were?"

"Matthew Stock of Chelmsford. I serve Sir Robert Cecil. The rector of this church visited me himself just last week. At my house in Chelmsford. He begged me to come."

The window closed slowly and then Matthew heard an unbolting of the door. Matthew saw a young, fair-haired man in a cassock staring at him curiously. "It is impossible for Father Graham to have been in Chelmsford when you say. He was sick. At his sister's. Only yesterday was he able to rise from his bed of affliction."

Matthew was taken back by the young man's words but thought arguing the point would be futile. He had certainly seen Graham with his own eyes and it was impossible for any man to be in two places at once. "Please let me see Master Graham. My business is urgent."

Still the young man hesitated uncertainly.

Matthew asked him who he was and what he did in the church.

"Alan Hopwood, if it please you. I am Father Graham's assistant."

Matthew made a stern face. "Well, Master Hopwood. Am I to see Father Graham, or must I obtain an order to do so from him whom I serve—Sir Robert Cecil?"

Hopwood's resistance seemed to collapse under the force of this second evocation of Cecil's name. "Come in," he said.

Matthew stepped into a narrow passage beyond which he could see what appeared to be an office or study. Hopwood closed the door firmly behind Matthew and shot the bolt before leading him to the end of the corridor.

"If you wait in here I'll see if I can find the man you seek," Hopwood said in a more ingratiating tone than before.

Matthew walked into the minister's study and sat down. It was a small room with a fireplace and a tall bookcase, and a conspicuous absence of religious adornment. Matthew remembered that Graham had identified himself as a staunch anti-Papist, which meant he was doubtless of the Puritan persuasion, although orthodox enough to hold a living in the established church. There was no little irony in the fact that a Papist miracle had occurred in a church in which the minister was so antagonistic to that creed. Matthew wondered if Poole's resurrection had won any converts to Rome, or merely made more enemies for the Jesuits, of whom Poole was a martyr.

While Matthew waited for Hopwood's return, he examined the books in the case. Those in English, mostly tracts, were sermons and discourses on Biblical topics, commentaries on the scriptures, or works of history. The majority of the books had titles in Latin or Greek, neither of which he understood, except for a handful of legal and medical terms in the former, but then what Englishman or business or public affairs did not have such a smattering? Matthew's own schooling had been small, although he read and wrote the queen's English with ease and although a man of plain speech and uncomplicated faith, he had accumulated in his forty years a good deal of practical knowledge of men and their ways, and of course with respect to cloth, its manufacture and sale, he was something of an expert, having been a clothier by trade practically his whole life.

After what seemed to Matthew a goodly time to wait for Hopwood's return Matthew decided to go find Graham himself. He was annoyed that having been so firmly pressed to come investigate the stealing of Poole's body, Graham had not taken the trouble to make himself available—or at least to inform his assistant of Matthew's expected arrival. He walked out into the corridor and noticed several other doors that led off the passage. Trying the first he found himself in a vestry. The second proved to be the door into the sanctuary itself.

Graham's Puritan sympathies were evident inside the sanctuary as they were in the minister's study. In the southern facing apse a pair of stained glass windows depicting Our Lord and three of his apostles let in a variegated light and illuminated a simply furnished altar above which hung the image of the crucified Christ. The statues and hangings now decried as relics of Popery had been removed, except for a statue of the church's namesake who keeping with his role as patron saint of shoemakers was equipped with a shoe in one hand and a cobbler's awl in the other. Clearly, there were some traditions that even the winds of religious reform could not readily sweep away.

Matthew stared for a few minutes at the altar, mouthed an earnest prayer for the success of his mission, and reflected briefly on how much he detested religious broils. Why could the warring sects not make peace, not follow the counsel of Him from whom they claimed to spring? Why must they be so contentious, so lacking in common charity? He had no answer.

He walked the length of the church, looking up at the open-beam ceiling and admiring the workmanship of the church's builders. The beams were oak, rough hewn, intricately laced, darkened by time and the smoke of candles. A structure designed to last until the Savior should come, perhaps. Along the stone walls were memorials of the church's benefactors. Matthew noticed the dates. St. Crispin's was indeed a venerable church.

To the right of the church door was a winding stair Matthew supposed led up to the belfry. He started when he heard a noise at the front of the church and turned. Hopwood advanced toward him, a worried expression on his face.

"I can't find Master Graham anywhere," he said. "And the noon service starts very soon. There's sure to be a multitude, there always is since Poole's body was stolen."

"I was just about to go up to the belfry," Matthew said. "Have you looked there?"

Hopwood appeared doubtful, but agreed there was a possibility that Graham was there. Hopwood said the rector had a special interest in the bells, especially the largest of them, which was called Great Harry. "It was cast in the time of Henry VI," Hopwood said with pride.

Matthew started up the stairs. Behind him, he could hear Hopwood's labored breathing and sensed the young cleric's impatience. Matthew thought it was unlikely Graham was in the belfry too, but he was confident the tower would afford a sweeping view of the churchyard. Unsure of how much he could trust Hopwood, Matthew had decided to keep his own purpose a secret until he could get Graham's sense of Hopwood's trustworthiness. As far as Matthew was concerned anyone associated with the church was suspect, expect perhaps Graham himself, whom Matthew felt would be hardly likely to initiate an investigation of his own perfidy.

The stairs made several twists before opening into the bell chamber. There were five bells hanging there, the large one obviously Great Harry and four smaller. It was the bells, of course, that first caught Matthew's eye. The second thing he noticed was the body slumped beneath one of the lancet windows.

"God in heaven," cried Hopwood, "It's Master Graham."

Hopwood rushed forward and knelt down by the crumpled body. The young man made a gagging noise and turned his face away, moaned, and shielded his eyes with his hand. A man with his throat cut was no pretty sight for Matthew either but his horror was secondary to his astonishment, for the dead priest was not Stephen Graham—at least not the Stephen Graham Matthew had met in Chelmsford.

"He's dead . . . he's been murdered," Hopwood cried, looking up at Matthew, his eyes wide. "He's been receiving threatening letters, warning him to stop preaching against the so-called miracles. The cursed Jesuits have done this. Look, there's the weapon itself."

Hopwood pointed to the corner where there was a bloody knife. Matthew walked over and picked it up. He realized before he touched the haft that the knife was his own. There were no two knives alike in Christendom. It was the knife that had disappeared from his kitchen.

In his confusion, Matthew frankly admitted that the knife was his own. He started to explain the rest—how someone claiming to be Graham had come to Chelmsford and urged his presence. But he had hardly begun his tale when Hopwood, already pale as death himself at the horror, turned even paler, stood up, and ran down the stairs, whether in an excess of grief or fright Matthew could not tell.

Trusting that Hopwood would return presently, Matthew decided to use the time to inspect the dead man. Unless Hopwood was mistaken in his identification, this was most certainly not the Stephen Graham Matthew had met. This man was older, by a good ten years, his face was round and fleshy and smooth-shaven whereas the face of Matthew's Graham had been long with a prominent brow and well-trimmed beard. A disturbance in the dust by the window evidenced a struggle. Matthew remembered the face he had seen in the belfry just before he entered the church. Had it been Graham's or his murderer's?

His thoughts were interrupted by the sound of voices and heavy footsteps on the stairs. He recognized Hopwood's shrill treble. "He's up here, this way!"

Thinking that Hopwood referred to the corpse Matthew turned just as Hopwood came into view, along with two of the three officers Matthew had seen guarding the churchyard. "That's the man, officers. He said his name was Matthew Stock and has virtually confessed to the murder."

Matthew started to protest but hardly got a word out before the officers rushed forward and pinned his arms behind him.

"He admitted the knife was his own," said Hopwood. "I left him alone in the rector's study. He said he was here at Master Graham's behest, said that the parson had come to Chelmsford last week, which he never did since twenty members of this parish will swear he lay too sick to go abroad nor get up. And he boldly admits the knife yonder is his own."

"The man who came to see me was not Father Graham," Matthew began.

"See, masters, now he weaves a new tale, made I warrant of stuff as false as the last. Examine him and you will surely find he is the one who threatened Master Graham with present death only last week."

One of the officers released Matthew to inspect the knife while the other demanded to know Matthew's real name and origin, for he said Matthew's dark complexion gave good evidence that he was a Spaniard or Portuguese and surely a spy, if not a Jesuit like Poole.

"I am nothing if not an honest Englishman," Matthew proclaimed. "A clothier and constable of Chelmsford, Essex, and employed by Sir Robert Cecil, if the truth be known."

"Oh, now it is Cecil he claims to serve." Hopwood let out a hysterical laugh; his eyes were wide and glaring. "He made the same claim when I foolishly let him in the church not a half hour past. Had I had my wits about me Master Graham would be alive at this moment."

"No, he would not have been," Matthew said, turning to the officer who had asked his name and of the three men seemed by his appearance and demeanor to be the most amenable to reason. "I saw someone in the tower before I entered the church. It was neither Master Hopwood here nor the dead man yonder. It must have been his murderer."

"That's a bald-faced lie," Hopwood said. "There was no other in the church but Master Graham and myself. The doors were locked to keep out the curious and to protect us from murderers. What more evidence do you need, officers? When I returned to the rector's study I found *him* descending from the belfry—"

"I was just about to go up," Matthew interjected.

"He insisted I go up with him," Hopwood said.

"That's true," Matthew said. "And why would I have invited him up to find the body of a man I killed? Why, that makes no sense at all."

"Aye, and perhaps you thought to blame it on Master Hopwood here," said the taller officer.

"Or make me the second victim," Hopwood said, looking desperately from one of the officers to the other.

The taller officer nodded to his companion; Matthew felt the grip tighten on his wrist and he was led downstairs and told to say nothing more if he knew what was good for him. Hopwood followed behind until they came to the church doors.

Outside the crowd of pilgrims had swelled with the addition of other persons who had come for the noon service. In a shrill, trembling voice, Hopwood announced that the service had been canceled, the minister murdered, and the murderer taken and present before them. "You have had your way, you Popish swine," Hopwood screamed. "But your man is taken. Here he stands. The officers have him. And I am still alive to decry your superstitious fraud."

Hopwood's outburst was greeted by angry shouts, some directed against Hopwood by Catholic sympathizers, some directed against Matthew as the murderer of a Puritan hero. Matthew was almost glad to be in custody. Had it not been so, he was sure he would have been torn apart by the howling mob of true believers, now stirred to such a frenzy by Hopwood's announcement it seemed nothing but a troop could establish order there.

5

*I*N her chamber at the Blue Boar, Joan made an effort to sleep. The light bothered her; sounds from adjoining rooms and from the street below distracted her. Somewhere nearby a dog barked and would not be stilled for all its master's eloquent cursing. But worst was the gnawing of unease; it would give her no peace.

She was sorry she had sent Matthew off to St. Crispin's without her. It was not that she feared she would miss something he would not dutifully report of later. Rather, a nagging doubt about what they were doing in London would not cease plucking at her sleeve, like a tenacious beggar who will give no rest to the passerby until a coin is pressed in his palm. Her friends called Joan independent and headstrong, charges she did not deny and in which she indeed took a secret pride. She did not suffer fools gladly and could not abide flattery, which brought her to her grounds of suspicion of Stephen Graham, the man who, she had declared to Matthew, smelled more of court than cloister.

She plainly did not trust him—not if he swore upon a stack of Bibles that every word he spoke was gospel truth. Not that she wasn't mistrustful of churchmen on principle, the godly minister of her own parish church being an exception to the rule. For she deemed the breed, for all their homilies on Christian humility and charity, to be a rancorous, preening, self-serving lot, preoccupied with their livings and sinecures and neglecting their flocks to scale the slippery slopes of ecclesiastical preferment. As for the noisome debate between those of Rome and those of Geneva, Joan had no more patience than did her husband. In good standing in her own parish church and a regular attender as the law prescribed, Joan believed herself to be sufficiently a Christian woman, given that she was a mere mortal and no "saint" in any meaning of the word she could make sense of. In sum, if the established Church of England was good enough for the queen, then who was Joan Stock to find it wanting?

It had not been Stephen Graham whose pleading had brought her to London therefore, but the mystery he described. Now that did intrigue. She believed in the resurrection of the dead as an article of faith. But it was a general resurrection the scriptures spoke of, not a particular one, and she saw no reason why a Papist priest should merit an earlier resurrection than any of her family or friends taken in death and buried in Chelmsford's own churchyard. On that point, she and Graham were one—that the miracle of Christopher Poole was a fraud. Was it a Papist plot as Graham supposed or, as Joan thought equally possible, a Puritan scheme to put the Papists in bad odor with the authorities and produce an even greater oppression of their religion? And what, pray, did Sir Robert Cecil have to do with it all?

Her brain so boiling with this thought and that, she got out of bed and opened the casement to better hear the hour bells. She was astonished when in a few minutes of waiting she heard five bells struck.

Matthew had promised to return by one or two and so was very late and Joan felt suddenly worried. It was more than a nagging concern about a loved one who fails to return when promised and thereby instills a dread of misfortune. It was a sudden, gripping anxiety that enveloped her and made her believe that if she remained in their bed-chamber a minute longer she would suffocate, let the window stand open as it might. Her anxiety was, she recognized even as she experienced it, a *glimmering*. That was what she was wont to call such seizures, which all her life she had had. Glimmerings came and went—inklings of disaster or danger—to herself or others—her full under-standing of their significance often waiting upon the result.

Now this glimmering was of considerable force, and she sat herself down on the bed while her body trembled and a blackness came over her like the hangman's hood. She knew in an instant that Matthew was in more than common difficulty.

She prayed as hard as she might to be free of the glim-mering and it passed shortly, but not her concern for her husband. A hundred perilous circumstances paraded before her eyes—the ways a man might die or be abused in a strange city. Each imagined scene was more horrible than that that went before.

Finally, she could stand no more, neither the visions nor the waiting. Throwing her cloak about her, she went down-stairs and in case Matthew should return and find her gone, she told the innkeeper that she was off to St. Crispin's.

"What, Mistress Stock," the man said good-humoredly. "Church at this hour?"

Joan gave no reply, but was out the door and into the street as his question came, hanging in the air behind her.

Before she even saw the belfry of St. Crispin's she heard the crowd and a clamor like that at a bearbaiting. Then she turned a corner and ran square into them, jamming the streets, necks craning to see above heads and hats and chil-dren perched upon their fathers' or mothers' shoulders. Joan thought that for a crowd of miracle-mongers it was an unruly crew, with much pushing and shoving and one clus-ter of citizens railing at another and exchanging names, few of which savored much of holiness to Joan, unless the epithets carried a sweeter odor of sanctity in London than they did in Chelmsford.

She made her way forward through the crowd, enduring the complaints of those around her at her boldness. Once, jabbed in the ribs hard enough to make her cry out, once, nearly knocked to the ground in a fistfight between two apprentices, one Papist the other Puritan, over whether the Pope was the anti-Christ.

Then she saw the church and churchyard behind an iron railing and a half-dozen officers vainly trying to prevent the zealots from advancing on the church porch, where several gentlemen stood, begging the crowd to disperse and no one paying any attention but pressing forward with more vigor.

Nowhere did she see Matthew. Her apprehension grew. Something had happened. Something more than Christopher Poole's resurrection. Finally she managed to catch the attention of a ruddy-faced woman with a small child in her arms; the woman struggled to stay upright, guarding the child with her fat arms.

Joan asked her what the uproar was.

"Have you not heard?" asked the woman, wide eyed. "Of the bloody murder?"

Joan replied she had heard of the miracle but of no murders.

"It was the parson!" exclaimed the woman as her child squirmed and drooled in her arms. "He who was rector of the church. A goodly person not taken in by Papist trickery and for his pains murdered in cold blood."

"Murdered by whom?" Joan asked.

"They say by a man from the country who gained entrance to the church by claiming he was come to London at the parson's behest, but his whole purpose was to slit the godly man's throat and then lop off his head."

"Did they say what this countryman's name was?"

"Oh, I heard nothing about that," said the woman. "And what difference does it make, since he no doubt used a false one? For my money, he's a Papist spy and now the neighborhood is up in arms against the Papists amongst us for the parson's murder. Many thanks to God that the miscreant was taken and so must face the judgment of the law and torture to make him tell who his confederates are."

A shove from behind moved Joan involuntarily away from the woman before she could learn more. She continued to move toward the church porch hoping against hope that the countryman the woman referred to was not Matthew. Yet how could he have become involved in a murder? Graham had invited them to London, had he not? The scope of Matthew's intent was no more than to look around the church and churchyard. He had been gone from her side for only a few hours. But now it seemed this same cleric was dead—by a murderer's hand. Someone from the country. Someone who had declared himself summoned by the victim?

Then Joan noticed that one of the gentlemen she had seen before on the porch was now standing next to the wall only a few yards from her. Hoping to get a truer account from this person, Joan set forth, elbowing her way, coming at last to him and asking him what went on to cause so great a stir?

The young cleric, who seemed strongly excited by the commotion around him, gave her a look to suggest that only a child or simpleton could ask such a question. "Why, it was I who found Master Graham's body. Alan Hopwood. It was I who fetched the officers to arrest the murderer."

"What was the man's name?"

"Stephen Graham, rector of the church here."

"No, I mean he accused of the murder."

Hopwood looked at her curiously, tipping his pale face to the side as though to see her best he must see her at an angle. "Why should that interest you? Did you know him?"

"Perhaps," she said. "Oh, do tell me his name."

"Marry, it was Stock . . . Matthew Stock."

"But that's impossible!" she said.

"Far from impossible," Hopwood said. He screwed up his eyes to give her a harder look than before. "Stock told me his name, although I have no doubt it is as false a name as the man himself."

Joan replied angrily. "Matthew Stock is my husband, sir, and he came to the church today on Sir Robert Cecil's business. He is no murderer. Why if he is not the honestest man in Christendom then I do not know him from Adam and I have been his wife for twenty years."

"You are his wife!"

"I am indeed."

Joan no sooner reaffirmed her relationship but Hopwood grabbed her by the arm and began to steer her toward the church, bellowing as he did that the officers should come for he had encountered Stock's accomplice.

Realizing what was happening, Joan struggled to free herself, while there was such a hubbub around her that no one seemed to notice the significance of Hopwood's alarm, nor was it clear that had they noticed they would have done more than gawk at him and his female prisoner.

Joan had been dragged nearly to the church porch when a tall man ahead of them suddenly turned and, colliding with Hopwood, caused him to lose his purchase on Joan's arm and allow her to escape.

She pushed through the throng, not looking behind her and imagining in the din of voices that she could still hear Hopwood proclaiming against her. Fleeing the way she had come because she could not determine how to do otherwise, she in time left the rancorous mob behind her and decided to return to the Blue Boar. At least there were people there who knew her and might give her some idea of where her husband had been taken. The next step was to alert Cecil of Matthew's misfortune. In her mind Joan knew that Cecil would put everything right, but in her heart she felt a profound unease. Her glimmering had proven itself to be prophetic. Accused herself, Joan now felt like a hare trapped in a thicket, with howling dogs on all sides.

Stearforth had been observing the events at St. Crispin's from the upstairs window of a tavern across the street from the church for several hours when as luck would have it he spotted Stock's wife conversing with Hopwood. The spectacle had given him satisfaction enough, for although he had not conceived of so excellent a device he had been the executor of it and he could not believe how smoothly everything had gone. For once, Stearforth's timing had been perfect. Well, it had been Motherwell's timing but perfect all the same. Stearforth regretted less now that he had had to pay the sexton double what he had originally offered. But to see Stock's wife sucked in, seized by Hopwood and very nearly taken into custody as her husband had been earlier—yes, that was gratifying indeed.

Of course Hopwood had bungled the arrest; the woman had escaped. But the important thing was that she had now been seen by Hopwood and apparently perceived to be as guilty as her husband.

The sudden appearance of some friends drew Stearforth from these reflections. Would he not come to have a drink or two with them for fellowship's sake? Yes, he would drink but he would buy, rather, for he was celebrating. He was not willing to tell them what and, because they knew Stearforth's humor was to affect a mysterious air, they accepted his offer without further question and the three of them went downstairs and drank for another hour.

After dark, the crowd outside the church began to disperse and Stearforth made his way directly to his employer's house. This time there was no waiting. He had no sooner identified himself at the door but he was shown immediately to the great man's study.

"It's done, even as you ordered, sir."

His employer was in his nightgown and slippers, heavy faced and immobile. He seemed to be a part of the chair he sat in.

"Sit down, Humphrey. Tell me all the particulars."

Stearforth told everything he had witnessed and what surmised, glad that things had worked out so satisfactorily that the truth required no varnish.

"Stock has been arrested then for the murder?"

"He has, Your Grace, and been taken to the Marshalsea."

"Oh, very good."

"Hopwood was a more than adequate witness. Finding Stock's knife, he concluded that Stock was the murderer. And Stock evidently admitted the weapon was his. Of course, when he began to tell a wild story about how Graham came to Chelmsford—"

"You have done well, Humphrey. What of the wife?"

"She came to the church. Undoubtedly looking for her husband and fell into Hopwood's clutches. Then she escaped."

For the first time the great man's face darkened with disapproval. Stearforth said, "She'll give us no trouble, sir. I am sure of it. After all, what can she do, her husband taken, herself suspected as an accomplice and sought for, and without friends in the City? If she's no ninny, she'll hie back to Chelmsford and set up shop as a widow, claim she knew nothing of her husband's affairs."

Stearforth laughed, but his employer's face remained serious. "You underestimate the little woman, Humphrey. Believe me, she's a peculiar housewife. Of subtle mind and iron will. Beware the fox that's taken in the trap. It has naught to lose and will bite off its leg if need be to escape."

"What shall be done with her then, sir?"

"It would be good if she would return to Chelmsford," said the employer, "but she will not."

"Shall she suffer the same fate as Graham?"

"No, Humphrey. Let us consider, rather, how we can get her out of London, far away, so that her leaving will seem to be an escape and further support the charge against her husband. Indeed, we may be able to use her absence as an advantage in dealing with Stock, assuming that he will have to be dealt with."

"Do you have further instructions for me?"

"Yes, Humphrey. Find Mistress Stock and watch her carefully. I don't want her to fall into the hands of the authorities where she can attest to her husband's story. Let me know what she does and when she does it. As for Stock, I have taken pains that he shall not lack for company in prison. My plan moves ahead with dispatch. These successes show that God is with us, dear Humphrey. And blessed be he for it."

6

WHEN Joan had returned to the Blue Boar she started to tell her story of Matthew's arrest and its complicated cause to the innkeeper, a genial, receptive man she counted as a friend, but he supposed it was all a jest, knowing Matthew to be a solid citizen, not likely to find himself on *that* side of the law. So what was to be done at such an hour, but go to her chamber and worry and pray and later when she fell from sheer exhaustion into a restless sleep to dream dreams of glowering judges, grim prisons, and hideous torturers all gathering around her innocent husband?

Before daylight, Joan woke, dressed, and taking from the kitchen below only a cup of milk as breakfast, she was in the street and on her way before even the carters stirred. She knew it was futile to inquire at the prisons. She did not know to which Matthew had been taken. Besides, she knew her very inquiry would expose her to arrest, now that Alan Hopwood had undoubtedly alerted the authorities to the fact that the murderer had a wife who was, by God's blessed son, as resolute a Papist conspirator as her spouse.

Joan's hope, therefore, was Cecil. Cecil, who would tell her in which foul hole Matthew lay. Cecil, who would use his considerable powers to secure Matthew's release.

Her immediate object, then, was to find this savior, although she well knew this might prove no easy task. Always in motion, he might be esconced at the royal court at Westminister with its labyrinthine passages, or hawking, his only sport, at his magnificent country home, Theobalds. Or he might be a guest of some lord or lady in the country. And yet if Graham's words had been true—that the queen was near death—wouldn't her principal secretary at least be in London, or near at hand? And where else but enjoying the delights of a house not more than six months done and the plaster hardly dry?

This elegant domicile—Cecil House—was located on Ivy Lane, a little street running down from the Strand to the broad river. An imposing structure of brick and timber, it had a noble front and back parts extending to the Thames. Joan knew that a direct approach to the gate would invite rebuff at such an hour. Her better opportunity was to somehow make her way around to the back where contact with some early-rising servant might help her to the information she sought.

A wall of smooth stones ran the length of Cecil's property, but she knew from earlier experience where there was a postern door by which servants and tradesmen came and went. She made her way to this and entered into the sloping garden at the rear of the house where she could see dim lights and hear voices. None of the servants Joan knew but she trusted that she could find someone who would tell her where the master of the house could be found, if not for goodness sake, then tempted by some gratuity from her purse. As the wife of a prosperous clothier, Joan dressed well and she knew that she would at least not be put off as an improvident supplicant in the eyes of servants no doubt wary of those who crawled over the back wall rather than coming in the front door.

She waited some time in an arbor before she saw a lantern being borne her way. As the light grew larger, she saw that its bearer was one of the manservants of the house by the livery he wore; she would have preferred to have encountered one of the scullions or lesser cooks or a more companionable female to query.

He was small and narrow shouldered, short of manhood but somewhat beyond the little boy, and he whistled as he approached, for fear of the lingering dark or perhaps only to amuse himself. He stopped suddenly at Joan's voice and seemed afraid.

"You there, boy. Do you belong to the house?"

But of course he did; he answered her sharply, almost defensively. He held the lantern he bore higher, to bring her into the circle of light. He asked who she was and what she did in his master's garden. There was a tremor in his voice. His face was white and smooth.

"I have a message for Sir Robert."

"Master Staunton receives my lord's messages."

"I know. But I must speak to Sir Robert directly. It's urgent, boy. Sir Robert will not be displeased to know you have helped me to him."

The youth, whom Joan could now see could not have been past twelve or thirteen and had the smooth look of a household servant, continued to regard Joan suspiciously.

"How did you get into my lord's garden?"

"Through the gate yonder."

"You shouldn't be here."

"Well," Joan said impatiently, handing the boy tuppence. "Necessity brought me to it. I swear my mission is a matter of life and death. One of Sir Robert's friends is in great danger. If you take me to him there's more in my purse for you. Not to mention what thanks your master is likely to give."

The boy took the coin. "Sir Robert isn't here."

"Where is he, then?"

"At Richmond Palace. The queen lies abed, sick unto death. All the counselors gather about her."

Joan's heart sank. Invading Cecil's private garden was one thing; penetrating the environs of the palace at Richmond was another.

"But I know for a fact he comes to the City," said the boy.

Joan gave him another coin, a whole shilling. He looked at it by the light of his lantern and seemed impressed.

"A company of foreigners are in the City—ambassadors from somewhere—Poland, I think, or Muscovy. It falls to my master to show them the sights this very morning—the Tower and the Bedlamites."

"You're telling the truth, now?"

"As God lives. I heard it from the head groom himself who was to have a brace of Sir Robert's horses prepared for the nonce."

She asked what hour this excursion was to take place, but the boy could not answer. He watched her expectantly. "You're a good lad," Joan said. "Sir Robert shall know of your kindness. Trust me that he will not be ungenerous."

"Who shall I say inquired of my lord if I am asked of him or another."

"Say, Joan Stock of Chelmsford—on her husband, Matthew's, behalf. The name will not be unfamiliar I warrant you."

Matthew might have lain on the straw bed, but it was so busy with vermin that he preferred the stone walls as a bolsterer. Sometime before dawn he had slept and when he awoke it was still dark in his cell and his bones were so wracked from his crouched position that he could hardly stand.

As he woke he noticed that Middleton, his cellmate, was already up and staring from the little barred window. It took Matthew a moment to remember where he was and as the realization flooded back he felt a grip of fear in his heart that was nearly intolerable. He had been in prison before, in dismal Newgate, on another false charge, but then a lesser one and his great protector Cecil had known of his predicament.

Matthew's one consolation was that Joan was free, at least. That was an improvement on his last imprisonment.

Middleton, seeming aware of being observed, said: "It is dawn. Twice I've heard the cock crow, and yet there is no light."

The day before, upon Matthew's arrival in the cell, Middleton had told Matthew of his crime—a savage murder of a shopkeeper and his wife against whom Middleton had had some grievance. Middleton had already been tried and sentenced. For Matthew the chilling part of the story was Middleton's remorselessness. He seemed content with his fate, as certain and grim as it was, thankful only that in his case justice had been swift. It had been less than a month since the murder. The bodies of his victims were hardly cold in their graves. But although Middleton had spoken defiantly the day before, this morning he seemed more subdued.

"Do you believe in God?" he asked, turning suddenly toward Matthew as though he had pondered the subject all the night and only now felt moved to utter it.

"I do."

"I shall meet Him presently."

Middleton spoke matter-of-factly. As if he spoke of meeting an old acquaintance or new connection in a tavern or some other place of common resort. "I doubt he shall think much of me."

"God?" Matthew asked.

Middleton nodded. He spoke urgently. "I tell you, Stock, if there's a way to avoid my end, do it. Death comes to us all, but I would fain die in bed as on the gallows and have my taking off a surprise rather than calendared."

Matthew had exchanged stories with the condemned man, protesting that he was falsely accused, a victim of a conspiracy, and the servant of a certain great lord who could illuminate all. Middleton had not disputed Matthew's claim of innocence. Although guilty himself, he did not disallow that a man could be trapped by a clever adversary. Middleton knew of several cases. He would have incriminated the son of the shopkeeper and his wife if he had thought of the devious strategem aforehand. Middleton had laughed about it.

"If you know anything that can help you, hold it not back," Middleton said now, more serious, standing with his arms folded and leaning back against the wall. "Don't let honor shut your mouth. Or promises of confidence. Nothing is worth more than life. Your great someone would not keep silent on your behalf. Don't be a fool to do so for him if you can save your neck. Say what you must. Lie if you must. Tell them what they want to know and more and be done with them. Sin hangs heavy on the best of men. If God will forgive some sin he will forgive all lies you tell to save your neck."

Matthew was about to respond to this cynical counsel when he heard the sound of boots in the corridor outside the cell, then a key rattling in the lock. A rough voice Matthew recognized as the turnkey's ordered Middleton to stand out. There were several men with the turnkey, one of whom carried a torch. Matthew noticed that one of the men was a cleric, and he suddenly realized why Middleton had plunged into so philosophical a mood. Matthew turned to look at Middleton. The condemned man had not moved from the wall but seemed rather to press himself against it, to dissolve into the stone. The turnkey repeated the order and when Middleton did not respond, two of the warders charged in and took him by force. Middleton let out a pitiful groan as he was dragged out, his shoes scraping the stone. A moment later the cell door clanged shut.

At the first blush of dawn Joan left Cecil's garden and headed back in the direction she had come. She prayed Cecil's young servant had known whereof he spoke. If not, she would be wasting valuable time. She knew going to the Tower with its formidable guards was out of the question. She might easily be taken there, charged, thrown in prison herself and no use to Matthew at all. But the Hospital of St. Mary of Bethlehem—or Bedlam as it was familiarly called—was more accessible. Situated near Bishopsgate on the north side of the City, it had no guards or walls, but the lunatics that were housed there were paraded in the street before the building for the enjoyment of the public, composed of common folk and more substantial persons as well.

In no more than a half an hour, Joan stood without Bedlam, apprehensive but determined. Two men washed down the cobbles in front of the building. The lunatics had not yet been brought out. Down the street stood a parish church; on the opposite side a fair inn, with the sign of the Dolphin. Behind the hospital was a foul-smelling ditch and beyond still the marshy expanse of Morefields where the citizenry went to practice archery. Even farther to the north, Joan could see several fine houses that might have pleased any gentleman's eye for their construction and noble fronts.

She had witnessed the spectacle itself on an earlier visit to London. The lunatics, men and women, were paraded in a wide place in the road called Bishop's Cross. Some made animal noises; some claimed to be kings or queens and were sometimes fitted out with crowns and moth-eaten robes. A perennial crowd pleaser was Jeremy Marsh, who was so afflicted in his brain that he thought he was a dozen or more people and changed from one voice to another in mid-sentence. Others begged alms of the onlookers. Their guardians were always close by. Joan didn't know whether the lunatics kept the money they garnered or gave it over to their guardians. The crowd was generous; someone was making a good living.

Since she knew she had time before Sir Robert should come with the ambassadors, Joan proceeded to the Dolphin, open for business even at this early hour. She found herself a table near the front where she could view the street. She ordered a bowl of wine and sat sipping it, waiting and watching. By eight o'clock, the street cleaners had returned inside and a crowd had begun to accumulate at Bishop's Cross. It was another pleasant day in London and Joan knew that this might make for a larger audience for the lunatics' antics than normal. In the course of waiting, she saw several coaches arrive, but none she recognized as Cecil's, which she knew well from having ridden in it during her last sojourn in the city, when Matthew had been busy solving the murders of young men in the Inns of Court.

She finished her wine and her continued presence was beginning to draw looks of wonder and annoyance from the tapster behind the bar. She ordered another cup of wine and yet another. Finally the Bedlamites emerged, single file. The street about Bishop's Cross was crowded with spectators. Feeling light-headed from so much drink on a virtually empty stomach, Joan paid what was owed to the tapster and ventured into the street, fearing that in so large a crowd she would miss Cecil should he come with his ambassadors.

She made her way through the gathering crowd, noticing that now indeed by their antics and outlandish costume the Bedlamites were variously calling attention to themselves by their behavior, while the crowd variously applauded or hooted, some of the sane ones pretending themselves to be lunatic to incite those who were so indeed. In her passage through the multitude Joan noticed several clusters of gentle-folk among the common faces, and at least one she thought might be Sir Robert, until drawing closer she found him to be someone else.

It was the better part of an hour when foot weary and despairing she spotted the man she sought. He was standing with several tall gentlemen dressed as Germans, he between them, a frail, hunchbacked man of fewer inches than Joan with prematurely graying hair and refined features.

At once she made a move to approach but the crowd was so pressed together that progress was impossible, nor, she knew, would her vocal appeal rise above the cries of the merry lunatics or the noisy throng they entertained. For a while she lost sight of the diminutive knight, but never of his companions, who were tall with outlandish hats. Joan pushed and shoved, while those around her regarded her intrusion with typical London disdain and hissed crudities at her for what they called her boldness.

You must get his attention, she said to herself. *You must*

*come to where he is and pluck him by sleeve or beard if
need be or scream in his face if need be. Anything—that
you must do for Matthew's sake.*

Yet it was only the Bedlamites who garnered Cecil's attention, and in her frustration Joan realized what she must
do and do with dispatch before, weary of this curious enter-
tainment, the queen's principal secretary and the ambassadors moved off to some other part of the city and her
chance would be lost.

She penetrated the ring of onlookers into the area in
which now a dozen of so men and women danced and grimaced and then began her own twirling and strange gibber-
ish. She played the madwoman and the fool, mimicking the
gestures of the Bedlamites, the contortions of body and
limbs. She made faces and extravagant gestures. She bab-
bled incomprehensibly. She twirled dizzily until she could
hardly keep her feet. She ducked and stretched. She forsook
her sanity and dignity, praying no more than one in her audience would recognize Joan Stock of Chelmsford in this
demented creature she enacted.

As she twirled her eye caught the momentary surprise of
those who moments before had been fellow spectators at
the sudden emergence of one of the afflicted from their own
number, garbed neither in shreds or fustian but good solid
cloth, but then she noticed, twirling, that they regarded her
no differently than the others, with a mixture of awe and revulsion.

She stopped her twirling, shrieked maniacally, finding in
the feigned behavior a release for her own pent up anxiety
about Matthew, and began a sinuous dance in the direction
of Cecil. Within moments she was directly in front of him,
but could not catch his eye, for at the same time two of the
lunatics, their faces wildly distorted and their hair disar-
rayed, dominated the scene, bowing and scraping in a gro-
tesque parody of courtly obsequiousness that had brought
mocking laughter from all who looked upon it but especially Cecil.

Frustrated at her failure to be noted, despite her own

mortifying display, she pushed the woman aside and took her place, falling upon her knees before Cecil and seizing upon his hand and kissing it until she had forced him to look into her eyes and recognize her.

Cecil's face betrayed amazement but no recognition. Joan screamed above the tumult of spectators and lunatic, "Matthew has been taken. At St. Crispin's church. For God's sake, Sir Robert. Help."

Cecil pulled her hand away and turning aside motioned to two armed men standing behind him. Joan heard his sharp command. "Arrest this woman. She's a continual annoyance with her suits and threats."

Joan did not struggle. Stunned by Cecil's rebuff she allowed herself to be taken by the men, limp as a puppet in their grasp, not really caring where they took her or for what reason.

7

MASTER SECRETARY CECIL sat in a plush, tall-backed chair that almost enveloped him, like a turtle in his shell. He was explaining himself in that patient way he had, speaking slowly in the resonant voice whose largeness belied his deformed little body. He gestured with his slender white hands.

"I recognized you straightway, but thought my seeming to do so would serve neither of our purposes. I am sorry, Joan. Believe me, I meant you no harm. My men treated you gently?"

"Like a lady, once we were out of sight of the ambassadors," Joan said, still hurt by the rebuff.

"And others," Cecil murmured. He glanced toward the mullioned window. As though watching for someone.

"Others?"

"Spies. Everywhere I go these days. The queen's impending death has set the whole country's teeth on edge. A new order is about to fall upon us. Every man scurries to find a place in it."

He thrust himself forward and rested his chin on his fingertips. His large dark eyes took her in. "Now tell me, what has happened to your husband?"

Joan told the story, beginning with Graham's visit to Chelmsford. Cecil interrupted to mention that he knew the cleric, by name at least, but had never heard him preach and would not recognize his face. Nor had he heard of his murder. "The man was in a fair way of being elevated to bishop, but he was no one I commended. There was too much bite in his sermonizing, or so I was told. I don't know about the Bacon crew. Of the so-called resurrection of Chrisopher Poole I have naturally heard. London can talk of little else, save for the queen's condition."

"Graham said he came upon your orders."

"Then he lied. I never gave him any. You two deserved a rest, not another mission in London."

"I was of the same mind—and so was Matthew—but we came thinking otherwise."

Cecil made a shrewd face. His fingers moved to the tabletop and he began to drum them nervously. "I smell a plot in this, Joan. But go on."

She told him how they had come to London and how Matthew had gone off to the church to Graham and to see the grave—and how when Matthew did not return she went in search of him only to find him taken for Stephen Graham's murderer.

Cecil seemed now even more distressed. He said, "This Poole's cousin is Margaret Whiteside, Lady Elyot. A cultivated woman in whose company I have often found myself during the past few months. She's no Papist but her cousin was, yet she loved him dearly and arranged for his burial at St. Crispin's. The resurrection, as it is called by pious believers, is as great an embarrassment to her as it is to me since it reflects on her own loyalty. I need not say that the fact that I have been lately in this woman's company touches my own person. My enemies would like nothing better than to see me discredited—both with the queen and with him who is likely to be her successor."

He meant the king of Scotland, Joan knew that. James was a resolute Protestant, fastidious in principle, although of his practice there had been nasty rumors. Yet surely there would be no room in his new realm for a murderer of godly ministers.

In an instant she realized how broad in scope was the treachery of Cecil's enemies. But what did a mere clothier and constable have to do with such weighty matters of conflicting sects and kingly powers?

"But why Matthew?" she asked, feeling the terrible burden of having been used by strangers.

"Doubtless because of me."

Cecil rose from the chair; his little body moved deftly to the window. "Your husband is no longer an obscure clothier of Chelmsford. At court at least, his service to me is known—to my friends and enemies."

She asked what enemies he meant.

"Certain of my cousin Bacon's faction—those who adored my lord of Essex before his fall. Who wished him well and might have conspired with him in the queen's overthrow. Those gentlemen you saw me with at Bedlam—"

"The German ambassadors."

"Dutchmen, rather. But I did not mean those. The English gentlemen."

"Yes, sir."

"Those are my friends, several my servants. At least two I know of are presently in the pay of my enemies to report where I go and whom I see."

She said, "But why don't you send them packing, imprison them?"

Cecil turned to her, smiled sadly. "It is better to know your enemies—more particularly to know their spies—than to be in ignorance. I at least know who they are and thereby may watch both my actions and my tongue when I am in their presence. I fear only what I do not know and that is who in particular is behind this present plot."

The *plot*. She considered the word, its meaning. He spoke of it as a commonplace thing, a known quantity. He didn't seem afraid as she was. He seemed to sense her lingering confusion.

"My ruin. That's their aim. As I said, it is known at court that Matthew has served me well. Consider how this strange concatenation of events must appear. First, a lady with whom I am known to keep company pays the burial expenses of a man who for his religious persuasion is little better than a traitor. The man's body is snatched, doubtless by his coreligionists, so that the Roman faith might be strengthened and at the same time the taint may be more deeply stained into this same lady's name. Then, lo, my secret servant, Matthew Stock, is discovered to have murdered the very man most vocal in decrying the fraud. You see how I am implicated on two counts—because Lady Elyot is my friend and because Matthew Stock is my servant? No, Joan, it is not your poor innocent husband whom the devil wants, but me. I am the target. It was for this reason that I pretended not to recognize you in the street. Although I had not heard of Graham's murder nor Matthew's arrest, the very mention of St. Crispin's church made me wary of how I might respond in front of my so-called friends."

Cecil sat down again and resumed his characteristic pose, resting his chin on his fingertips, his fine dark eyes hooded in thoughtfulness.

"But what is to be done—about Matthew I mean?"

"There's the rub."

"He must not languish in prison—or, God forbid, be hanged for a crime he did not commit."

"He shall not," Cecil said.

"Then you will order his release?" It was more a plea than a question.

"Ah, that I cannot do," he said.

She stared at him in disbelief.

He raised a palm to stay the anger she had not expressed but felt rising within her. "Let me explain."

"Oh please do, sir."

"The case stands thus. If I order Matthew's release—and I assure you it lies within my power to do so without so much as a word of explanation as to my motives—I will do nothing less than give my enemies comfort and undeniable proof that Matthew is my tool. See, they will say, he protects his minion. He impedes justice, which wants not reasonable grounds for Stock's arrest. Thus he proves his own complicity in the plot to kill an honest minister whose only crime is godly zeal against Roman superstition."

"But if you do nothing," Joan said, "Matthew will be tried, and surely it will be a public trial with much ado about how he has served you in the past. You will still be implicated—and be made to seem a betrayer of your friend and faithful servant."

Cecil smiled again, but shrewdly, not benignly as before. "Oh, dear Mistress Joan, you have excellent political instincts for a housewife. Would that I had a dozen such women—or even a half dozen—to advise me in matters of state. But don't despair. Between exposing myself as Matthew's champion and a vain effort to keep myself aloof there is a middle road."

"Which is?"

"To work with all the cunning in my power to identify the real murderer and the bold conceiver of this plot before Matthew comes to harm or our relationship becomes a matter of public interest. I know of no other effectual way of saving Matthew. For consider, if I intervene on his behalf I will be condemned. Trust me that further evidence will accrue against me. I will be seen as a Papist sympathizer and plotter. My honest dealing with Spain will be exploited. The queen will spew me from her mouth. The king to come will regard me as hiss and byword. My enemies will triumph and England will be the worse for it."

"But Matthew would be saved," she could not help saying. He was her husband, her life. Let England go hang if she lost his precious soul to the executioner's rope.

"Alas, it would not turn out as you expect. For if I order his release and what I fear transpires, he would only be confined again, now perceived more guilty than before. As the queen's principal secretary I can draw him out, but as a condemned traitor I have not the power to save even myself. No, Joan, we are in the hands of no mean chess player. He anticipates our every move and cries check whatever we do."

"Then what is to be done?" she cried in desperation.

"We shall move to avoid his check—until such time that we can ourselves cry mate."

Joan thought about this. She knew little about chess except that it was a game of complicated rules and stratagems, played by men of great intelligence and cunning. And yet if her husband was to be one of the pieces, moved willy nilly on the checkered board, she would insist on playing too.

"Tell me," she asked, "how can I help?"

Cecil smiled and reached across the desk to take her hand. "You don't disappoint me, Mistress Joan. The truth is that you can be of great help—to your husband and to me."

"Only speak it, Sir Robert."

Cecil thought for a moment. Then he said, "It is known that Matthew has been in my employ. Your own service, while to my own mind not a whit less valuable, is less well known. As I have said, my own moves will be watched and reported. I will do what I can to see that no harm comes to Matthew while he is imprisoned. But there is something you can do. This same Stephen Graham whom Matthew is said to have murdered has a sister who lives in the suburbs, the wife of a ship captain. She may know if her brother had enemies—or if he was involved with some patron at court. I suspect that Bacon circle behind this intrigue, but will forbear accusations until proof is at hand. When I know who engendered this plot I will find means to bring him down."

"I will go find Graham's sister forthwith," Joan said.

"Take care, Joan. These malefactors may have killed her brother for no other reason than to implicate Matthew. If so, it is an act of unquestionable evil."

"I shall take every grain of care that's warranted," Joan said. "But Matthew must be freed. Tell me where I can find this woman, please."

* * *

By Matthew's reckoning there were fifteen or twenty men in the room. Most were officers or constable's men, the rest manacled prisoners like himself, two revealed to be gentlemen by their dress, one of them, with a handkerchief pressed to his nose to avoid contagion. Behind a high desk a sallow-faced magistrate sat. Below him a young clerk wrote busily at a little table. The chamber had a high raftered ceiling and around the periphery were benches upon which officers and prisoners hunched, their faces all turned upward toward the magistrate, although several of the prisoners looked to be asleep and one of the officers did doze, despite the noise of talking and wrangling in the room. The magistrate suffered the commotion because he was deeply engrossed in a conversation with his clerk, leaning down from his desk so that Matthew could see only the round hat he wore and nothing of his eyes.

Matthew waited a long time before his name was called while the other prisoners were taken before the bar, charged with their crimes—a battery, three robberies, and two murders—and then dragged off again. Then he was yanked to his feet roughly and pushed toward the magistrate's desk by the prison warder in whose charge he was. At the same time Matthew saw the constable's man who had arrested him come forward along with the curate Hopwood and a stout old man he had never seen before but with so scarred and villainous a face that his own mother would condemn him to hang out of pity's sake for his ugliness.

The magistrate, to whom the clerk had earlier referred as Sir Thomas Bendlowes, peered down at Matthew as a falcon might have surveyed his prey in a field.

"Matthew Stock?"

"I am," said Matthew, his voice trembling.

"Clothier of Chelmsford?"

"And constable of the town."

Sir Thomas murmured something to the clerk but Matthew could not tell by the man's expression whether the constableship was a mark for him or against him.

"You are charged with the murder of Stephen Graham, rector of St. Crispin's Eastcheap. How plead you?"

"Not guilty, sir."

He had answered quickly, guilelessly, the outburst of innocence, but his truth sounded like a lie, even to himself. Had he no faith in his own story?

"Arresting officer?"

"Michael Barrows," said the constable's man.

The magistrate nodded; his clerk wrote in a great book.

"Any witnesses?"

"These men here, sir," said Barrows nodding to Hopwood and the old man, who was standing a little to the rear of Hopwood.

The magistrate turned his head toward Hopwood and nodded as though indicating that he should proceed with his account. Hopwood looked eager to give information.

"This Stock came yesterday asking for Master Graham," he said. "As a stratagem he told some story about how Master Graham had been in Chelmsford the day before—"

"It was two days before," Matthew interrupted. "And the man was not Graham but an imposter."

"Be silent," roared the magistrate so that the whole room complied. "You'll have time to say your piece before you're hanged." Matthew's warder slapped him on the back to reinforce the magistrate's order and hissed, "Hold your tongue if you want to keep it."

Hopwood continued.

"He said our rector had been in Chelmsford, which thing he never was, for I know for a fact he was sick abed at his sister's house since Sunday last, shivering with the ague. Only on the morning of his murder had he returned to the church, worse the luck for him."

"Well, proceed then," said Sir Thomas Bendlowes. "What else did you see?"

"He prevailed upon me to let him in, claiming to act upon the authority of some gentleman at court whose name I forget. Then whilst I went to fetch the rector he made himself free of the inside of the church and cut the rector's throat from ear to ear. All this was in the bell tower."

Hopwood had turned to regard Matthew with an expression of disgust and horror. Matthew could see that the curate's scathing look had its designed effect on the magistrate, whose pinched face was now even more severe than before.

Matthew felt compelled to protest Hopwood's accusation but remembered Sir Thomas Bendlowes's warning and knowing that his protest would avail nothing but the magistrate's dislike and the warder's violence, he held his tongue.

"Then you saw Stock kill the priest?" queried the magistrate.

"No, sir," Hopwood said.

"Then how do you know it was he who killed the priest and not some accomplice of his? Might there not be others?"

"Stock admitted the knife that killed the rector was his own. It was as good as a confession," Hopwood proclaimed in a shrill voice.

"There is another witness," said the constable's man. "Motherwell."

Barrows turned and motioned for the old man with the scarred cheeks to come forward. As Matthew turned in the same direction to see who this witness might be he noticed a familiar face in the crowd. It took him but a second and the recognition gave him the first cause of hope he had had that day. It was Richard Staunton, one of Cecil's under secretaries, a youngish man of gentle manners who had often spoken to Matthew kindly. From across the room Staunton flashed him a look of recognition and brought a single finger to his lips in a gesture of silence. Matthew gave a little nod in response and then turned his attention to this new witness.

"This is Motherwell, sir. Sexton of St. Crispin's."

"Speak man, what did you see?"

Motherwell stepped forward a little and peered at Matthew. "Indeed, this is truly the one, as I am a Christian."

"Which one?" demanded the magistrate.

"The one I saw murder Master Graham."

"You were in the bell tower?"

"I was, Sir Thomas."

"And you saw this man kill Graham?"

"May God feed my soul to the worms if it is otherwise," Motherwell said. "This Matthew Stock came up to where Master Graham was inspecting Great Harry."

"Great Harry?"

"The largest of the bells, sir."

"Then?"

"Why he slipped cowardlike up behind him. When the rector wasn't looking, Stock cut his throat. As though he were slicing a fresh cheese."

"The man lies. I never killed anyone," Matthew cried. "A man came to Chelmsford claiming to be Graham. He asked me to come to London to inquire into the theft of Christopher Poole's body. Yet it was not the real Graham, but another—doubtless the real murderer."

The magistrate glowered. "You offend justice in praising your own victim, Stock, but would do better to confess your crime and your accomplices' identities. Improbable contradictions do nothing more than support the testimony of these honest churchmen."

The magistrate nodded to Matthew's warder. "Bind his mouth. I will suffer no more interruptions."

The warder threw his arm around Matthew's throat, choking him while another officer stuck a gag in his mouth and began to bind it with a leather strap. Then the warder released his choke hold and Matthew began breathing again.

"My witness is as true as God's word," said Motherwell piously.

"What were you doing in the bell tower?" asked the magistrate. "And how was it you did not go to the rector's aid?"

Motherwell lowered his head in seeming shame. "Well, the truth of it, sir, is that I was sore afraid. I was doing something at the other end of the belfry when Stock came up."

"Doing what?"

"Well—"

"Speak, man. What was it you were doing there?"

"Marry, sir. I have this cursed condition of my bladder. Sometimes, sir, I can no more hold my water than my old wife her tongue, before she died, that is."

There was some laughter at this response, but the magistrate called out for silence again and then ordered Motherwell to proceed as before.

"Stock was upon the rector before I was aware and because I was afraid for my own life I kept hidden until he had fled. I looked after the rector and found such a deal of blood and so wide a swath that I knew there was naught to be done."

"But you are sure this is the man you saw kill Master Graham?"

"As I hope for heaven," said Motherwell.

"The question then is *why*," said the magistrate. "Yet that need not be answered today. The testimonies against the man are sufficient—and as for reason I doubt not that it has to be with Graham's outspokenness against the queen's enemies, which I suppose this man to be, for if his coreligionists can think to kill a queen at the Pope's behest, I see no reason why they should stint at killing a minister of the Church of England who has denounced their fraudulent practices and thereby won souls for Christ."

"The man has a wife," said Hopwood. "It is likely she is an accomplice, for she came to the church in search of her husband the very day of the murder."

"Did she?" said the magistrate, interested. "Then I shall write out a warrant for her arrest, for if man and wife be one flesh and the one be a murderer it follows therefrom that the other is an accomplice at least. Bind this man Stock over for the next assizes. He shall stand trial for his crime. Meanwhile his accomplices shall be found out."

Matthew felt himself being dragged off. He cast an eye to where he had seen Richard Staunton before but now Staunton was gone and in his place was the man who had represented himself to be Stephen Graham smiling triumphantly. Bound and gagged as he was, Matthew was helpless to even point an accusing finger much less denounce the plotter and he felt hot tears of rage fill his eyes.

Stearforth had slipped into the magistrate's chamber in time to hear Motherwell give his testimony against Matthew Stock and was gratified by the results, wishing only that the sexton had made a more presentable appearance. Was it possible that one so vile featured, so stamped with the look of Cain, should be given credence in a hall of justice, his professed piety and mighty hypocritical oaths notwithstanding?

But Sir Thomas Bendlowes had seemed to believe Motherwell's words, even though Stearforth had held his breath when the man had inquired how Motherwell had happened to be in the belfry at the same time Stock was slitting Graham's throat. Pissing in the corner, indeed! Fearful that he himself would be slain, indeed! Motherwell was at least an inventive knave—not one to be caught napping by a question aimed at discovering his bald-faced mendacity. Yes, there was that to be said for him. What man, after all, was completely devoid of virtues?

Now, to Stearforth's way of thinking, there was only one thing wanting in Stock's arraignment, which was some explicit mention of Sir Robert Cecil as he whose commands bade Stock come to London and St. Crispin's Church.

Stearforth raised this very point with Richard Staunton only a few moments later when Matthew had been removed and the two men could find a quiet corner.

"That pasty-faced dimwit Hopwood mentioned something about Stock's professed patron," Stearforth said. "Referred to him as some great gentleman at court. Bendlowes did nothing to draw the matter out."

"I'm surprised our mutual friend does not have Hopwood in his pocket to such a degree that he can put more exact words in Hopwood's mouth," said Staunton, whose elegant suit of clothes was drawing as much of Stearforth's attention as was the man's freshly trimmed beard and mustache.

Stearforth laughed. "That pious fool would fall through such a hole, though he held on for dear life and had his buttocks stitched to the lining. But, never fear, though we might have wished Cecil's complicity broadcast from the rooftops, Stock's side of the story will come out in due course. Believe me, he'll talk as his trial draws near and he sees himself without help, save what he can muster by clinging like a drowning man to every would-be rescuer. I suppose your master appreciates the vulnerability of his own situation?"

Staunton shrugged. "He asked me to come down here and observe the proceedings against Stock. He said nothing about being worried, one way or t'other."

"Ah, a very cool gentleman indeed, the queen's principal secretary," remarked Stearforth. "But he's no fool, as all the world knows, and since he knows his pet is taken, he cannot help but be alarmed as to what Stock may declare in an effort to save himself from hanging. You must make sure that he does talk, Staunton."

Staunton looked up at Stearforth with an expression of mild annoyance, and Stearforth knew he must be careful with this proud, disdainful servant, who having betrayed one great master could hardly be trusted to prove faithful to another.

Staunton flashed a superior smile and said, "Never fear. My master has commanded me to duties beyond those you have imagined. I shall see that Stock spills every unsavory detail, implicates every great person, and in sum, is made the very wrench by which Cecil is unbolted from the queen's esteem. Within a week the scandal will be trumpeted throughout Europe."

"And if it does not work out so?" Stearforth asked, finding his companion's confidence irksome.

"Then Matthew Stock shall meet his own death, which death will then be laid at the feet of Cecil. You see, dear Stearforth, everything has been thought of. Whichever way it turns out, Cecil loses. And likewise our redoubtable constable as well."

8

I_T was not a long walk from Cecil's House on the Strand to where Graham's sister lived. Cecil had provided her with directions, told her the woman's name, shook her hand warmly and wished her Godspeed. His eyes had been moist and sincere.

Joan walked speedily, her thoughts in turmoil. Everything was happening too quickly. She felt borne along on a flood in which she flailed around blindly. Presently she came to the neighborhood of scattered cottages with thatched roofs and whitewashed walls set in open pastures intersected with lanes lined with still-bare poplars and hedges. Behind her she could see the City, the grim squat Tower, St. Paul's rising importantly, and at lesser elevation churches of more modest size memorializing a dozen saints and asserting man's aspirations into a mottled heaven of clouds and patches of azure.

She spent a good hour trudging up and down the narrow lanes looking for the cottage she sought, since so many of the dwellings looked alike or were half-hidden behind the hedges.

Elspeth Morgan's cottage was at lane's end. Joan stood at a picket fence and regarded the cottage. Beyond it to the right was an open pasture where a half dozen cows grazed and farther still a man, a cowherd she supposed, sat with his back against a tree staring in her direction. A path of flat round stones led from the fence to the cottage door, which as Cecil's informant had said was painted a bright green to match the shutters. A curl of thin smoke wafted upward from the stone chimney. Joan approached the door and knocked twice.

Almost at once the door was opened by a woman in her late twenties, dressed plainly in a russet skirt, white apron, and frilly cap. She had pretty features, Joan thought, a flushed complexion and smooth brow, but her gray eyes were wary, as though she expected someone else. Peeking from behind her skirts were the faces of two children, a boy and a girl of about the same age. The children's faces were also stern, little images of the mother. All seemed oppressed by more than grief at a brother and uncle's death.

The woman said, "What is it you want?"

"Are you Elspeth Morgan?"

"I am she."

"Sister of Stephen Graham?"

"Yes."

"My name is Joan Stock. I knew your brother, and I have come to pay my respects."

This announcement failed to have any effect on Elspeth Morgan. There was a tenseness in her voice; she continued to stare warily at Joan, and Joan wondered if she had already heard that a Chelmsford clothier by the name of Stock had been charged with her brother's murder.

"Were you a member of his congregation? I don't remember you."

"I'm a stranger here. From the country."

Joan's words seemed to put the young woman more at ease. She told her children to go into the kitchen to play, then she invited Joan to enter.

Inside the cottage the furnishings were few and simple, but there was an orderliness in their arrangement that bespoke competent housewifery. At one end of the low-ceilinged room was a door leading into the kitchen, which Joan could see part of. There Elspeth's children went to play with a fat brindled cat, teasing the creature with a ball of yarn.

"Won't you sit down?"

Joan accepted the invitation, relieved to sit after so much trudging through the neighborhood, and smiled pleasantly at Elspeth, who remained standing even though the room was supplied with several chairs beside the one Joan occupied.

"Your brother's death is a great loss to the church."

"It is."

"I understand he was a wonderous preacher."

"You never heard him preach?"

Joan realized she had made an error and immediately worked to correct it. "Oh, of course. More than once."

"He spoke from memory," said Elspeth, staring beyond Joan now as though she saw her dead brother in her mind's eye.

"He was a wonder," Joan agreed.

"Then you *never* heard my brother preach," Elspeth said looking at Joan with the searching gaze of one who has caught another in a lie. "For he always read from a text. He was more careful for every word. He would never have trusted his memory."

Joan did not know how to respond to this. In the kitchen the children had stopped playing with the cat and stood looking into the room where their mother was.

"Who *are* you, Joan Stock, and why have you come?"

Realizing that there was no point in obscuring further her purpose, Joan decided to be blunt and take whatever consequences followed.

"My husband is Matthew Stock of Chelmsford. A clothier and constable of the town. It is he who is charged with your brother's murder, but he is as innocent as a lamb, though he now finds himself in the company of wolves."

In the few seconds it took to convey these facts, Elspeth Morgan's expression changed from suspicion to amazement and then to anger. If her severe features were unwelcoming before, they were more so now and Joan felt almost afraid of what her honest admission had wrought.

"If you are who you say you are, you have your gall to come here. What, has your husband not done enough, but you are come to do worse, to aggravate my grief with your husband's name?"

Joan said, "He is innocent, falsely accused."

"So say all malefactors when they are called to account for their crimes."

"And is it not sometimes the truth, even though they declare it themselves and none believes them but God?"

"Not often, I should judge," answered the young woman after considering Joan's rebuttal. "Please be good enough to leave. See, my children know you now, the wife of a murderer. You're frightening them."

Joan glanced over to the doorway where the children were still looking in. Neither appeared to be terrified, only made curious by their mother's anger at a seemingly inoffensive stranger.

"Will you hear my husband's side of the story?"

"Why should I? He'll be heard before a magistrate."

"Yes, but will *you* be there to hear it?"

"I have my children to look after. My husband's master of a ship."

"I know."

"How do you know?"

"I was told by a certain great lord, my husband's master."

Joan was careful not to mention Cecil's name although she was sorely tempted. She knew she needed a passage through Elspeth Morgan's hostility and was at a loss to know what it might be.

"It's an easy thing to refer to a nameless lord—to claim a connection," Elspeth said. "I have known many such servants, and have found none to be worthy."

"Please, please listen," Joan said. "Suppose my husband is all he is claimed to be and more. Yet I am no more my husband than you are yours. If your husband were to turn pirate, the sin would not fall upon your head. You would remain yourself, as I am myself. We twain are wives of husbands and women too, sisters—you a daughter and a mother as I am."

For a moment Elspeth seemed to take this in although her hostile expression did not soften. Then, suddenly, she turned her face toward the kitchen. With a wave of her hand she sent her children away from the open door and in a few seconds Joan could hear them teasing the cat again.

Elspeth said, "I am preparing supper for my children. I have little time for conversation. If you have something to tell me, pray be quick, and then go. You appeal to our common womanhood, and women we are indeed. Being that we are so, I will listen, but don't expect me to believe just because we are women. Men tell lies and women are no better, though they be sisters, mothers, and whatever else."

"Well said," Joan replied, gratified that Elspeth was prepared to be reasonable. She began telling the young woman how a man had come to Chelmsford claiming to be her brother, a man who told the Stocks all about the so-called resurrection of Christopher Poole but she was not far into her tale before she noticed the skeptical cast of Elspeth's gray eyes, as though Joan were some vagabond come to the door hawking cheap goods.

"My brother was sick abed the day you say this fellow came to Chelmsford, using his name."

Joan considered this. She caught no sign of the lie in Elspeth's expression. Why should she lie about a thing like that? Joan remembered her own suspicion of her visitor's character. So that was it. Yes, an imposter. "It was another man, not your brother. But my husband and I had no way of knowing."

It was Elspeth's turn to consider. She studied Joan's face, her own less hostile than before, as though having come upon a common truth the women now could relate to each other in a different way. Elspeth said, "You say he wanted you to come to the city and disclose the fraud?"

"Yes."

"Why you? Why should he seek help elsewhere?"

"My husband is constable of the town. He has some skill in discovering that which others would fain keep to themselves for want of honesty. We thought it nothing strange that your brother—or the base fellow pretending to be he— might want his help. So we came to London, my husband to your brother's church, to be falsely accused of his murder."

For a few moments Elspeth sat very still studying Joan, as though in the older woman's countenance alone the truth could be had. Then she said, "What manner of man was it who said he was my brother?"

Joan described the imposter the best she could, including the manner of his dress, his posture, his expressions.

"Good God," Elspeth said, when Joan was finished. "You have described Humphrey Stearforth."

"Who is he?"

"A servant to Lady Elyot. My brother's living was in her gift. Stearforth was intercessor between her and him. He was often at the church and at least twice stood within this house. By your description and the knowledge you say he had of my brother's business, your visitor could have been no other."

"But why would he represent himself as your brother?" Joan asked.

"Why should Satan have tempted mother Eve?" Elspeth said, her expression darkening. But Joan could tell this new antipathy was not directed at her but at Lady Elyot's servant. Joan urged Elspeth to tell her more about Stearforth.

"He is, as you describe, a well-spoken man of goodly appearance. About thirty, I think, with neatly trimmed beard and good suit. Indeed, the doublet and jerkin you describe he wore himself during his last visit in this house."

"You likened him to the devil."

"A good likening, to my mind."

"Apparently, he betrayed your brother."

"No surprise there," Elspeth said.

"He came to your house?"

"Accompanied my brother, before he was sick. Stephen went to carry something to an old friend in the neighborhood. Stearforth remained here. Stephen was no sooner gone from the house than Stearforth comes into the kitchen where I am, throws his arms around my waist, and tells me he burns for my love."

"But he knew you were a married woman!"

"That means no more than one bean in a stew to him, for he thinks he's a great courtier. He began to woo me despite my protests and had my little son not come into the kitchen at the moment he would have had me on the floor."

"I hope he did you no harm," Joan said.

"None to my body, yet I was mightily offended and told him so. I reminded him of my marriage vows. He laughed and said vows were silly stuff, made to be broken if opportunity presented itself. He claimed such a philosophy was all the rage at court. He said there women took lovers as a matter of course; their husbands knew of it and were too occupied with their own mistresses to care. He argued that marriage was no sacrament and that priests invented it to maintain power over the laity."

"How did the matter end?" Joan asked.

"I slapped his face with all my strength and threatened him with a poker, which he seeing, it straightway cooled his ardor."

"I wonder he was not afraid of what you would tell your brother of all he did."

"So I threatened, but he mocked that too. He said I might tell Stephen all I liked but if I did, he would tell a different story. That it was I who seduced him, being as I was a wife whose husband was long at sea and naturally ripe to be plucked. He said I was a plain woman and that it strained belief that he, a gentleman and handsome, would risk his honor on such a drab as I."

"This man is beneath contempt," Joan said frowning. "Would that he were here as we speak. I should give him leave to hang. Did you tell your brother?"

Elspeth's face colored. "I meant to, not willing to give Stearforth the satisfaction of showing that I was afraid. But afraid I was in truth. I reasoned that even though Stephen believed me there would always be a place in his mind that wondered if Stearforth hadn't told the truth—that I was the temptress and not he. It was more than I could bear, the thought that he might suppose me a whore in wife's apron. So I kept silent and thank God Stearforth never came again."

"Pray he never does," Joan said. "The man is a blasphemer and lecher too—and from what you have said it is not unthinkable that he is your brother's murderer."

Despite her hatred for Stearforth, Elspeth seemed taken back by this suggestion. "But why would he kill my brother? Stearforth is no Papist. He seems to have no religion at all. What could he gain?"

"I don't know—at least not at present," Joan said. "But tell me, did your brother have enemies?"

"Well, the Papists hated him because he told the truth, because he said Poole's body had been taken by them to make a miracle where none was."

"What of his own flock? Pastors sometimes offend by their preachings."

"Not Stephen. He was the soul of gentleness. He never offended one, save he was of Rome. There he spoke with thunder and lightning. It was for that reason when Master Hopwood came from the church to give me word of his death and said that a Chelmsford clothier was arrested for the crime I took the clothier to be a Papist or his tool."

"Ah," said Joan. "Matthew never was a Papist, but a solid member of the queen's own church. Even his father was none of Rome, and he lived in Queen Mary's time."

Elspeth said she believed all that Joan had told her and smiled a little. Then she beckoned her two children in from where they played and introduced them to Joan. The boy was Simon, the girl Catherine, and they were six and seven. Joan blessed each child and said the boy would grow tall surely and the girl be as fair as any and the children looked less severe than before.

Joan asked Elspeth once again if she could remember anything her brother said while he stayed with her that might serve to clear her husband. Elspeth was silent for some time; she seemed deep in her thoughts while Joan prayed Elspeth would retrieve some word or token useful to her purpose. At length, Elspeth said, "Stephen kept a book, a diary, which he wrote in from the time he was a small boy. Even when he was sick in the bed yonder he had it with him and would write in the midst of his very fever. I was often curious to know what he wrote there but he said it was private—between him and God. He asked me to destroy every page should he die before me."

"And did you?"

"I don't have the book. He took it with him when he went back to the parsonage. It must be there yet. Master Hopwood said he would deliver my brother's books and other possessions unto me, I being his sole heir since he had neither wife nor child."

"*When* did Hopwood say he would do this?"

Elspeth shrugged. "He said in due course. I told him there was no need to make haste. This is a small cottage and there is little room. To be truthful, I planned to sell his books and give his clothing to the poor of the parish."

"You must have that diary," Joan said. "It may contain a clue."

"Clue?"

"To his murderer."

"But he never intended for me to see it. He asked that it be burned."

"That was when he didn't know he would be murdered," Joan said. "As I see it, that alters the matter."

Elspeth said she wasn't sure. "He was most definite about it. 'Burn the diary after I am dead.' "

"After I am dead, not after I am *murdered*," Joan insisted. "Look, Elspeth, did your brother not love justice?"

"Most assuredly."

"Would he wish it frustrated by ignorance?"

She shook her head.

"Then surely he would not mind his diary perused by one who loved him if in doing so his murderer's name might be brought to light."

Elspeth considered this, then said she would do it. "It's late today. I have my children to care for. I'll go the first thing in the morning."

Joan thanked her, promised to return at noon the next day, and rose to go. Elspeth apologized for her inhospitableness and pressed Joan to take a cup of ale and some sweetmeats before leaving. But Joan said she really must be gone, for she hoped to go to Lady Elyot's house before day's end. She wanted to see the man Stearforth herself, confront him, and confirm for herself that he was the same flattering rogue that stood in her kitchen telling her one lie after another.

She walked out into the sunlight and turned her face toward the city. At the same time she noticed that while the cows still grazed in the pasture opposite Elspeth's cottage the cowherd was no longer to be seen.

Late in the afternoon, Joan located Elyot House. It was built in the shape of the letter H, of two stories with many mullioned windows reflecting the pale March light. Undismayed by either the size of the house or a gate locked against her, she went down the alley beside the house and soon found the postern gate, which stood agape as though it had been left open purposely for her, an impression she took as a good omen. Across the gravel courtyard she politically avoided the main entrance and the great likelihood of being turned away and came around to the rear where there was an entrance to the kitchen.

She mounted a half dozen steps and knocked firmly.

It was a while before anyone answered although she could hear voices within and a good deal of rattling of pans and scuffing of feet. She gave the door another round of knocks and presently it was opened by a lanky horse-faced man in livery whom she assumed by his age and air of authority to be the butler or steward.

She told him she was looking for Humphrey Stearforth.

"For what purpose?" asked the man brusquely. Behind him a gravelly female voice cried out for Haws. The tall man twisted his head around and answered that he would return anon and then turned back to Joan with an expression to suggest he really didn't have time to stand in the doorway talking to strangers.

Joan said that she had an important message for him.

"What sort of message?"

"A personal one," said Joan, beginning to grow annoyed at the imperious butler, if that's what he was.

"I can give it to him," said Haws.

"That I prefer to do myself."

Haws looked at her narrowly. "Well, he's not here anymore."

"If you had told me earlier we would both have spared ourselves pains," Joan replied sharply. Haws smiled but not pleasantly. His teeth were large and yellow and they protruded from his mouth. She had never seen a man who so reminded her of a horse, with his very long face and jaw and wide-set eyes that seemed to challenge the viewer to choose one to meet.

"Can you tell me where I can find him?"

Haws made no reply. He leaned against the doorpost and folded his arms in a gesture of refusal. Joan sighed and reached into her purse, explored its contents with her fingers and made contact with a coin of the heft she thought would open the mouth of the miscreant before her. "For your memory," she said looking at him stonily to show how much she detested bribery and at the same time pressing the coin into his outstretched palm.

He flashed another horsey smile. "I'll tell you what I know. That's all I can do. Stearforth was employed here until a fortnight past when the mistress discharged him."

"Why?"

"Light fingers," Haws said, manipulating his own as

though the sign had universal significance. "I heard he had made himself free with her private letters and told tales out of doors. Lady Elyot dislikes that in a servant, as what gentlewoman would not. And so she booted him out. Last Wednesday I saw him in the Strand. He looked very prosperous. I asked him how he did—for form's sake, you understand, for I hate the man with all my heart."

Joan didn't bother to inquire the reason for Haws's professed antipathy. She supposed him the kind of man who hated a great number of people and was hated in turn, but she was curious about Stearforth's present business. Had he found a new employer, perhaps somewhat less scrupulous about her privacy?

"Ah," said Haws, nodding his head up and down. "He was mysterious about that. Of course I asked him how he did and what he did. He answered that he did very well but would say only that he had a new master, of more substance than his last. That he was busy about his master's business and discretion forbade him to say else about it."

"You say you saw him at Paul's."

"By the bookstalls."

"Examining books?"

Haws laughed. "Talking to several other men."

She wanted to ask what men. In her mind's eye she was already at Paul's herself, watching for Stearforth, thinking that if she didn't see him she could ask one of these other men Haws mentioned. But the strident female voice that had called from within earlier repeated the demand that Haws was wanted. Now by the mistress of the house herself, and Joan knew her interview with the butler was over.

Haws closed the door without another word. The rudesby, she thought. She regretted now that she had been so generous in her bribe. He really hadn't given her that much information. And yet if Stearforth did haunt Paul's, he might not be that difficult to find. His face was engraved upon her memory.

* * *

She had been feeding her children and when Elspeth answered the door she thought it might be Joan Stock returning with a question she had forgotten to ask. But he who was standing there when she opened to him pushed the door so she couldn't close it.

"Good day, Goody Morgan. Don't be so quick to be inhospitable. I'm no stranger to your house. Surely, if you can entertain a murderer's wife you can abide my company."

Stearforth was dressed in an old cloak and smelled of the field and cattle. She noticed he had mud on his boots. The next thing Elspeth thought of were her children. They had come into the room in response to the knocking, just as their mother had and were standing there looking up at the towering man they had seen before. Sensitive to their mother's apprehension, they regarded Stearforth warily as he strode into the room with his muddy boots and took the best chair for himself, stretching out his long legs, making himself comfortable in a way their father did when he came home from the sea.

Elspeth spoke sharply, although there was a quiver in her voice. "What do you want here? You've no business here, now my brother's dead. Your business is with his successor, or with Master Hopwood."

"Hopwood is his successor, but I have no business with Hopwood, either. I am no longer Lady Elyot's servant. I've left to seek opportunities elsewhere. And indeed I've found them."

He looked at her boldly under his heavy brows, as though waiting for her to ask who his new employer was. In fact, she was curious, but also determined not to please him by asking. She would not satisfy his pride any more than she would his lust. She stood with her jaw set, her arms folded across her breasts, staring down at him.

After a moment Stearforth turned his attention to the children and beckoned them to come to his side. He lifted the girl into his lap with one hand and with the other drew the boy close to him. "It's a hot day for the month. I wouldn't mind a drink. What have you?"

"Nothing for you," she said, trying to keep her voice even, trying not to show fear.

"Oh, come now Elspeth. What's past is past. Forgive like the good Christian you claim to be. You misconstrued my meaning last time I was here. I aimed at no more than a little harmless flirtation. If you thought I meant more you misread my character."

"I doubt I misread your character or your intention," she said.

He bent forward, retracting his long legs. "I said I was thirsty. Get me something to drink and do it now."

As he spoke he clutched her son tightly to him so that she could see the look of surprise and pain on the little white face.

"You go into the kitchen and play a good housewife's part or shall I show the boy a thing in my pocket?"

"I'll go," she said, her voice breaking. "Just don't hurt my son or daughter."

Behind her she heard Stearforth laugh genially and tell the children how queer their mother was that she had such difficulty understanding the queen's English. Why one would think he had ill designs upon her and the children, when all he intended was good. He asked the children if they knew what good was and received no response.

Elspeth poured some ale in a cup, her hand trembling so that she nearly spilled the ale. She hurried back where Stearforth was. He was still clutching the children. The girl was sobbing quietly.

He had to release her son to take the cup. He took a long draught and said: "You know, I am often in your neighborhood now. I could stop by frequently if the mood struck me. What did you tell Stock's wife?"

"Nothing," Elspeth said.

He regarded her skeptically. "Give me some credit, Elspeth. Do you take me for a fool? I watched your house a good hour while you spoke with the woman. Don't tell me you sat in silence. It's unthinkable that two women should do so."

"We talked of my brother. She tried to persuade me that her husband was innocent."

"And of course you believed every word."

"I told her to leave."

"After an hour?"

"Shortly after she arrived, after I found out who she was. But she would not leave."

He watched her while he raised the cup and finished the ale. Then he wiped his mouth and beard with the back of his hand and let the girl run to her mother's side. He rose and walked outside. "Be wise, Elspeth. If the Stock woman returns let the constable know of it. Her husband might as well be dead, so great the evidence is against him. She herself is sought by the law—as an accomplice. You are doing your children a disservice by entertaining her in your house, and dishonoring your late brother's memory. Why, the law might suppose you were implicated in your brother's death. You are his heir, are you not?"

Elspeth said nothing. The outrageous and shameful accusation struck her dumb. She concentrated her fury in her gaze, while he stood calmly looking up at the sky, like a seaman searching for a star to steer by.

"You have handsome children, Elspeth. It would be horrible if something were to happen to them. Some accident I mean. Maybe I or one of my friends will keep a watch on the house. Just to make sure nothing ill befalls the children. You understand. Oh, don't bother to thank me. Consider my concern a gesture of friendship, a way of making amends for the little misunderstanding we had."

He turned his eyes from the sky and looked at her intently. He smiled and said, "By the way, did Stock's wife saw where she was staying in London?"

"She didn't say."

"What a shame, then. Yet she will be found—and taken. Never fear. Justice will be done in Stephen's case. Remember what I said. I'll be keeping my eye on the house."

She watched him walk toward the lane. She called out after him, "Stearforth, did you kill Stephen? Did you murder my brother?"

He stopped and turned slowly. "Remember," he said, as though her question had no greater purpose than to inquire of his health. "I'll be watching you."

9

J_{OAN} left Elyot House, her eagerness to trace Stearforth to his current employer sending her toward Paul's, forgetful of how tired she was and how frightened, a stolid determination ruling her. What else had she to do but keep busy while Matthew languished in prison and the queen's secretary, frustrated by his ignorance of his enemy, meditated a revenge to come when Joan should have found the enemy out.

Even so late in the day a great crowd milled around the cathedral. The bookstalls there were full of customers and a motley assembly of gallants, gentlemen, tradesmen, foreigners (how they stuck out in their outlandish dress, yapping in their outlandish tongues), common merchants, and city officials testified to the extent that the city used the cathedral as a common meeting place as well as a house of God. There were women too, some very respectable-looking and usually accompanied by some man for safety's sake. Also a devil's plenty of whores sidling up to the men, mincing, leering from round painted eyes like puppets'.

Joan watched the scene for a while, at too great a distance to identify individual faces. She pictured Stearforth in her mind; under her breath she pronounced his name as though doing so might invoke his presence. She looked about her and, drawing nearer, searched the faces of strangers. She began to wonder. The man she remembered had been square-faced, heavy-browed, his beard nicely scissored, and black. His eyes were brown, or were they black? In Chelmsford he had held his hat in his hand; his hair had been pushed back and was thinning at the temples. His pronounced brow; that had been the distinguishing feature, how it dominated the face overshadowing mouth and jaw. But out of doors all the men wore hats and most had beards of the same fashionable cut as Stearforth's. Her confidence in finding the man she sought faltered.

She began an aimless patrol of the bookstalls and then moved up on the church porch where there was so great a multitude she could hardly penetrate it. It was supper time and the porch was a convenient meeting place for gentlemen bent on an evening's adventure in the darkening city where the only lights, except for heaven's, were borne in one's own hand. But nowhere in the crowd did she see a face that she would swear was Stearforth's.

Close to despair and concerned about the gathering darkness, she saw a beggar standing by the church door. As she approached, she saw he was a young man with only one leg and his right arm was withered. He was propped up against the wall like a broom. She wondered how he managed to get around.

She put a few pennies in his outstretched hand and he thanked her.

"God bless you," she said, lingering in front of him. "I wonder if you could help me."

The beggar, who was very dirty and had a face so covered with boils and pustules that she thought they must surely cause him pain, had taken the coins and put them inside his tattered cloak. He looked up expectantly.

"What you will, ma'am."

"I'm looking for a man. His name is Humphrey Stearforth."

The beggar's face took on a puzzled expression. "I know no one by that name."

"He's a tall man with sable beard, beetle-browed somewhat, a good dresser, a great talker."

The beggar laughed. "You've described half the gentlemen that haunt these precincts. What do you want of him?"

"For a piece of work," she said, taken by surprise at the directness of the question but supplying a plausible answer in an instant.

"A piece of work," nodded the beggar sagely. "Mark you, if it's the kind of work I suppose it is, there's a plenty of young men who'll do it and ask not the reason but only a fee."

"I suspect Stearforth is such a man," Joan said, "if I could but find him."

"Now failing that," said the beggar, "you might consider an alternative."

"Alternative?"

"I mean another handy gentleman looking for a cure for idleness. Would this work be of a legal nature, may I ask?"

"Oh, I need no lawyer," Joan said, thinking she had had quite enough of that breed since Christmas when she and Matthew were enmeshed in the murders at the Middle Temple.

"A soldier then," said the beggar, making a little motion of his hand as though he were thrusting with a knife.

"No, I would describe him as an intelligencer. One quick of wit, fleet of foot, not overly scrupulous, and totally devoted to whoever pays his fee."

The beggar laughed. "Now that sounds as much like a lawyer as any other profession, but since you declare you will have none of that kind, I think I have a man who might serve your turn, and if does not he can name twenty more that shall. Indeed, he may even know this Stearforth of whom you speak, since he would seem to be of the same tribe."

Joan asked the man's name and where he might be found.

"Why, his name is Moseby. He will do anything for money, anything or I am no true man but a skulking dog. Moseby can be found here of days, and some evenings. Although I haven't seen him around this even. Try in the afternoons. He rises late from his bed and then comes to Paul's to search out invitations to supper."

"How will I know this Moseby?"

"Trust me to point him out. I swear he makes his dinner of pigeon droppings, then stands about looking as though he had business. He has one good suit which he wears from one month to the next, a surly manner, but he knows how to do work and keep his mouth shut and in his trade that's practically everything."

"Moseby, you said? Does he have a Christian name?"

"Moseby is the only name I know him by and consider myself fortunate to know that, for he's not of a mind to tell his name to many."

"I lay at the Rose, under the name of Mistress Gray," Joan said. She gave the beggar another tuppence and decided that she had made an ally in her quest. If Moseby was the man the beggar said he was he was likely to know Stearforth.

She returned to the Blue Boar, told the innkeeper she must return to Chelmsford, and went directly to the Rose, a smaller Inn not far from Paul's. She took a chamber and told the innkeeper her husband was arriving by ship within a few days and would call for her. She told the lie with a lump in her throat. God knew whether she would see Matthew in a few days or ever, for although he was but a few miles away he might as well have been in France for all the loneliness she felt.

Matthew had protested all the way back to his cell that he was innocent, but his guard merely assured him that all accused murderers professed the same and he should hardly distinguish himself by such a plea. "Now if you would stand out, fellow, admit you are guilty as sin. Make peace with heaven, if not with man, and be done with this noxious caterwauling."

"I saw the man I am supposed to have murdered in the magistrate's chamber," Matthew said as the jailer ushered him into his cell and slammed the iron door behind him.

The jailer laughed. "It was a ghost, you saw. Then that proves your guilt. No ghosts haunt the innocent."

"But he *wasn't* Graham, don't you see?" Matthew yelled after the fleeing form of the jailer. "He was an imposter. The imposter was in the judge's chamber. It was a trap to get me to come to London, to put me in the place where—"

He stopped when he realized that the jailer was gone. And that he was not alone in the cell. He turned around to see the other prisoner, his new cellmate, Matthew presumed.

"Thomas Buck," said the man, who was taller than Matthew, trimmer and younger, with a carefully cropped beard but in ragged clothes. He spoke with a London accent and his speech was clear and deliberate and his eyes had the expression of one who had not been imprisoned for a long time.

Buck extended his hand for Matthew to shake, and seeing no reason not to, Matthew complied. He felt the soft flesh. Buck was a gentleman, despite his garb, an impression further enhanced by the smooth lines of the man's face.

"With what are you charged?" asked Buck.

"Murder," said Matthew. "Falsely."

He watched Buck's face to see his response, expecting disbelief of the sort the jailer had displayed.

"I believe it," said Buck. Buck sat down on the stone floor and motioned Matthew to join him. "I am in the same position. Falsely accused by my wife's brother."

"Of murder?" asked Matthew.

"Theft. The swine said I took certain goods of his, which I believe he never had. He has always hated me, ever since I married his sister and she died shortly thereafter."

Matthew was curious to know how the wife had died,

but was thinking how to ask when Buck supplied the answer as though he read Matthew's mind.

"Of sickness—a fever. It struck one day and she was buried the next. She was round with our child at the time." Buck's voice broke in the telling of his misery. Matthew, who was suspicious before, now felt more at ease with his fellow sufferer.

"Tell me *your* story," Buck said.

Matthew did. He told Buck all about the parson who had come to Chelmsford who was no parson at all, who was an imposter whom he had seen only an hour before in the magistrate's chamber mocking as Matthew was arraigned.

"So the real parson never came, then?" said Buck.

"I met him first when he lay dead and bleeding in the church belfry. My own knife lay a few feet away. My initial was etched in the haft. The curate was in my company when I found the body. He raised the hue and cry against me and there was another man, a pocky old fellow with white hair and villainous eye who I think was the sexton of the church. He falsely said he saw me do the murder, but before God, I never did. The sexton lied."

"Why should he do that?" Buck asked.

"Why? Who knows—perhaps he did the murder himself, or was paid by the real murderer to accuse me."

Buck thought for a minute then said, "Well, Matthew, if I can be so bold as to address you by your Christian name, you've made a believer out of me. Your story has the honest ring of truth in every part. I don't wonder the magistrate was taken in by this wealth of specious evidence. It was even so in my own case."

"Why how was that?" asked Matthew, interested.

"My brother-in-law suborned witnesses against me. He found a shopkeeper in Chelsea who claimed I brought the stolen goods to him to sell them, which thing I never did since there were never any goods to steal, much less sell. But I will make myself free of these charges in good time and live to see all of my accusers hanged for their perjury."

Buck nodded his head confidently and stared off at the

stone wall opposite him. Matthew couldn't resist asking his new cellmate how this turn in his fortunes was to be effected.

In responding, Buck lowered his voice as though he feared the jailer might be lurking in the passage beyond and said, "I've had good advice."

"From whom?"

"Why a friend, a friend who knows how to deal with these magistrates and jailers, who understands the game, so to speak."

Matthew wondered that Buck could so casually dismiss his predicament as a game. Theft was as much a hanging offense as murder. The young man and Matthew shared the same fate if they could not refute their accusers.

"I am not going to deny my guilt," said Buck after a few moments of silence.

"Not deny it? Then how do you intend to be free of the charge."

"A trade, friend Matthew, a simple trade." Buck turned to Matthew and looked at him intently. There was so little light in the cell that Matthew could not detect the man's eyes but they seemed at the moment especially large and luminous with practical wisdom. "My brother-in-law is a wealthy man, whose wealth is gotten in part by avoidance of certain taxes and impositions he is ever at pains to keep concealed. Therefore, have I been advised by this friend I mention, to offer in exchange for my own liberty information about my brother-in-law to damn him in the eyes of the law and draw into the same net a dozen seeming-honest citizens of the town whose private dealings would not stand up to scrutiny. Which information I am prepared to give. In return I will walk out a free man and my brother-in-law and his henchmen can go to hell."

Matthew heard this plan with no little admiration for the planner. It was certainly logical, and it had an element of justice in it, for the malicious brother-in-law and his accomplices would get their deserts for their perjuries. What the magistrate could not correct because of his inability to see into the human heart, the accused man would rectify by a simple negotiation—a lie for a lie—and somehow the result would be a higher truth.

Or would it?

Matthew was pondering that question when his fellow inmate spoke again.

"In a matter of a few days I'll be free. Say, Matthew, you're a good man. I can read it in your face and I believe every word you've said about your innocence. It's a shame you can't use such a stratagem."

"How do you mean?"

"Why, I mean do as I do, plan as I have planned. Is there not someone whom you could lay the blame upon? It stands to reason that there is. You're accused of murdering a churchman, of being a Papist agent. It requires little wit to see that were you guilty as charged you would be acting under orders—orders from someone higher up, so to speak."

"Go on," said Matthew.

"Well, my meaning is that were you to offer to reveal the identity of that person, say in exchange for your skin, you might find your offer taken."

"The authorities are not likely to let me go free for supplying that information. Why, they could gain the same results with torture."

"Ah," said Buck excitedly. "But all the more reason, friend Matthew, for you to make the offer. You'll save them the trouble of torturing you. And you, in turn, will be spared the pains. It makes perfectly good sense to me. They'll have the truth from you, you know. They have ways of making a man talk his head off, though he has thrice-stitched his mouth with oaths to God and angels. I could tell you a hundred tales, horrible to imagine."

Matthew had no interest in hearing such stories. Thoughts of torture and death had been too much on his mind as it was, but he was intrigued by this man Buck— and also suspicious. Was Buck a well-meaning friend, eager to share a means of escape with him out of the goodness of his heart, or a false friend, interested only in encouraging him to betray Cecil?

"I would be loath to perjure myself," Matthew said.

"Perjure? Why not, if that is the only way justice may be done? Consider, Matthew. Perjury is condemned because it impedes justice."

"It is condemned because it is the same as bearing false witness, a thing expressly condemned in the ninth of the Commandments."

"Tush, tush, Matthew, now you speak as a churchman yourself. But be sensible. Grant me that perjury, in the eyes of the law, impedes justice."

"I cannot deny it does."

"Well, then, if justice already be impeded by false testimony of another, how is justice betrayed by false testimony that merely corrects the first? I say the end justifies the means."

Matthew thought Buck was beginning to sound like a lawyer. He professed his inability to follow Buck's logic, although he understood it very well. Buck went on undaunted.

"Perjury as a remedy for perjury's ill is no crime or sin, Matthew. I mean no more than that. The principle is irrefutable. A practical man cannot deny it. Think deeply, then, who might have put you to the task of murdering the parson?"

"I cannot think of one," Matthew said.

Buck emitted a sigh of exasperation. "Well," he said. "In due time perhaps a name may come. Indeed, I may provide one to you at length, should your imagination fail you. Let me be your teacher in these mysteries. That you are an honest man is more than obvious here. You need someone more schooled in practical wisdom rather than in these Christian homilies you treat as eternal laws. Trust me."

Matthew looked at his cellmate where Buck sat in the shadows and nodded as though in agreement.

* * *

Joan ordered supper sent up to her chamber, picked at her solitary meal, felt a powerful need of sleep. She was in her nightgown when she heard the knock at her door. She threw her wool cloak about her and asked who it was, hoping it was the host or his boy who had brought up her supper and not the constable's men come to arrest her.

"Moseby," said the voice on the other side of the door.

For a moment she made no sense of the name, then remembered. But was it Moseby indeed or an impersonator? A name was a thing easily acquired in a city of strangers. One could put it on, take it off, lend it out, like a mask.

"I don't know any Moseby," she said, deciding caution in such a case was better than boldness.

For a moment there was nothing but silence beyond the door. Then her visitor spoke again:

"Jacob Moseby. If you are the woman who sought me at Paul's earlier today. A friend told me where you lay and I came after."

Joan opened the door. Out in the passage stood a man with the wary look of a fugitive, a hesitant and vulnerable man, no leather-vested officer as she had feared. "Come in, then."

Moseby stepped into the chamber. The beggar's description had been uncannily accurate. Moseby was lean and pinch-faced; he wore a tattered cloak and a broad-brimmed hat with a high crown. A silver earring dangled in his left ear and the dark strands of hair descending from beneath the hat were lank and oily.

In an instant Joan decided what she would tell this lean and hungry man before her. She would say nothing of murder and arrests, would not so much as mention her husband's name or the name of the dead priest or of his church. She knew Moseby's kind. Little that happened in the City passed them by. Such men were the perfect calendar of the news, and they lived on the edge of the law so that the very hint of prison or authority sent them to ground. She didn't want to scare him off before she discovered for herself where Stearforth was or whom he served.

"Are you discreet?" she asked, making a doubtful face to draw him out.

"As a dead man."

She nodded and pointed toward a chair for him to sit in. She walked to the bed and sat down on its edge to enlarge the distance between them. Strange men were ever dangerous company for a woman alone; Joan had not forgotten that simple truth. She would not tempt him with a mere foot or two, not as she was half dressed, the door fast behind them, and a bed in sight to put mischief into a brain already disposed to it. There was but one candlestick in the room and it held a lone taper that flickered; in the hearth the ruins of an earlier fire gave off a glow. So much for the light by which she studied Moseby's face.

"Well, I do have work for the right man," she began, slowly as though she were still doubtful about her visitor's qualifications. "He whom I would employ must know the City."

"Like the back of my hand," he said.

"And its more often-encountered citizens."

"I am still your man."

"Particularly one."

"Only say his name. There's a goodly chance I know him well. If he frequents Paul's churchyard, why I am blood brother to every second gentleman and a close cousin to the rest."

"Marry, you *might* be the man I need," she said. "Do you know one named Humphrey Stearforth."

Moseby quivered a little at the name. It was an obvious sign of recognition, but he acted as though he had to search his inventory of names to be sure.

"I might know such a fellow."

"Do you know him or not?"

"I said I *might*. It would depend on why he was wanted."

"He owes me money—more, he wronged my daughter."

Moseby smiled slightly at this and Joan wasn't sure whether he had detected the falsity of her hasty invention or merely understood her professed motives. Stearforth was a lecher, among his other crimes. Perhaps he was infamous for it.

"You want me to avenge your daughter's sullied honor, or merely get your money back or both?"

"Let's begin with the first," Joan said, thinking quickly. "But I don't want you to kill him."

"That's good," said Moseby. "Murder is not exactly my humor. I prefer more subtle shifts."

"I'm sure you do," said Joan drily. "To be truthful, I have something more elaborate in mind, something that requires a certain deftness—and also absolute secrecy. And for both these skills I am prepared to pay generously."

Moseby nodded and folded his arms. "How generously?"

Joan named a sum, having no idea what such treachery demanded on the market. Moseby countered with a higher number and they settled on a figure in between.

"Your first duty is to find him."

"No sooner commanded than done. The next?"

"To bring word of it to me, along with an account of his habits—where he lies of nights and for whom he works and the nature of that work."

"Give me but a day."

"You have it," Joan said, rising from the bed.

But Moseby continued to sit in his chair. He seemed more relaxed now, now that their bargain had been struck, and he looked at Joan with an expression of mild interest.

"Our business is concluded for now," Joan said abruptly, suddenly flushing under his direct stare which seemed to take in not only her face but her entire body. "My husband will return shortly. He knows nothing of what I intend for Stearforth and would not be pleased to find a strange man in his room."

Moseby let out a little laugh and stood up. "I don't think you have a husband," he said. "I doubt you have a wronged daughter. I suspect it was you who were wronged and want revenge for yourself."

Joan was about to counter this version of events before she realized it was superior to her own. She forced a smile.

"Then you will appreciate my determination. A woman's vengeance is not to be taken lightly."

"There are other consolations," Moseby said moving toward her.

"I said my husband would return shortly."

He reached out and put his hands on her shoulders. Quivering, she looked up into his face. "Do you want the money or not?" she said. "The walls are thin. If you want more, you shall have to fight for it and suppress my cries for help. I promise you I have prodigious lungs for screaming. Do it. Put me to the test."

At this threat he pulled back and smiled again as though the whole thing were a joke.

"Bring by noon tomorrow what information I need and you shall be paid. Do that much for me and we shall see what other services follow."

"Where shall we meet—here?"

"No, in the City. You name it."

She was relieved when he named a place she knew that was sufficiently public, a tavern only a few steps away from Paul's churchyard. When he left she bolted the door behind him and scolded herself for the dangerous game she had played. Matthew would have had a fit had he known of it.

10

*T*HE next morning Joan awoke early to go to Elspeth's cottage. The shipmaster's young wife had promised to secure her brother's diary, and Joan supposed Elspeth would have had sufficient time during the previous afternoon to accomplish her mission. Joan planned to be back in the City in time to meet Moseby and receive his report. If Fortune smiled, as that Good Housewife sometimes did, Joan might have as much information as Cecil needed by nightfall.

But when she arrived at Elspeth's cottage she felt at once something was amiss. Nothing seemed outwardly changed. The cottage looked as it had the day before, and across the lane the same congregation of dappled cows grazed indolently. But she saw no sign of the cowherd who tended them.

She knocked at the door for some time and heard stirring within and what sounded like whispers, but no one answered. She called out Elspeth's name and thinking that she was gone and it might be the children she heard she called out their names too. Still there was no response. She would have supposed them all gone had it not been for the smoking chimney, the whispers she had heard, and her own intuition that the cottage was inhabited.

She stepped off the doorstep into the soft earth of an old flower bed and walked around to the back of the cottage. She found herself in a kitchen garden yet to be tilled and planted for the new season. About twenty feet from the cottage was a privy made of weathered boards. The door stood open. She walked out to look inside, then went back to the cottage. There were no windows in the rear of the structure but there was a back door. She pressed her ear against its rough wood and listened. At first there was a hollow silence; then she heard a titter of childish laughter.

It was unthinkable that Elspeth would leave her children alone in the cottage, or that the children, being there, would laugh were their mother in danger. Joan went around to the front of the cottage and walked toward the lane, but only walked far enough until she believed the hedge concealed her. There she waited for a long time, peering through the thick foliage.

After a while, Elspeth's little son came out. He was carrying a pail in his hand, swinging it back and forth, and she could hear him singing, but didn't recognize the words. Behind him came the cat Joan had seen the day before, walking deliberately across the yard as though it were stalking the child. When the boy noticed the cat, he put the pail down and called the animal, but the cat scurried past him, coming so close to where Joan was concealed behind the hedge that she thought surely the boy would see her.

But the boy was intent on his pursuit and scurried around in some low-growing bushes as the cat continued to stay out of his reach. With a moment's reflection, Joan decided to confront the mystery directly. She stepped out from behind the hedge, leaned down, and swept the cat up in her arms. Surprised at her sudden appearance, the boy froze and looked up at her, his eyes round, glistening. He started to move away but she held him.

"Oh, please don't go," she said.

The boy stopped again, but seemed on the verge of escape. He looked up at her, his little white face a mixture of curiosity and fear.

"Is your mother home?"

The boy shook his head. His eyes told Joan the truth.

There was no point in giving the child the lie. Joan nodded. "Well, I trust she will be home soon if you're worried about being alone. I won't ask to come in, just to stand here by the hedge. Would you like your cat?"

The animal had been content in Joan's embrace and was no more reproachful for being extended toward the child, limp and glassy-eyed. The boy made no movement. He continued to stare at Joan warily.

Joan was at a loss to understand this new manner in the family. Had she offended Elspeth in some way to bring this disdain upon her? Surely, Elspeth was inside the cottage, perhaps peering from the window even as Joan spoke to the woman's son.

Then she looked beyond the child and saw Elspeth step out on the doorstep in full view. Frowning, she called her son to come in. Her voice was shrill, almost hysterical, as though Joan represented some great danger. When the boy didn't move at his mother's command, Elspeth crossed the yard at a quick pace, seized him by the hand, and started to pull him back. "Go away, Mistress Stock. Leave us alone."

"But what have I done?" Joan protested.

"Enough to give us more trouble than we deserve. Now let us be. Go back to Chelmsford."

"I can't leave my husband."

"Let him look to God for his salvation, if he is deserving of it."

By now Elspeth had her son in tow and was halfway back to the cottage. Joan called after her. "Your brother's diary. Did you find it?"

Elspeth didn't answer. She was already within the cottage again, the door shut firmly behind her.

For some time Joan stared at the cottage, perplexed by this sea change. What was Elspeth thinking?

* * *

Matthew's suspicion of his new cellmate was not allayed by the man's first comment of the day, which was to ask whether Matthew had given any thought to his proposal of the night before.

"Touching what?" Matthew replied with a yawn, as though it was too early in the morning to recall what had been talked of hours earlier, when the truth was that he remembered every word.

The other man grimaced with annoyance. "My device of shifting blame to another. I recommended it to you. Consider it, friend Matthew. It might well save your life."

"Ah, I wouldn't know where to begin," Matthew said. He rose from against the wall, his bones protesting the movement and yet aching for it. He felt the pain of worry in his heart, penetrating like a searing needle.

"Easy," Buck went on confidently. "Answer their questions. If they ask who gave you orders to knife the parson, say it was this lord or that. I wouldn't be surprised if they don't suggest some names to you. Graham was hated by the Papists, which makes all Papist sympathizers suspect and there are a good dozen of them at court. On the other hand, the plotter may be a Puritan wanting to give the Papists a bad name. In this world anything's possible."

Matthew thought about this. It was true. In this world anything was possible. Corruption was universal. A good man was hardly to be found in these days of shame. The whole world was worse than it had been before the days of Noah. "I'll think on it."

"Please yourself," said Buck with a reassuring smile. "But think hard and soon. You may have but one chance; once you are tried, time to strike a bargain will be passed."

Breakfast came, such as it was. The guard passed two bowls of gruel through the iron bars and then two slices of moldy bread that Matthew doubted would tempt a rat from his corner.

"Fine fare for one who is wont to dine with gentlemen," said Buck with a heavy sigh.

Matthew nodded, thinking of Joan and what she might be

doing—and eating. He sniffed at the gruel, felt the texture of the bread and gave both to Buck, who for all his professed delicacy of appetite consumed both with the greatest relish.

The tavern was full to overflowing. Joan was unable to find an empty stool. She got a cup of wine from a passing drawer and took up a position just outside the front door where she could spot Moseby when he appeared. Her feet were tired from the long walk to Elspeth's house and yet she was too excited to be preoccupied with her discomfort. She felt she was on the track of something important. Elspeth's sudden and mysterious hostility confirmed it.

It was long past noon when Moseby appeared and in fact she had difficulty recognizing him at first, for he was dressed differently—and better—in a doublet of Lincoln green and hose of the same color, plain worsted but without patches. He wore a short cloak and a velvet hat. She had no doubt the villain had put the money she had given him on his back. She could only hope he would have something to show for his efforts.

Moseby saluted her with an ingratiating smile and led her back into the tavern. He had no trouble finding the stool Joan had sought in vain in an inconspicuous corner. Joan was glad to sit.

After he had ordered a tankard of ale for himself, she bent forward conspiratorily and asked, "Well, what word of my man Stearforth? Will I be revenged or no?"

"He is employed."

"By whom?"

Moseby shrugged. A drawer brought the tankard and Moseby looked to Joan, as though it were her duty to pay for it. Joan paid, annoyed both at Moseby's assumption that she would and his artful delay in telling her what she wanted to know.

"I know where he can be found. If revenge is all you want, I can arrange that well enough."

"I'll take my revenge in due time," Joan said. "But I would know whom he serves. And where he lives."

"He has a room in Fleet Street. He lives with a widow named Porter. He serves someone in the City, a great person, or so my informant tells it, for they do not remember when he has had so much money about him. He pays for all, where before he pled the pauper as often as a round of drinks was served."

Joan sighed with exasperation. "Would this great person have a name, or does he go by *that* appendage?"

Moseby laughed and plucked at his chin. "To tell the truth, Mistress, I have not come upon his name, although I have seen the two together in the Strand—Stearforth in a good suit of clothes and his companion in a better."

"And how do you know he with whom you have seen Stearforth is his master and not some underling?"

Moseby made a shrewd face of one whose genius has been grossly underestimated. "I cannot tell. But if this personage be an underling, then we have far mismeasured the degree of Stearforth's success."

"What if you follow this man to *his* place of residence?"

"That would take much time. I might have to linger in Paul's churchyard for, oh, two or three more days."

"Then linger if that's what is required," she said, exasperated.

"It will cost a bit more—all the lingering you speak of."

"I am hardly surprised. In London everything costs more, doesn't it?"

"Well now, madam, surely that's God's truth, it is indeed," said Moseby, grinning wolfishly.

She reached into her purse and offered him a certain sum. They haggled over the price while Moseby drained the tankard and explained how difficult it was to find anyone in London, much less follow him through the streets to discover his dwelling place.

"I'm sure you can do it, if anyone can," she said dryly, handing him the sum he had wheedled out of her.

She left Moseby ordering another tankard and proceeded

on a venture she expected would produce more immediate results. She hoped that somewhere between the tavern and St. Crispin's it would occur to her just how she was to secure Stephen Graham's diary, now that his sister had become an enemy.

It took her a good two hours of scouring shops and stalls to find what she wanted and when she found it all she bundled it back to the inn. Esconced in her chamber, Joan began to remake herself. She applied herself to the task with cool efficiency, changing her own good clothes for the poorer, covering her head with an old woolen scarf, and, in short, adding a score of years to her appearance by these contrivances. Then she practiced walking with a stoop, propping herself up with a cane with one hand while in the other she held a fresh loaf of bread she had bought from a baker in Cordon Street.

By late afternoon she was at St. Crispin's, staring up at its rather severe front and considering her chances of encountering the curate Hopwood who had seen her before and might recognize her in her disguise. But she would have to risk that possibility.

She approached the side door and knocked. In a short time, the door was answered and she looked up to see not Hopwood, as she feared she might, but a stout, graying man who said his name was Motherwell, the sexton.

"I'm come with a gift of thanks for Master Graham."

"He's dead," Motherwell said bluntly. "You've not heard? Murdered he was. All London knows of it."

Joan made an expression of dismay, and tried to control the nervousness in her voice.

"I had not heard, sir," she said, knowing that the sexton was hardly entitled to the honor of being addressed so but knowing too that it would flatter him. "I came to bring him this loaf—in return for a service he did for my son."

"And what service would that be?" asked Motherwell.

"Why my son in Shrewsbury gave him his diary to

peruse—to see if anything therein were out of keeping with Holy Writ."

Motherwell looked confused by this explanation, and Joan went on.

"My son would enter the church, you see, and he expressed many pious thoughts in this little book, which I brought to Master Graham petitioning him to read therein—only to determine if there were any blasphemy in it."

"Oh, I see," said Motherwell. "It's a book, then, that your son let the parson have. Well, there are a devil's plenty of books in his study here and all must be carted off to his sister's house, and I must do the carting. I suppose you might step in, then. If you find it among all his, 'tis all one with me, who has thereby one less book to cart."

Joan entered, hardly believing in her fortune, and followed the sexton down a long hall and into a spacious well-lighted room that by its books and other furnishings had been the murdered cleric's.

"What manner of book was it?" asked Motherwell from behind her after she had spent a few moments perusing the books in shelves and stacked on the floor.

"Well, it was a diary of sorts," Joan said, without looking behind her. "It was not large, bound in brown leather. I recall." She wished now that she had had a better description of the book from Elspeth Morgan.

"I have much to do elsewhere in the church," said the sexton, self-importantly. "You may look as you like and take the book with you. You can find your way out, I trust."

"Oh yes," said Joan. "I surely can, and many thanks to you, sir, for your kindness. My son would be greatly grieved not to have his book back again. It is as dear to his heart as is his mother."

With relief, Joan heard the door shut behind her. The unpleasant-looking sexton had been as courteous as she would have wished, and yet there was in his face something that alerted her to danger. She looked at the shelves of books and the piles of books on the floor. It was clear that already Motherwell had begun his work of packing

Graham's possessions for removal. She wondered where to begin her search. She remembered what Elspeth had said about her brother's writing habits. He had written in his diary each day and always kept it with him. It followed in Joan's mind, therefore, that she was unlikely to find the book wedged between the learned tomes that crowded the shelves. Indeed, if the book was so portable it was not likely to be large, and probably without inscription on its spine.

In one corner of the room was Graham's desk—a flat table without drawers. A carved box sat on the top containing a variety of quills and a bottle of ink and next to this a stack of pamphlets all, Joan discovered on quick glance, dealing with various religious controversies in which Graham had been embroiled. Some had been authored by Graham himself and attacked the Church of Rome on one hand or one of the more strident opponents on the other. She also found a broadside describing the resurrection of Christopher Poole upon which Graham had scribbled derisive comments.

She examined all the books heaped upon the floor, of which there must have been three score or more, then went to the shelves, thinking the diary might have been placed among the larger volumes, but did not find what she so earnestly sought. Then it occurred to her that a book of so personal a nature might reasonably be concealed. The question was where.

Joan considered that the diary would need to be accessible to the minister, otherwise writing in it would be too inconvenient. That meant the diary was in this room, which meant . . .

She remembered Elspeth's account of her brother's habits. He had written in his diary while lying in bed, she had said. Had he done so out of necessity, because there were no proper writing surfaces in Elspeth's cottage, or because he preferred to write in bed?

The room she now stood in was the minister's study and nothing more. But surely his sleeping chamber was nearby.

She remembered seeing a staircase off to the right as she had been lead into the study. Venturing beyond the room into which she had been admitted by the sexton was risky, but she knew too that having entered the parsonage once, she was not likely to gain admission again.

In the passage beyond the study she was gratified to hear all silent in the house. The sexton had said he had some work in the church proper. Well and good, Joan thought, so he stayed there. She went to the stairs.

The upper story of the house consisted of a narrow passage off of which there were several doors, leading she supposed to bedchambers. The first of these was a sparsely furnished room of which Joan had the sense it was rather for guests than regular occupants, for there were no personal articles anywhere to be seen and the room had the musty smell of disuse. The other room was obviously that inhabited by Graham. There was a large cabinet against one wall and a poster bed against the other; a little table by the bed upon which stood a lamp and about a dozen books; and two curved-back chairs, one at the table and the other against a wall, below a wooden crucifix, the room's only religious adornment. Heavy curtains covered a single window.

Here the sexton was clearly yet to begin his task, for nothing seemed disturbed from what it undoubtedly was when Graham left it on the morning of his murder. Joan at once examined the books by the minister's bedside, finding them all, where the titles were not Latin, works of religious disputation. Nor was the cabinet forthcoming in revealing the diary. There hung the minister's garments, not his priestly robes which she knew to hang in the sacristy, but what he wore outside the church, two decent suits, several shirts and pairs of shoes. But there were no books there, nor could any exploring of the cabinet's recesses discover any.

Exasperated by these futile efforts and unnerved by what she now knew would appear to be a suspiciously lengthy stay in the house, not to mention the impropriety of her invasion of the dead man's very bedchamber, she was about to go before she decided that the bed itself might be well worth her more exacting scrutiny.

The bed was spread with a coverlet of floral design. She felt all along its surface looking for telltale lumps but had no success. The goose down mattress yielded gracefully beneath the pressure of her fingers. She got down on her knees to peer beneath the bed and saw nothing there but dust. She was rising again when she noticed the little drawer inset into the headboard.

She was excited by this discovery even before opening the drawer and finding that it did indeed contain a book. It took her only a second to confirm that this was Graham's diary. The penmanship of the pages within matched exactly what she had observed written in the margins of the broadside.

She was inclined to begin reading from the back but decided not to press her luck in the house. She started for the door when she heard heavy footfalls in the passage. She heard masculine voices, one of which she recognized as the sexton's. It took her a moment longer to place the other as Hopwood's.

She quickly went to the cabinet and concealed herself in its deepest recess behind Graham's clothes. She closed the door again, her heart pounding so loudly that she was sure it could be heard. The door to the chamber opened. The voices, muffled before, now came through the oak panel with alarming clarity.

"Empty," said Motherwell.

"You say she wanted her son's diary?"

"That's what she said."

"Strange, Graham said nothing to me about it."

"Strange only if he told you everything he did."

The last voice was Motherwell's, and the sarcasm was biting. There was a silence in which she could only imagine Hopwood's response. Yet how could it be but disapproving, given the sexton's insolence? But when she heard Hopwood speak again there was no reproof in his voice.

"She was an old woman?"

"Yes, bent over. Carried a loaf of bread in a basket. A gift for the parson, she said. I saw little of her face. But then I had no reason to look."

"You had never seen her before?"

"Perhaps. Who can tell? One old woman is much like another, save she have a beard or a great goiter. This had neither."

"She was looking for a diary?"

"Her son's. Said she had brought it to Graham so he could see whether there was anything blasphemous in it."

"Strange that the son should care. A diary is private business, not likely to offend in that regard."

Hopwood's voice trailed off. Joan knew the men were leaving, yet she held her breath. She clutched the diary in her hand. Her hand sweated.

Hopwood followed Motherwell down the stairs, as though Motherwell were in charge. The old man was huffing and puffing again, as much as he had done when he had come up. As he descended, Hopwood thought about this diary business. Graham had kept a diary. Hopwood had once seen him writing in it. Perhaps that was why the woman had brought her son's book to Graham. Hopwood could understand why she might have wanted it back. If not dangerous to public morals, diaries might well contain a deal of unsavory gossip at the very least, mortifying disclosures, and confessions of private vice.

"You're sure she didn't say anything else—she didn't mention the son's name," Hopwood said.

"She did not."

"Nor her own name?"

At the bottom of the stairs, the sexton turned with exasperation. "Master Hopwood, she told a plausible tale, I let her in Graham's study. Would that she had carted off a hundred books to save my own back from carrying them."

The two men moved into the study. "And you never saw her leave?"

"If I had seen her leave, there would have been no cause to carry ourselves upstairs."

Hopwood glared at Motherwell, who was seated at Graham's desk as though it were his own, and was tempted to censure his unruly tongue. Yet he felt the old fear and loathing of the sexton—a man of probable vice whose tenure at the church was a burden even Graham had often complained of, perhaps candidly in his own diary.

It was at that moment that an idea came to Hopwood that made him quite forget his fear of the sexton. It was not her son's book that the woman sought but Graham's.

"Cursed woman," he said.

Motherwell looked up quickly, lifting an eyebrow in surprise at this outburst from the usually mild-mannered Hopwood.

"That was Joan Stock you suffered to enter," Hopwood said. "And Graham's diary she was after. Fool, you might have taken her when she was here and saved the constable and his men a world of trouble. She is as thick in Graham's murder as her husband."

"But this was an old woman."

"Trust me, Motherwell, your old woman was Stock's wife. Come, let's go upstairs again. If she's not left the house I trust she's concealed herself somewhere to avoid us. We but looked in the doors. There's corners to examine and beds to look under."

The two men moved quickly to the door and upstairs, but when they came to the dead man's bedchamber they looked under the bed and found nothing but dust and within the cabinet, only Graham's clothes, the whiff of old wool and sweat, and a loaf of bread in a basket.

11

MATTHEW had no soul for confinement, no mind made for wandering while the body encompassed by a dank cell could hardly stand upright, much less walk free. If his captors had given him some mindless work to do, that would have been something. Or light to read by, or a book to hold, even without sufficient light. But there were only the four stone walls, a stone floor, and foul, matted straw, a pail to relieve himself in, and the fearsome loneliness of being confined with a false friend.

Buck seemed imperturbed by his own imprisonment, which had only the effect of convincing Matthew that the man was no true prisoner. Buck spent much of his time sleeping, even during the day, propped up against the wall as though it were the softest of pillows. He ate the prison swill ravenously and told Matthew endless stories about his escapades, many of which Matthew was sure were the purest of fictions. With obvious calculation he would return from time to time to his seductive theme—how Matthew was a fool for taking the blame for a murder he did not commit when he might escape the rope by implicating his most revered employer. "Who cares not a whit for you," Buck said. "Who would as soon see you hanged as his carbuncle lanced or his pox cured. You're no benefit to him alive, but better off dead and silenced, that his own part in this villainy might not be known."

Matthew made no effort to defend his silence. When probed by Buck, Matthew represented it as confusion. And the truth was that he did not know what to do. Since his brief view of Richard Staunton, he had waited for further contact from Cecil. Every time the warder brought his food, he expected a note to be hid beneath the dish. Every footfall outside his cell he hoped was Staunton bringing news of his present release, for he had no hope that the great man would descend himself to come to such a vile place.

Beneath all these tortured thoughts was the fear that Buck's words might be true—that Cecil had abandoned him to his fate, that he would not see Joan's sweet face again or hear her voice or his daughter's or sing his little grandson to sleep. The thought of these losses filled his eyes with tears and he looked at where Buck sat digging for wax in his ear and wondered if he had misread the man. Perhaps Buck was no enemy, only a well-meaning friend with the very solution to his dilemma.

But his better opinion of his cellmate passed quickly when Buck rose and began to talk again—about corruption in high places, about dishonesty among the merchants, about vile practices in the church. Buck's strategy was all too palpable. Matthew might be abandoned by Cecil, but Buck was no friend.

And yet, Matthew thought suddenly, even an enemy might be of use.

"Friend Matthew, what do you spend your time thinking of? You're as silent as a monument in the churchyard."

"I've been thinking of the plan you proposed."

"And I hope to God have decided it is a good one."

"I think it might be the best one, given I have no recourse but to contemplate my own hanging."

"You'll talk then?"

"Yes."

"And name whom?"

Matthew hesitated. "On that point I'm still uncertain. There are various gentlemen whom I might implicate."

"Marry, my friend. It's best to choose wisely. Now you take my case. There were several of my brother-in-law's friends I forbore incriminating, thinking they might show gratitude for the relief."

"Did they?"

"One did." Buck showed Matthew the ring he wore on one of his fingers. "The ring was but a pledge for more, which he presently supplied."

"See then my hesitation. I would not offend where I may yet benefit."

Buck laughed and slapped Matthew's knee in a gesture of fellowship. "Now you're using your brain, Matthew. No more thought of hanging when your prospects have so improved. But tell me, who *is* the man?"

"Cecil," Matthew whispered.

Buck's smile broadened showing his rather fine white teeth. "Ah, the queen's darling, her factotum. He who thinks so much of himself?"

Matthew nodded.

"Why it's perfect!" Buck exclaimed ecstatically. "Your fortune is made. It's all too probable. It's well known that Cecil takes money from the Spaniard, that he keeps company with the cousin of Christopher Poole, the most subtle resurrecter that ever plagued England. That he should have secured your services to do away with a vocal opponent of the Roman heretics is all so plausible that it will no sooner be broadcast than believed. Oh, Matthew, you'll be more than free—you'll be celebrated. England's poets will sing your praises. You'll be the subject of every broadside and traveler's tale. The queen will honor you for having delivered such a traitor to her knowledge. We shall address you as Sir Matthew within the month at least."

Buck fell silent for a few moments as though catching his breath after this torrent of words.

Matthew said, "I am confirmed in my purpose. My problem now is to know how to negotiate with my captors. If

I tell too readily, I'll have nothing to bargain with. If too late I may cinch the knot at my own throat."

"You need an intermediary," said Buck, nodding his head sagaciously.

"A lawyer or priest?"

"Neither. Someone, rather, who can appraise the situation on both sides, who is disinterested as was Solomon when he pronounced which quarrelsome mother was the true, and yet one who has your own interests foremost in his heart."

"He hardly can be disinterested if he favors me," Matthew said.

"Well, he should *seem* disinterested to the casual observer. Solomons come rarely along. Most judges are as venal as those they judge. Now I have just the man for you."

"Who?"

"Your humble servant, Thomas Buck."

Saying this Buck leaped to his feet and bowed low before Matthew.

"Trust me as you would your own brother."

Matthew stood up too. He looked at Buck, who was effervescent with enthusiasm.

"You would do this for me?"

"Haven't I told you I was a friend from our first meeting?"

"You did."

"Well then, of course I'll mediate between you and the magistrate. The burden of all my tale is how I am experienced in such matters as yours. Look, I'll call the warder and let him know you have a confession to make. You'll be before the magistrate within the day and doubtless a free man by tomorrow this time."

"Oh, but I think this is moving all too quickly," Matthew said with a heavy sigh. "I'll wait until tomorrow."

"Wait until tomorrow? What womanish indecision is this? I speak bluntly, only because I care for you. Tell your tale, secure your release from this vile hole, and make your fortune forever."

Matthew shook his head in confusion and sat back down.

He watched Buck as the man paced up and down the cell, finally called the warder, whispered something, and was removed without any explanation. In a short time he returned. Matthew asked him where he had been.

"Attempting to secure more creature comforts for you," Buck said flatly. "You reject my counsel, yet I remain your friend. I am not without influence here in the prison. Wait until you see our dinner. No more of that slop they call food."

Buck's words proved true. Within the hour the warder arrived with plates upon which were several pieces of savory fowl, cheese, and freshly baked bread that so stimulated Matthew's shrunken stomach that he almost wept at the first delicious exhalation of the aroma. There was wine, too, not the ditch water he had been made to drink before. Matthew thanked Buck profusely for his help, pledged him with his cup, and gorged to his heart's content.

They were no sooner finished when Matthew heard a voice at the cell door. He looked up and saw Richard Staunton peering in. Matthew jumped to his feet.

"You told Sir Robert of my case?" Matthew asked before his visitor could speak.

"Pray keep your voice low, Master Stock," Staunton said, looking around him circumspectly and covering his mouth with a handkerchief. "I have told Sir Robert."

"Will he work my release?"

"He cannot, I'm afraid. There's nothing he can do."

"What do you mean there's nothing he can do?" Matthew almost shouted. "I languish here. I will be presently tried for my life. Yet I am as innocent as he in Graham's murder."

"My master thinks otherwise."

"What?"

"My master is grateful for your past service, but is neither able nor willing to save you from your just doom," Staunton pronounced. "He condemns the murderer, especially he who would kill one of the Lord's annointed."

"But he knows I have been put in this place by his enemies. So that I will implicate him."

"You would be wise not to try it," said Staunton. "Sir Robert must protect himself. He protects more than himself, but also the queen's good name."

"I am expendable then?"

"My master bids you make peace with God and assures you he will provide for your good wife after your death."

"Provide for my wife?"

"It's more than is required of him, being as you are a murderer. The proof is incontrovertible."

Matthew turned his back on the well-dressed secretary and in a moment he heard the man departing, saying something to the warder about the stench of urine in the prison.

He looked down at Buck, who by his self-satisfied smile had overheard the conversation. Buck said, "There is no master so ungrateful as he who has most to be grateful for in a servant. His thanks are brief and treacherous. Whom he commends one day, he condemns the next. Have you not just now seen evidence of Sir Robert's love for you?"

"I have," Matthew said gloomily.

"Then will you do as I have advised?"

"I will," said Matthew, sinking down in apparent despair although he was inwardly glad, for if there was ever a doubt about Buck's duplicity it had vanished forever. What kind of fool did Buck—or for that matter, Cecil's false servant—think he was?

Stearforth had followed Joan Stock back to the City, and lost her somewhere in the crowd near Paul's Cross. After an hour or two of searching, he decided to go to St. Crispin's on the chance that was her destination.

Upon arriving at the place, Stearforth observed Motherwell approaching from the other direction and was glad, for to Stearforth's mind what Motherwell lacked in moral virtue he made up for in his dependable corruptibility. Seeming happy to encounter Stearforth for his part, the sexton immediately informed him of the strange visit of the woman Hopwood had surmised to be Stock's wife. "Hopwood thinks she came to filch Graham's diary," Motherwell said.

"Damn her to hell," exclaimed Stearforth. "Why did the imbecile let her in? He should have cried out for the watch and had her taken or at least exposed her and barred the door."

"Well, Hopwood, as you know, is a dog brain," said Motherwell, not eager to reveal the fact that it was he who had admitted Joan Stock to the rectory.

Stearforth motioned to the sexton to follow him. The two men continued at a brisk pace down the street until they came to a tavern where Stearforth was a frequent patron and where he knew the host had a private room for just such conferences as he now intended.

"Sit down and start talking," Stearforth said.

"About what?"

"About this diary Hopwood babbles of. It belonged to Graham. And what if it did? What would Stock's wife think to find therein but the wrangles of churchmen and pious and hypocritical effusions? Has she turned to religion or what?"

"I know nothing of her religion," Motherwell said, not happy to be ordered about by his younger companion. "Or of Graham's diary. If he had one, I never knew of it. Nor why it should be worth more than the paper it's written upon."

"Well," said Stearforth, "the Stock woman thought it worth the risk of a disguise and invasion to have it, so it must be worth more than we supposed. Now let me think."

Stearforth paused, massaging his beetled brow and staring off into the middle distance. He continued. "It must have something to do with her husband's case, that's clear. If so, then perhaps Graham wrote something that might give her an idea—"

"Of who killed Graham?" interjected Motherwell. "That's impossible. Graham would have said nothing about *me*."

"Not you, idiot. You were only the tool. Graham may have written something about me—or something about one greater than I. Surely, whatever Stock's wife might be, she's no fool. We must get that diary back again."

"And put an end to the woman's meddling," said Motherwell, with happy anticipation. "Tell me but where and when and then let us proceed to a discussion of my fee."

"Patience, Motherwell. You're too quick to draw that blade of yours. Let me first see what he whom I serve would have, before we unleash you upon Joan Stock."

"I shall wait like a good dog therefore," said Motherwell.

It took Stearforth half an hour to make his way to his new destination, contemplating all the while what he would do to Joan Stock, once he had her in his power. But all of course would be at his master's approval. That was essential now that Stearforth was sitting where he was, in a position of favor at long last. No, he would do nothing without approval. Then, if things fell out badly, he would not be to blame. He would have done exactly what he was told, and he would have the reward of his obedience without the risk of the plot's failure.

He was admitted into the great solemn house as he generally was these days, a considerable improvement from at first when the employer's butler required him to stand at the door while he determined that it was the master's pleasure to have him admitted. The same butler, obsequious now that he sensed Stearforth's star on the rise, hurried before him, leading the way to the handsomely appointed rooms where his employer did his private business. Stearforth was gratified to find him alone, although at supper.

His employer looked up and said, "Stearforth, is it? Well come have a chair, man. See, my cook has prepared sufficient for at least a dozen men of healthy appetite."

Stearforth's eyes quickly swept the table which was abundantly laid, but he thought it politic not to accept the invitation too readily. He was famished but a hungry servant was generally despised, and he was not about to lose ground by speaking his mind.

"Many thanks, Your Grace, but I have already dined today. At a friend's."

The man at table looked up at Stearforth with a shrewd expression and smiled with his thin lips. "Nonsense, Stearforth. No tall man like you can stand to reject a good meal. Sit down I pray you. Here, I'll have Jonathan fetch you a plate and knife."

The butler, who had stood patiently by while this conversation was in progress, now hurried off to do as he was ordered. Stearforth sat down, took a napkin from the table, and tucked it in the top of his doublet as he saw his host had done. Before him on the table was the good part of a roast pig, covered with herbs and garnished by boiled turnips and leeks. A flagon of wine was also at hand and a silver goblet to drink it from. Stearforth was so delighted by the repast and the honor of being invited to sit with his host that he nearly forgot the purpose of his visit.

The butler returned with plate and knife. Stearforth watched as the man expertly carved from the roast pig and laid a generous amount of the succulent meat upon the plate and not a few of the turnips and leeks. Stearforth took the knife and stabbed the meat, brought it to his mouth, and chewed with inexpressible relish. God in heaven, he thought. Was it not good to the tongue, and was not this the life he had dreamed of since a poor student at Oxford?

While Stearforth ate the other man went on at some length of a recent audience with the queen. He spoke of her appearance, which was, he said, much decayed—so much so that hardly one could be found who knew her that thought she would last out the year.

Stearforth had asked for a second helping before he had had enough and his mind came back to the matter that brought him.

"Stock's wife has been busy at St. Crispin's."

"Praying for her husband?"

"Preying upon Graham's library."

"What? She's turned scholar?"

"Thief—and probably spy as well. Graham had a diary. Joan Stock sneaked into the parsonage disguised as an old woman begging to have her son's diary returned."

The other man looked up quickly. "How do you know all this?"

"Motherwell told me. Hopwood let her in, believing her tale."

"Hopwood is a fool. No wonder the church falters."

"She was in and out of the house before either Motherwell or Hopwood knew what she had come for."

"And found the diary."

"So it is supposed."

"I'm afraid Mistress Stock is becoming a thorn in my side, Stearforth. But we shall put her to use. Her husband is slow to accommodate our wishes. He insists on protecting Cecil, despite plain signs that Cecil cares nothing for him and would gladly see him hanged. I'm afraid Stock's integrity will be our undoing unless we can persuade him to cooperate. There's a way to do this."

"How, sir?"

"Take his wife. Secure her in some place where she cannot escape and none can rescue her. Then tell Stock she'll live only upon his confession and accusation against Cecil. Here, Stearforth. You had a healthy appetite after all. But have some of this pudding too. It's excellent."

Stearforth tried the pudding and saw that the other man was right about its quality. He knew he was also right about what to do with Stock's wife.

Buck and the other man, whom Matthew had seen at the magistrate's hall, took him to a little room in the upper part of the prison that had a window and fresh air and was evidently part of the living quarters of him who was in charge of the prison.

The other man was a short, stout Yorkshireman by his accent. He had a livid scar running from his right eye to his lower lip and the officious manner of a secretary, yet he treated Matthew with surprising courtesy, while Buck had now dropped any pretense that his confinement in Marshalsea was anything but subterfuge. Matthew was told yet another officer of the court would come presently and in the meantime would he like a little something for his supper besides salt fish and moldy bread and a potent ale brewed by the warder's worthy wife.

Matthew said he would, and this same wife, a small-boned woman with high cheekbones and stern gaze presently came in and brought him the promised supper, a hearty stew, more of the fresh-baked bread he had had before, and a good round orange to crown the feast. He was also given a basin of fresh water to wash in and some scented soap and a towel and a razor to shave with, which amenities he had not enjoyed for a whole week, so that a rich growth of gray stubble spread upon his cheeks and he itched in his shirt as though every louse in Christendom had taken up residence there.

He thanked the warder's stern wife for her courtesy, washed and shaved. He saw no harm in availing himself of these privileges. Two could play the game of deception even if one was less practiced in it.

Feeling much better after his second decent meal of the afternoon, washed and barbered and wishing only for a clean shirt to amend himself completely, Matthew waited for the magistrate's clerk while Buck and Harking—that was the scarred gentleman's name—played cards on a little table in the corner and made conversation of a most trivial sort, bantering about whether the French were more licentious than the Italians and, once, raising their voices about the proper whelping of dogs, of which Harking evidently was a great fancier. Matthew noticed that although Buck was obviously of higher place in the social order than Harking, he dealt with him in an open and familiar manner. Harking was also very merry, as though the present events were of no more moment than a casual encounter of three old friends.

Matthew did not object to this delay. He had a chair in the corner to sit in and would have drifted off into sleep had his pulse not been quickened by anticipation of just what he was to offer up as a token of his compliance without doing Cecil any real hurt.

It was nearly dark and the room had been furnished with candles before anyone came. There were two new persons rather than the one expected: a tall, stooped man named Conley dressed in a lawyer's gown and his younger assistant who was not introduced. Buck came over to where Matthew sat and said in a low whisper. "You're not to worry, my friend. Remember what I told you. Throw yourself on their mercy. Tell them what expedience dictates and so be done of this unpleasantness."

Then Matthew was brought over to the table where Buck and Harking had been playing cards, made to sit down, and Conley sat down opposite. Buck and Harking stood watching at some distance. Conley's assistant brought out from beneath his cloak a tablet. He too sat down, drawing a pen and ink bottle from his pocket.

Conley asked Matthew what his name was and where he dwelt and what he did. To all such questions Matthew answered truthfully. The assistant scratched away with his pen as Matthew spoke.

"You are charged with the murder of Stephen Graham and before the magistrate pled not guilty to the offense," intoned Conley, looking at Matthew accusingly.

"I did."

"And now wish to plead otherwise—to confess to the crime?"

"Well, sir, that depends," Matthew said, looking from Conley to Buck, who was observing the proceedings from a place in the corner.

"Depends upon what?" asked Conley curtly. "Either you plead one way or t'other. There are no two ways about it." Conley turned his head to look at Buck, as though he were responsible for this confusion.

"It depends on whether information as to who bid me do

the killing is worth some leniency in my case," Matthew said, fearing at once that in making such a claim he had been too bold.

For a few moments Conley said nothing, but fixed Matthew in an icy stare of hostility or contempt, Matthew could not discern which. Matthew's heart pounded. He found Conley's stare excruciating, but he was not about to drop his own eyes first.

"It is not my custom to negotiate with murderers," Conley said.

"It is not my custom to be regarded as such."

"You sell cloth in Chelmsford, I understand."

"I do."

"And are the town constable?"

"I am."

"Were you born and bred a Papist or are you a convert?"

"Neither, but an Englishman born and a dutiful communicant of the English church."

This response seemed to take Conley by surprise. He waited a moment before proceeding, studying Matthew's face. "Then you scorn the Bishop of Rome and all his works."

"As God is my witness," Matthew said, thinking with respect to these religious matters there would be no cause to dissemble, whatever he might say otherwise.

Conley shifted in his chair, lowered his brow even farther so that Matthew wondered that the man could still see him and said, "Who is he who bid you do the murder?"

"A man whose place at court is such that to describe his influence is to give his name—and yet not to give it."

There was another chilling silence.

"I see you have sojourned in the City long enough to learn the art of indirection," Conley said. "Am I to understand that you are prepared to name names but not to do so until some concession has been made?"

"You are."

"And may we know your terms?"

"I must have a guarantee," Matthew said.

"From—"

"From someone with power to enforce it."

"You want a patron?"

"In exchange for the one I have lost."

"He whom you are prepared to incriminate."

Matthew nodded. He turned his head briefly to see how Buck was taking all this and caught a fleeting smile of approval flash across the young man's face.

12

*T*HE innkeeper, a large florid man, looked at Joan strangely when she entered, although he had been open and amicable before. Then she remembered how she was dressed, how she must appear, still in her old woman's disguise—a version of her own mother while she was still alive. She pulled the hat off to reveal her face, mumbled something about having lost her good cloak to a thief, whereupon the innkeeper, smiling indulgently, said the same thing had happened to his own wife not two years since, and begged her to join him and the other guests for supper.

She said no, thanking him for the offer, and he replied he would have his boy bring up wood for her fire straightway.

In her chamber, Joan removed the diary from the cloak, and wishing not to commence her perusal until the boy had come and gone, she hid the diary in a narrow crack she found in the hearth and sat down to think. Belatedly, the full realization of the risk she had taken that afternoon came upon her. Why, the door might have been opened by Hopwood himself rather than the sexton and he discovering who she was might have seized her as an accomplice in Matthew's crime. Instead of sitting as she now was in the relative comfort of a London inn, she might have been in the Marshalsea herself, or standing helplessly before a stern magistrate or being interrogated by a prosecutor. Or worse, she imagined, what if Hopwood, recognizing her, had called the sexton who wore a dagger at his side and looked the man to use it. Would he have hesitated to plunge it into her chest had he thought her a danger to himself?

A knocking came at the door and a voice without identified her visitor as Jack, the innkeeper's boy. She unbolted the door and let him in.

The boy who entered looked to be thirteen or fourteen with freckled face and hair the color of straw. He wore an apron around his waist and in his arms he carried two sturdy faggots. He went directly to lay the fire.

"A gentleman asked after you just now," he said as he struck the match to the kindling.

"A gentleman? Did he give his name?"

"He said he thought you were the wife of an acquaintance of his and wanted to confirm it was you and not some other."

"Indeed, and what did this gentleman look like?"

Jack's description suited Stearforth perfectly, and Joan felt sick inside, as though she had eaten unripened fruit.

"Did you tell him my name?"

"I said your name was Mistress Gray."

"Yes?"

"He said that he must have been mistaken, for the woman he sought was named Joan Stock of Chelmsford."

The boy stood with his back to her as the little flame curled up around the faggots and became a bigger flame. She gave the boy a penny for the wood and said she would have sixpence for him if he saw the man around the inn again and brought word to her directly. She said good night and bolted the door behind him, her heart beating rapidly and the sick feeling still with her.

Remembering the diary, she retrieved it from its hiding place. She sat down before the firelight and opened the book to the last page, moving forward until she came across Graham's writing.

The minister wrote in a generous round hand, easy for her to read.

The last entry was dated the day before Graham's murder. It was more of a religious meditation upon the sacrament than a record of what he did and said. In fact, as she read, she wondered if the elegant sentiments of the meditation were his own, or copied from some other author, making of the diary more a commonplace book than a record of the maker's daily affairs. Her doubt on this point was resolved when she turned to the day earlier, for here was a summary of a conversation Graham had had with Motherwell, the sexton. The quarrel between them was over the burial plots in the churchyard, for which the sexton was discovered to have charged an extra fee, unapproved by Graham. Graham referred to the sexton as greedy, unscrupulous, insolent. He had threatened to complain to Lady Elyot. How Motherwell had answered to this threat was not recorded. Had it been with that knife that Stearforth had stolen? But how would Motherwell have the knife, but by Stearforth, and why should Stearforth be concerned about Motherwell's keeping his place? No, revenge made no sense. If Motherwell did the murder, he did it upon Stearforth's instruction; if Stearforth was the murderer, he acted upon the orders of some greater. And who knew where it all ended, how high up it went?

The entries before were clearly written during the parson's sickness and consisted of prayers and appeals for health, inventories of his physical symptoms, and harangues against his enemies, who had sent him threatening letters and who he believed may have poisoned him. These made dreary reading and Joan found herself skipping large sections of these bilious and morbid reflections.

Finally, she came upon a passage that interested her greatly. It was dated approximately a month before Graham's death. She read the words out loud. Her fear was gone now:

Met Master S. in Fleet Street where he gave me good day and said his mistress had asked after my health. Said all the town talked of Poole's resurrection and that he thought it was a great fraud. Approved of my sermons denouncing it as the same and gave me a crown for the poor box. Said all Papists were traitors to England and ought to be hanged.

Joan hurried over the next section which consisted of an anti-Roman diatribe and then found Master S. mentioned again. But of course Master S. had to be Stearforth.

Master S., secretary to Lady E., came to my house for dinner with two other gentlemen, Sir John Putney and Master Davidson, friends of his grace the archbishop. Sir John commented that the archbishop looked favorably on my nomination to a bishopric, not sure which but know that Ely will soon be vacant. Also remarked that the Council had taken interest in my response to the matter of Christopher Poole. Sir John noted that my election, however, would not please the Bacon party, who favored one of their own, he would not say who.

There the entry ended for that date. Joan thought about Graham's words. *The Bacon party.* That would be Lord Bacon, whose friendship with the fallen Essex had put him and his friends in bad odor at Court. She knew that much about politics. A candidate of their own for bishop. She understood little of ecclesiastical policy except that it was as obscure and twisted as that of the lords temporal and was inextricably connected to it. Here was a goodly matter to reflect upon. If the followers of Lord Bacon, who all the world knew, were at odds with Cecil, preferred another candidate over Graham, that meant that the unnamed gentleman was Graham's enemy. But would such rivalry among men of God move them to murder? It seemed unthinkable.

But all this reading by firelight had given her a headache.

She closed the diary, intending fully to conclude her reading the next day, and inserted it in its hiding place.

She went to the door to make sure she had bolted it securely, then prepared for bed. Nor did she forget her prayers for Matthew's rescue, the triumph of truth, and the confounding of her enemies, not only Humphrey Stearforth but also the unnamed lord temporal or spiritual who seemed ultimately behind these mysteries.

Sometime later Joan dreamed. Scenes from her day, hopelessly confused, then a clearer more sustained vision of her own house in Chelmsford. She sat stitching with Graham's diary in her lap. Or a book like it. Suddenly she heard a noise from out-of-doors. She rose to go to the window. It was one that looked not out on High Street but on the back parts of the house that gave away to a field where there were a sprinkling of outbuildings, a garden, a pasture. Matthew approached from a distance. She could tell it was Matthew by his gait and swing of his arms. A broad-brimmed hat shielded his face.

At the same time she became aware that across the pasture was a lone figure dressed in a long frieze coat and a peaked cap of the kind cowherds wore. He was following Matthew, although her husband did not seem aware of him. Then she saw for the first time that the man carried a sheep crook over his shoulders. He grew nearer to Matthew but still her husband showed no awareness.

Joan opened her mouth to call out to Matthew, but the sound that came forth was no more substantial than a whimper although she tried with all her might, growing increasingly anxious for her husband without knowing why.

She turned from the window and ran downstairs, thinking to warn Matthew more directly, but by the time she came to the door it was already opened and a man was standing in her kitchen.

It was not Matthew, but the cowherd. She looked over his shoulder to see if her husband was to be seen, but he was not. Then she looked at the cowherd. In her dream she almost expected to see Stearforth or Motherwell, but he before her had a face she had never seen before, a long face with weary eyes and thin lips. He made neither explanation nor apology for his intrusion, but stood there as though he were the true master of the house, the sheep crook upright like a soldier's pike.

"Where is my husband?" she said. "Where is Matthew?"

But the stranger made no response, and Joan awoke, wondering what the dream had meant. Like any good Christian, she believed in the prophetic powers of visions of the night, believed that they were sent by God, or occasionally by the devil. Which was this?

Her contemplations were disturbed by a sound, and it was a moment before she recognized the source. Someone was at the door of her room. What hour must it be? She had retired early, without supper. She reckoned it must be near midnight, for she knew she had slept awhile before the dream awoke her and the fire was no more than a pile of glowing embers on the hearth now.

The knocking came a little more incessantly, yet it was not the pounding of an alarm as might have been given if the house was afire.

She rose from the bed, threw her cloak around her and went to the door. She asked who her visitor was before she even considered forgoing the security of the door's iron bolt.

She heard Jack's voice. "It's I, Mistress Gray, with more word about the man who asked of you."

Joan remembered her offer to pay the boy for further word of Stearforth's activity and without further concern unbolted.

She had opened the door no more than a crack before Jack came stumbling in. Stearforth was behind him. He seized her in an ironlike clutch and stifled her protest with a rough hand over her mouth. Behind him she saw Motherwell. His knife was drawn and he held it at Jack's neck. The boy's face was a mask of terror.

Motherwell shut the door. He carried a brace of candles

so Joan could see all now, the hostile faces of the invaders and the paleness of Jack's face.

"I'm going to take my hand from your mouth," Stearforth said. "But if you scream, the boy will die."

Joan looked at Motherwell and knew that Stearforth was not exaggerating. She nodded her head in compliance. Motherwell took an even tighter grip on Jack and pressed his dagger so hard into the boy's flesh that she thought she saw blood run on his skin.

"Dress," Stearforth commanded after he had released her. "And be quick."

"Not with you men looking on," she said.

"You will dress and be quick about it, regardless of who looks or who doesn't look," Stearforth said. "My friend will finish the boy and proceed to you thereafter."

The tone of Stearforth's voice warned her against further objections. She went over to the bed where she had laid out her gown and turning her back on the intruders she did what she had been ordered to do, although with such fear and trembling that she was hard put to tie or button.

"You're taking me to prison then? At least I will see my husband."

Behind her the men laughed.

"A prison of sorts," said Motherwell.

"Just don't hurt Jack," she said.

"Oh, we won't," Motherwell said.

Finished dressing she turned about and was startled to see that Jack was no longer being held by Motherwell. The boy was now seated over by the hearth, his arms wrapped casually around his knees, and was looking on these activities with more curiosity than fear. Before she could inquire into the reason for the boy's release, Stearforth came forward and pulling a scarf from his pocket bound it around her mouth.

"The boy is a plausible actor," Stearforth said. "He has a good sense of which side his bread is buttered on, *Mistress Gray*. You promised him sixpence but I gave him twice that. For helping bring a runaway wife back to her husband. And so we shall."

"Here boy," said Stearforth, handing Jack the coins. "There's a bit more too, so that you may more quickly forget everything that has transpired here. Tell your master Mistress Gray departed for home earlier than she had expected."

"I shall, sir," said Jack, rising from the hearth. He cast a glance at Joan on his way out the door, but she could not discern whether his expression was one of gratification or regret.

At such an hour, the inn seemed a vacant house, and there were no witnesses to Joan's abduction. Even if there had been, she was not sure she could have given any signal of distress, so closely kept she was on each side by her two captors.

In the street were a horse and cart. Stearforth pushed her into the back of the cart and climbed aboard with her while Motherwell drove. He drove slowly from necessity since the street was so narrow and the only light was from the torch affixed to the cart. She was facing the rear but she looked for landmarks as they passed; she wanted to remember everything. Who knew but she would have opportunity to find her way back again.

She grew worried when they passed through Ludgate and started to leave the City. Where were they bound and to what purpose? Joan reckoned that if Motherwell's intent was to slit her throat he might have done so on any London street or alley to good effect. She thought perhaps she was being taken to some outlying house, remote from other habitation. And what would be done to her there—murder or worse?

She knew that by the road they traveled they were not far from the river for she could smell it in the cold night air, all marshy and fetid. They must be near Wapping, she thought. Sometime later her suspicion was confirmed. Ahead of them she glimpsed a broad expanse of moonlit water and at a distance the outlines of a ship at anchor. Was she to be abducted then, rather than murdered? Conveyed to France or to some deserted isle to die of hunger and loneliness, or perhaps be thrown overboard as soon as land was left behind?

The cart jolted to a halt and Stearforth yanked her from the cartbed. Motherwell led the way with the torch. They walked along the riverside for twenty or thirty yards before coming to a boat concealed in the reeds. Stearforth ordered her to climb in, while Motherwell found oars beneath the seats and prepared to row. Stearforth shoved the boat into the stream before jumping in himself.

"We've planned an ocean voyage for you, Mistress Stock," Stearforth said. "To a place where no one will think to look for you. If your husband is of a cooperative mind you may see Chelmsford again. If not, burial at sea is very economical, I understand. And you avoid the indignity of disinterment in five years to make way for another rotting corpse."

It was not a great ship like some that came up to London, but a merchant's barque, of about a dozen yards in length with bulging sides, a high forecastle and poop, and two masts with sails furrowed. They approached under the stern and Joan tried to read the name but could only make out the the first two letters *P* and *l*. Motherwell maneuvered the craft to the side of the ship where there was a wooden ladder and secured the boat with a line. Motherwell nodded to Stearforth and Stearforth helped her to her feet and up the ladder.

On board she was nearly thrown off balance by the unfamiliar pitch of the deck, which shifted uneasily beneath her feet; and the stench of the vessel, a revolting mix of fish and offal, almost made her retch. From aft came a man who by his manner and authoritative voice, Joan took to be the captain. He was barrel chested and full bearded, and as much as Joan could make out of his face seemed not as cruel as she might have feared, but was fitted out with kindly, intelligent eyes and straight brows.

"Who do we have here?" asked the captain, addressing

Stearforth, whom he seemed to know from some other transaction.

"One who could use a little sea air," said Stearforth, moving to step between the captain and the sexton.

The captain drew Stearforth aside and the two men walked to the rail. They talked between themselves while Motherwell held back with Joan. Then the captain returned and said that he would take Joan aboard, but first he looked her up and down as though he were thinking of recruiting her for the crew. She took offense at this insulting examination but was in no position to protest. She struggled to speak and made motions to indicate that the gag should be removed.

"I think we can comply with that request, seeing that there's hardly a soul around but us," Stearforth said. He nodded to Motherwell and Motherwell removed the scarf. Joan did not scream. She knew Stearforth was right, but how pleasant it was to breathe through her mouth again, pleasant but for the awful odors. Would she not die if she had to endure such conditions?

Two sailors, young men in ragged, filthy clothes, emerged from below deck and gathered behind the captain. A wiry seaman with an eye patch stood a little farther off. By his air of authority, Joan supposed he was second in command.

"We've been at sea for nearly a year, except for my mate," the captain said stonily. "The men won't be happy to know they're putting to sea again."

"Perhaps we can make them happier. Take this."

Stearforth handed the captain a purse. The captain took it and emptied the contents into his hand. He took a moment to examine the coins, looked back at Stearforth, and said it was enough. "Will Calais suit?" he asked. "I'm not provisioned for a longer voyage."

"An excellent destination," Stearforth said.

"What do you intend to do with me?" Joan wanted to know. Stearforth laughed. "You'll see in good time, Mistress Stock. Much depends on the cooperation of your husband, which I trust this little sea voyage will all but guarantee if he's the doting husband I take him for." Turning to the captain he said, "It's my master's wish that she be made comfortable for the voyage so don't put her in the hold. We may well need her in good condition later."

The captain turned and told one of the two men behind him to escort Joan to his own cabin.

A door in the raised afterdeck of the vessel led to a narrow stairway and yet another door which when opened revealed a low-ceilinged cabin hardly bigger than her cook's quarters in her own house in Chelmsford. Its walls conformed to the outward shape of the ship and the wood planks were varnished to a high sheen. Bunks were built into the wall. There was also a table on which charts were spread, a smaller desk with burning oil lamp and several mechanical devices Joan surmised the captain used to find his way in the wide sea. The cabin was filthy like the rest of the ship.

Having been so closely guarded before, she was now surprised to find herself left alone by her escort, although she heard the door locked behind the man and she knew she was as much a prisoner here as she had been before. She immediately began to give her cell a closer inspection.

The charts upon the table were beyond her comprehension, but she found the captain's desk of interest. She noticed a knife with a long thin blade that she imagined the captain might have used to unseal his letters. This she tucked into the pocket of her cloak, hoping that the captain would not soon notice it was gone from its customary place. There was also a large book that proved upon opening to be the ship's log and here on the first page she read the name that she had only partly discerned before boarding: *Plover*.

Pleased by this addition to her knowledge she was preparing to inspect several drawers built within the desk when the door opened and the master of the vessel entered.

She saw now how tall he was for his head almost scraped the overhead beams, and the breadth of his shoulders seemed to fill the doorway. He regarded her sternly, as though despite payment for her passage he considered her presence an annoyance, or perhaps as ill luck.

"You'll sleep there," he said gruffly, pointing to one of the bunks.

"And where will you sleep?" she asked.

The captain nodded toward the bunk opposite.

"Not on your life," Joan declared. "I'm an honest woman and not accustomed to sharing my sleeping quarters with strange men."

"Have no fear," said the captain, removing his cap to reveal an unruly mop of hair as curly as an Italian's. "I am a married man myself and am devoted to my wife. You'll be safe enough here."

Joan started to continue to protest, not prepared to trust any man who was commissioned as her jailer, married or no, but the captain held up his hand to discourage further discussion.

"If my cabin does not please you, you may sleep with the crew. They are unmarried men who have tasted no female flesh these twelve months and will be as randy as hedgehogs. I cannot answer for their conduct, for they are vile knaves, every one. I have signed them on for want of a better crew. The choice is yours."

The captain stood with his arms akimbo while Joan considered her options. By the firmness of his expression she had no doubt the captain meant exactly what he said and she concluded that she might better handle the captain than his crew. She signaled her compliance with a nod.

"There's a chamber pot in the corner," he said. "We sail within these two hours and until then you can have the cabin to yourself. I trust you'll not prowl amid that which doesn't concern you."

"I hope you don't think I'm that kind of woman," Joan said.

The captain made no reply to this. He put his cap back on his head and with a little wave of his hand bid her good night.

Joan thought about the bunk. It did look inviting and even the slight roll of the deck had made her stomach queasy. But she was determined to make use of her opportunity. She went back to the ship's log and opened it. The captain was not a careful penman; he wrote in a reckless scrawl. The matter was not informative—dates, tides, points of embarking and arrival, an inventory of stores, crew members, an occasional passenger. But then she noticed something she had not noticed before. The captain had signed his name to the entries. Edmund was the first name. That was certain. But the second was less easily deciphered. *Morgan*, she thought he wrote. Edmund Morgan, master of the *Plover*.

Suddenly she was struck with an odd thought. Elspeth Morgan's husband was a shipmaster. Elspeth had said she hadn't seen him in twelvemonth. Could the master of the *Plover* be Elspeth's husband?

13

O_N the morning after his interrogation by Master Conley, Matthew left Marshalsea in the company of the same gentleman and also Buck, but by a back door, not the main, which was in plain sight of the street and as Buck hinted, well within view of Cecil's spies, who by his departure would be alerted to Matthew's intended betrayal.

Buck provided no explanation for his own discharge, nor did Matthew inquire of it. He was in manacles, and given to understand that he was not being released from the charge of murder, but only being transferred into the custody of Conley and another gentleman he would presently meet who would answer for his appearance before the authorities at a later time.

Matthew wanted to know who the gentleman was and where he was to be taken.

"All in due course, Master Stock," Conley said. "For now, keep you close beside us and never think of escape. Those manacles will affirm you a prisoner. And a reward for escaped criminals never fails to tempt our sturdy London yeomanry."

His two guardians kept Matthew walking at a brisk pace, and they traveled about a half a mile through the city before stopping before a stately house in the Cornhill ward that with its crenellated battlements and turrets looked like a small castle.

As he had been conducted from the prison by stealth, so now his guides led him into the house in the same fashion, by a back gate and door. From there, they immediately descended to a spacious cellar where he was placed in a locked room without windows or furnishings and told to content himself until he should be called for.

He stood there in his new cell, but without contentment. Removal from the Marshalsea was an improvement in his condition, the fresher air of outdoors energized his spirits and made him more hopeful of real freedom. Yet this new environment presented its own horrors, for where he was imprisoned by walls before he now felt himself entangled more than ever in a web of conflicting loyalties and shadowy powers. What had he got himself into?

And with whom?

Matthew had little time to debate these questions. Conley and Buck returned within a few minutes to let him out. He said his new patron would see him now.

"Am I ever to learn his name?" Matthew asked.

"You may call him *Your Grace*," Conley said.

The three men left the cellar and climbed yet another flight of stairs to come to a sumptuously furnished apartment with portraits and tapestries adorning the walls and a splendid turkey carpet upon the floor.

Of the two men already in the chamber, one was standing with his face toward a mullioned window so that Matthew could see only his back. The other was seated with his legs crossed and his hands folded in his lap. In his midforties, he was elegantly dressed in silk hose and doublet with a ruff collar of such ample circumference that his head seemed detached and too small for his corpulent body. He had the heavy face of a churchman or judge, a somewhat moody air, and a small delicate mouth that was out of keeping with his broad forehead, dark penetrating eyes, and bulbous nose with its flaring nostrils.

"This is Stock, Your Grace," Conley said, bowing, and along with Buck, taking up a position in the corner.

At this introduction the man who was standing turned slowly, and Matthew saw to his amazement that it was the false Stephen Graham.

"Come in, Master Stock. Sit down," said the seated gentleman, his small mouth widening into a smile. "May I introduce you to Master Humphrey Stearforth, whom I believe you met earlier—under a different name?"

Matthew accepted the offer, but kept his eyes fixed on Stearforth, who had the same mocking sneer upon his face as he did when Matthew had briefly seen him in the magistrate's court. So that was his name. Matthew repeated it silently.

"I understand from Master Conley that you are prepared to plead guilty to your crime. And, more important, to name him who put you up to it?"

"I may be, Your Grace," Matthew said. "If certain conditions are met."

"One of which is, I suppose, that the charge against you be dismissed, or at least reduced?"

"Yes."

"You appear to assume, Master Stock, that these matters are more dictated by negotiation than by law, the law being that if one man kills another he must answer for it. I can't imagine who has given you such a false impression."

"I have had counsel from your sagacious servant."

His Grace raised a questioning brow.

"I mean my former cellmate, Thomas Buck."

"Master Buck knows a good deal about the law. He should, having been so entangled with it during his few years. But let me explain how the matter stands with you."

This explanation was interrupted by the entrance of a servant with some letters, which His Grace took in his hands, sifted, and placed on his desk before him. All this time Stearforth said nothing but looked on silently, although the mocking grin had been replaced with a more malign regard of one who watches his enemy's body twisting on the gibbet.

"You stand accused of murder in cold blood," His Grace continued. "The weapon used to murder your victim was your own. There are two witnesses to your crime, the curate and sexton of the church."

"Both are false witnesses," Matthew protested. "Hopwood found the body after the fact, and the sexton Motherwell is a craven liar."

"Be that as it may," the man continued, unruffled by Matthew's protest. "They will appear to be credible witnesses, and appearances are everything in these matters. Moreover, you are now an escaped prisoner, thus confirming your guilt."

"But—"

"Remember, Master Stock, we are talking about appearances only. The truth is that the court will have no record of your release from Marshalsea. So you see your predicament is more serious than you supposed."

"Then why have I been brought here if my release was a fraud?"

"To dig your pit—and the pit of your employer the deeper. You are without recourse. But if you testify against Sir Robert Cecil—say that he hired you to do the murder to silence Graham—then the rope will be snatched from your neck."

"I see no reason it should be, if I am confessed of a murder. What will I accomplish more than dragging Sir Robert into the crime?"

"There are ways of getting around the law, Master Stock. Besides you have no choice. On the one hand, if you fail to accuse Cecil, your death is certain. At least with our proposal you may have a glimmer of hope that you will escape. I will also make it worth your while in other ways. As you can see, I'm not without the means. There's also an additional inducement. Stearforth, why don't you tell him?"

Stearforth, who as yet had not spoken a word, took a step forward and put his hands behind his back as though he were a butler waiting for his master's order of wine. "We have your wife now. She's where Cecil cannot find her. If you wish to see her again, you'll do as my master instructs."

"A wise man knows when he is beaten, Master Stock, and doesn't flail against a stone wall," said His Grace.

Matthew looked from the seated gentleman back to Stearforth and knew from Stearforth's malicious stare that he wasn't lying about Joan. Matthew's soul writhed with impotent fury. Who were these men who regarded truth with so much disdain as to frame this entrapment? Had they no fear of God's vengeance on the false witness, no sense of the harm they did to the commonwealth in endeavoring to undo one of the queen's good servants?

"Will you cooperate with us, Master Stock?"

"What am I to do?" he asked, trembling with a mixture of rage and fear.

"You will be my guest for a day or two. Then you will be returned to Marshalsea, but only briefly. On Friday you will be carried before the queen's Privy Council where you will confess to the murder of Stephen Graham and accuse Cecil to his face."

"And what if my accusation is not believed? I am an accused murderer, and even as an honest man am only a town constable and shopkeeper. How will my word fare against that of the queen's principal secretary?"

"Better than you suppose," said His Grace with the same composure. "There will be other evidence."

"What other evidence?"

"Marry, you have no need to know, Master Stock. Have you not learned that wisdom of your employer's family motto, *Patiens qui prudens*? But there will be other evidence, and your testimony will crown it. Even if the council is skeptical, Cecil's reputation will be sufficiently besmirched so to add credence to all rumors of his past intrigues."

"I shall not know what to say to the council."

"You shall be taught. Stearforth here is a graduate of our

noble University of Oxford. He is a skilled writer and has already composed your text. You shall learn it by heart, for it must be exactly spoken. The alternative to this is that Stearforth will write your epitaph—and that of your wife. You will be disgraced and buried in an unmarked grave. Now I offer you the hope of a glorious resurrection from such a fate. A chance for a second and better grave at the end of a long life rather than ignominy. What say you, Master Stock, can we come to terms?"

Matthew looked from one man to the next. Their faces were implacable; none appeared doubtful of what Matthew would say.

"You have left me no choice," Matthew said.

"Which was my intent," said His Grace smiling. "We have an understanding at last. Good Master Buck, unlock Master Stock's manacles. I don't think he'll try to avoid our hospitality, now that he is aware of his true position in the case."

He unfolded his hands and placed them on his knees. "And now for dinner. What do you prefer, Master Stock, a plump partridge or venison? My cook is ready for either or both."

"The partridge," said Matthew, who had no appetite at all.

Matthew dined with His Grace and Stearforth. Conley and Buck had departed on some other mission. His Grace ate heartily, but Stearforth merely picked, and Matthew could not bring himself to do much more than sip the wine, which although sugared, had a bitter aftertaste. While he ate, Matthew's host maintained a continuous stream of talk, most of it court gossip involving persons of whose names Matthew had not heard. The only constant reference was to the late Earl of Essex, the foolish courtier whose ambition had overreached reason and brought upon him disgrace and public execution, two years before. But the allusions were sufficiently positive to suggest that his host had been a follower of that lord, which meant that he was no friend to Cecil, no friend of the queen.

When the meal had ended, His Grace dismissed his dinner guests, and Stearforth took Matthew off to an adjacent room. He handed Matthew a parchment upon which there was practically a full page of writing. "This is your testimony," Stearforth said. "A room is being prepared for you in the house. Take this copy with you. Study it carefully. You'll need to have it all by heart on Friday. And to recite it with . . . sincerity."

Sincerity, thought Matthew. That would be a trick if he could do it. He looked at the paper.

The lines blurred. He couldn't read. Was the difficulty with his eyes or his conscience? He looked up at Stearforth. He couldn't believe the man's nonchalance. Here was a confession to a crime which Stearforth had committed—or caused to be committed, and Stearforth had authored it. Was there ever such an impudence since the world began?

"Do you feel no guilt at what you've done?" Matthew asked.

"Guilt? What is that, Master Stock, but a foolish impulse of one too easily intimidated by fear of divine retribution?"

"You're an atheist, then?"

Stearforth laughed. "A practical man, rather. That God exists I make no effort to deny, but to be honest, I rarely see his image in my fellow men, but of the devil, rather, and if the devil is God then I have good reason to feel justified rather than condemned."

"Did you kill Graham?"

"I? No."

"But gave orders to him who did?"

Stearforth made a low bow of acknowledgment. "Words that if you report them, I'll deny every syllable and comma."

"And what about me? And my wife? What did we ever do to you?"

"Not a thing," Stearforth said, laughing again. "Why

should you suppose you needed to do anything to me to deserve what has happened? Blame it rather on bad luck, or your own officious long nose. After all, I never forced you to come to London to inquire after Kit Poole's hoary corpse. That was your notion."

"But you put me to it."

"And what if I did? My retort is that you continued what I merely began."

"What happened to Christopher Poole's body? Did you steal it to bring me to this pass?"

"Why, you are more intelligent than you seem, Master Stock. But have you come upon this grave truth only now? Poole's resurrection was mere bait. Yet see what big fish have been caught thereby."

Matthew looked down at his confession. He could read it now; the words stuck out as though enlarged: *I did murder the priest, Stephen Graham* seared his brain. Stearforth had written another line of equal power: *Sir Robert Cecil paid me twenty pounds with promise of a house in Suffolk.* What, a mere twenty pounds and a house that might be a hovel to turn a decent man off! What a world it was that men could even be supposed to risk heaven for such mischief.

Stearforth left him alone to study the words he was to speak, but Matthew spent his time thinking about Joan, where she might be and in what danger and whether he would ever see her sweet face again.

In his house in Chelsea, Sir Robert Cecil sat in his handsomely paneled study and worried about the queen's torpor and prepared inventories of the royal valuables and memoranda of accounts due and payable. He loved the woman of whom he was principal servant, but he was also a realist. If Elizabeth outlived the month it would be a miracle. Everytime he was in her presence now he saw the skull beneath the skin. Thrice he had dreamed of her death in a single week. Soon she would pass from his life, the way his honored father (and her greater servant) Lord Burghley had, the way his beloved wife had. Cecil was surviving them all, his hair prematurely gray, his health, never robust, as crooked as his back, only his fertile brain a match for the exigencies of his high office.

When the knocking came at his door, he admitted his visitor and saw, with some anticipation, that it was Richard Staunton.

"How is Matthew Stock?" he asked.

"Well, under the circumstances, Your Honor."

Staunton came over to stand at attention before Cecil's desk. The light of the candles extended so far as to illuminate his legs and trunk. The face of the man was hidden in the shadows, and had it not been for the familiar voice, Cecil would have had cause to doubt his visitor's identity.

"How are his spirits?"

"Good."

"They're feeding him well?"

"Yes, sir."

"You assured him of my regard?"

"As you requested, your honor."

"And he still maintains his innocence."

"He does."

"Good."

Cecil sat back in his chair and felt a strong pang of guilt. Matthew Stock was more than one of his agents; Cecil considered him a friend. Indeed, he was devoted to the husband and the wife. And where was Joan? She had promised to make a report of her findings as soon as she had learned something. But it had been two days and there was nothing. If it had not been for the queen's failing health, Matthew's predicament would have had all of his attention, but his agile mind could not be everywhere at once.

"Did Stock say anything of his wife? Has she been to see him?"

"No, sir. He made no mention of his wife, but seems entirely preoccupied with himself. He spoke most rudely to me, insisting you owed him a great debt for services performed in your behalf and hoped to have speedy release as compensation."

"Did he say that?" Cecil asked.

"His very words, if my memory doesn't deceive me, Sir Robert. He spoke with great insolence to me and disparagingly of your honorable self."

"Prison will change a man, Staunton," Cecil mused.

"That's God's truth, sir. Will that be all for tonight?"

"I think so, yes."

Cecil watched Staunton go and kept staring at the closed door as though he could see through it.

Staunton left his master with a feeling of deep relief. Cecil had not been ungenerous to him during his twelve-month tenure as one of the principal secretary's numerous clerks, and betrayal did not therefore come easy to him. Yet it came, as Staunton felt it must. The old order was changing and Cecil was a part of that order. Every hour might bring the death knell for the ancient woman who was queen and where should Staunton be then, bound to a lord who might have no place under the king who was to come? Yes, where should Richard Staunton be then?

Staunton did not proceed to his own rooms in the house, but went out into the night and walked a quarter of a mile to the far more modest dwelling of his cousin Roger Achely in Lime Street, where receiving a good welcome of his cousin and his wife, Staunton sat down to a late supper for which he repaid his hosts by such news of court as he had.

When his cousin's wife pleaded weariness about eleven o'clock and absented herself to bed, Staunton gave his cousin copies of Cecil's letters he had secretly conveyed from the house and told him all of Cecil's concern for his imprisoned agent.

"Excellent news," said Achely. "You are doing well. Trust me that His Grace shall know of it and reward you handsomely."

Achely went to his cupboard and brought back a little

leather purse and handed it to Staunton. Staunton undid the strings and poured the contents into his hand. He counted out five silver pieces, newly minted and shining by the fire-light.

"A goodly sum," he murmured happily.

"Well within your deserts, dear cousin," Achely said.

This pleasant transaction was a cause of gratification to them both, and during the next hour they drank enough Rhenish to keep them standing at the chamber pot the rest of the night.

Sometime close to twelve of the clock, Staunton thanked his cousin for his hospitality and set out for home. His in-toxication greatly diminished his proper caution as he trav-eled through the empty streets. Yet he was not so besotted to fail to notice the two men walking behind him at a dis-tance. They were only shadows against the houses, almost figments of his imagination. Like him they bore no torch or lamp but depended upon a generous moon, but their path was so congruent with his own and their pace so steady, it was not long before his suspicion grew and varying his way, once even doubling back on his tracks to confirm his fears, he was sobered completely and began to run.

He dared not look behind him but he could hear the clat-ter of their feet in pursuit and was out of breath entirely when he entered the back gate of Cecil House terrified that his pursuers, robbers surely, would follow him inside.

Clutching his purse to his side he did not feel safe until, admitted to the house by a sleepy-eyed butler who regarded him and his winey breath with disapproval, he made his way to his own room and closed the door soundly behind him.

He went at once and hid the purse in a chest he kept concealed in the bottom drawer of his desk along with cop-ies of other documents he had made and hoped to pass to his cousin at regular intervals in order to ensure a constant supply of gratitudes for his betrayal.

He was making ready for bed when the door opened and

two men came in. He was commencing to complain of the rudeness of their entry when they fell upon him.

"You villains," he cried, struggling to free himself. "Sir Robert shall know of this and have you beaten roundly."

His threat was no sooner spoken than Cecil himself appeared in the doorway.

"Sir Robert knows of it and more," Cecil said.

Staunton realized at that moment that the men constraining him were the two who had followed him from his cousin's and he felt such a weight of terror that his bowels loosened despite himself.

"Jesu God. He's beshit himself," said one of the men, noticing the disgrace.

"His incontinence bespeaks a guilty conscience," Cecil said, looking down at Staunton's leg, and then to one of the men who held Staunton. "Let him clean himself. Then bring him downstairs."

The serving man to whom this order was given had drawn a pistol and was holding it to Staunton's chest. With his free hand he shoved Staunton toward his bed and watched with steely eyes as Staunton removed his hose and tossed them, into a corner. He cleaned himself with water from a basin, dried himself with a towel, and then put on fresh hose he took from a chest in the corner. At the same time the second serving man was complying with Cecil's instruction that the room be searched.

Later, Staunton fell on his knees to beg his master's forgiveness even before the stolen letters were discovered and presented to Cecil.

Cecil, who seemed only a few inches taller even when Staunton was kneeling, looked at him with a remorseful expression.

"How did I know?" Cecil said, putting Staunton's question into words. "You lied about Matthew Stock. He would never have said what you reported. That was what you wanted me to think."

Staunton let his head drop forward. "Please forgive—"

"Yes, I'll forgive," said Cecil. "But first you'll talk—

freely or from a depth of pain beyond your imagining. The choice is yours. Afterwards, we'll negotiate the terms of my forgiveness."

14

*T*HE motions of the *Plover* had rocked her into a fitful
sleep in which Matthew's face appeared, disappeared,
changed whimsically to other faces, but once, alarmingly, to
Stearforth's.

Then the ship's more vigorous pitch and roll jerked her
awake. The strangeness of the place seized her like a gaged
fist. She sat upright in the bunk and cracked her head on an
overhanging beam. The captain had hung an oilskin cloak
on it which looked disturbingly like a hanged man swinging
on the gibbet.

It took her a few moments to remember where she was
and why, and then deep apprehension replaced the strangeness and aggravated the growing turmoil in her stomach
caused by the restless motion of the ship.

She went to the mullioned window and looked out.
Through the early morning mist she could see the broad expanse of rough water and a spreading wake and flat, green
land on either side. The ship was still in the river but proceeding toward its wide mouth and beyond the channel, to
the sea. Joan had never been at sea and she knew from the
queasy feeling in her gut that it would be an ordeal. She

was also afraid of Captain Morgan. What orders had he been given concerning her, once they reached France?

She heard the clomp of boots on the stairs outside the cabin. The door burst open and Morgan appeared.

His face was reddened by the wind, and moisture glistened on his beard and forehead. He looked tired but determined and she once again felt the mixture of attraction and fear that she had experienced in their first encounter. He regarded her with a surprised look, as if he had forgotten she was his prisoner.

"Did you get any sleep?" he asked, as he removed his cloak and cap and threw them on the opposite bunk. He stood firm despite the roll and pitch. Like a tree, she thought, rooted in the deck.

"A little. It wasn't easy, under the circumstances."

"No, I suppose it wouldn't be. Cook will bring something for you to eat. Can you wait an hour?"

She said she could. The idea of food repelled her at the moment, but she knew she must eat sometime. How she wished she were on dry land again. And yet the captain's ingratiating manner pleased her. Evidently, he thought of himself more as host than jailer. She thought that a good omen.

"Must I stay in this cabin for the voyage?"

"I'd stand clear of the deck. You'd just be in the way. The voyage won't be a long one. Have you been to sea before?"

"Never. Not even in a small boat."

Through his beard Morgan's lips parted into a genial smile. He sat down on the bunk, removed his boots, and swung his body into a horizontal position with one practiced motion. Seeing him there, staring up at the beams overhead, his expression relaxed, Joan wanted to ask who was piloting the ship, and then she remembered that a captain could hardly be expected to be at the helm at all hours. Of course he would have the one-eyed mate take his place. That stood to reason.

Although relaxing, Morgan did not seem averse to conversation. She asked him how long he had been captain, on what other ships he had served, and then she asked what she really wanted to know: whether he had a wife, and perhaps children. She would like to have asked their names, but that would have been to give away too much. She still was not sure of him, how he might respond to her if he knew exactly who she was and why she was being transported against her will. But then she wondered if he did not already know that from Motherwell or Stearforth.

Morgan said he had been master for three years, having served on another vessel as first mate. Yes, he had served on other vessels; he had worked his way up, having started his career at the age of eight in a pig of a ship that went straight to the bottom within a week of his joining its crew. Most of his shipmates, being unable to swim or find a barrel or beam to float upon, had drowned; he had been fortunate. He could not swim either, but in jumping over the side he had come up near the floating corpse of the ship's carpenter, a hulk of a man, and the captain being then a mere boy with no more weight than a goose, was able to cling to the dead man's belt until a benign tide brought both corpse and boy ashore.

"I named my son after him. The carpenter, I mean. He had saved my life unwittingly."

"And what was his name?" Joan asked, thankful for this opportunity to find out what she wanted to know.

"Simon. Simon Danvers."

"He must be a fine little boy," she said.

"Oh, he is. A strapping lad. Eight."

Joan thought she remembered Elspeth had said her son was seven, but maybe the captain was mistaken. Or perhaps she was. *Morgan* after all was not that uncommon a name. There might be other sea captains who were *Morgans*. Her captain might be a cousin or brother, yet how many with a Simon for a firstborn son?

"Is Simon your only child?"

"I have a daughter."

"And what is her name?"

He looked at her for a moment as though to inquire why she should take such an interest. "Catherine," he said.

Joan thought: he *must* be Elspeth's husband. She marveled again at the coincidence. But then she thought, Why not? The link was Stearforth. But in what precise way? The question was whether the master of the *Plover* was really one of the conspirators or a mere instrument? That was what she needed to find out. If he was not a fellow conspirator, she had reason to hope he could become her ally.

Their conversation was interrupted by the appearance of one of the crew, who declared in sailor's cant that there was something amiss with the sails and the captain needed straightway above deck. With the same easy motion that he had used in getting himself into the bunk in the first place, Morgan swiveled out, thrust his feet into his boots, and in what seemed to Joan no more than a second was on his way out the door again.

Joan noticed at once that he had forgotten to lock the door behind him but she was not sure what advantage escape would offer, given the distance to land and her own disinclination to leap into the river. She could swim no better than Morgan's poor companions who had gone down with his first ship and she could not count on a floating corpse to clutch to.

Now the ship began to roll more violently than before and her suffering became nearly intolerable. She clutched at her stomach and wished for death, flinging herself back in the bunk and shutting her eyes, as though a self-induced blindness would shut out the sickening motion. She tried to imagine herself in her own bed, with Matthew by her side, but she could not avoid the reality that he was in prison and she in another and hers the cramped cabin of a ship plowing deeper and deeper into turbulent sea. She felt her gorge rise. Seized by a powerful need to retch, she leaned her head over the side of the bunk and gagged helplessly. But there was little in her belly to void but a sour-tasting drool. She had not eaten since noon of the previous day and then only some bread and cheese. Her body convulsed with dry heaves. She sweat as though she had been standing before a raging fire, her head pounded, and again she wished for death, so sick she was.

Firm ground was what she needed. Air, fresh air, was the next best thing. She remembered that Morgan had not absolutely forbidden her to leave the cabin. He had only advised against it. But was she to die for her compliance with a mere suggestion? If she was to die, then she would die with the open sky above her, not entombed in this floating coffin.

She struggled from the bunk and made her way to the door and from there up the stairs to the main deck. The first things she saw above her were the flapping sheets of canvas; the next the horizon that seemed awry as though the whole world had tilted. About a dozen of the crew labored to raise a sail on the forward mast. She braced herself against a railing, filled her lungs with the bracing sea air, and looked to see where Morgan was.

He was high on the afterdeck, his hand on the helm and a second man helping him turn the great wheel. Joan saw now what had occasioned the sickening motion. The ship was changing course. Ahead was the open sea, an expanse of green and blue and flecks of white where the wind scattered the spume.

The vessel completed its turn. The horizon became even again, and the stinging air lessened Joan's nausea. She looked toward the bow. The crewmen had finished their labors and were staring at her. Their looks were more hostile than merely curious. She could tell how unwelcome she was. One, a big-chested man with bare arms, separated himself from the others and walked to the ship's side, where reaching into the coarsely made breeches he wore, he pulled something from inside and while looking at her but standing at an angle to her he urinated over the side.

The other men laughed. Joan turned away in anger and disgust.

"I advised you to stay below, Mistress Stock."

Morgan's voice at her ear startled her. She wouldn't have

thought he could make his way from the helm to where she was with such speed.

"I needed air," she said, still seething from the insult offered to her by the big sailor. "I was sick."

Morgan nodded understandingly and made a serious face. "My crew is an uncouth lot. You're well to stay out of their way. They may decide you're a witch."

"I hope I do not look like one," Joan said, bristling at this new offense to her dignity.

Morgan laughed. "It's not how you appear, but what you are—a woman. The men take your presence as bad luck. We didn't expect these rough seas, which have come on a sudden. The voyage over was as smooth as glass, but see now how the *Plover* is tormented."

Morgan looked up into the rigging; Joan followed his gaze and saw it wasn't the rigging that occupied his attention but the glowering heavens.

"Is there to be a storm, then?"

"There surely will be," said Morgan. "And for that reason I must ask you again to go below. Did cook bring you your breakfast?"

"No."

"Then he shall. And mine too, for God knows when I shall eat again if those clouds fulfill their promise."

She wanted to ask whether given such stormy prospects it wouldn't be wise to put back to land, but she knew his answer would be no. Besides, there was hardly time, for already he was ushering her below deck again.

He had not left her alone for a minute when the cook entered. He came in without knocking. He was a very fat man in a fouled apron, and he averted his eyes from her as he put a covered bowl and a flagon down on the table and went out, without having said a word in greeting or in response to her thank you. She uncovered the bowl and inspected its contents, finding neither its greenish watery appearance or fishy odor appetizing. Even had she done so, she probably would not have eaten, fearing that some obnoxious ingredient or poison might have been added by the superstitious crew. Besides, she decided practically, why eat if the seas roughened as promised and all was to be vomited again?

There was a seat by the stern window and she sat down there and looked out. The waves were higher now and she could barely make out the coast in the distance. The thought that she was at sea, really at sea, divorced from the solid earth and bobbing precariously above God knew what depths with strange monsters lurking beneath filled her with unspeakable dread. So despairing she was that she forced herself to think of Matthew, although his condition was no better. She wondered what he must be doing now, what he must be suffering. She wondered if he had been made aware of her own captivity and was sure he had. It would be another thing hanging over his head: his wife's danger if he did not do what he was told. Curse Stearforth, she thought. And that damned villain Motherwell.

Nor were her thoughts particularly kindly toward Sir Robert Cecil, whose golden words of concern for his faithful servant were all very well, but by his own admission considerably short of what was needed to work Matthew's deliverance.

Stearforth, now jailer and servant, brought Matthew a fresh suit of clothes. They fit badly but offered him a chance to air his own, which reeked of the prison and his own fear. Then he had been left alone in a bedchamber, locked in as he quickly confirmed, to learn his confession, word for word as His Grace had commanded.

Matthew had decided earlier that professing a poor memory would be a plausible delay, and yet he knew sooner or later he must recite as ordered or he was done for—and Joan too. It was hard to imagine why his captors would spare either of them if his feigned compliance was discovered. It was time he needed, time to think, time to escape.

Stearforth returned in the early evening to escort him to supper. He was relieved to find that Stearforth would be his only companion at table. His Grace was eating elsewhere,

Stearforth said somewhat mysteriously, although with the implication that the company would be considerably more elevated than the present.

All of which was well and good with Matthew. He had no stomach for another of His Grace's self-indulgent discourses on court life. Stearforth was abhorrent too, but somehow his down-to-earth vileness was more palatable. A liveried servant brought in a succession of dishes, the chief ornament of which was a goose of such succulence and expert seasoning that Matthew had never had the like. There was an assortment of other meats, and Matthew concluded that whatever His Grace lacked in true grace, he did not want for an excellent larder and cook.

Matthew ate ravenously. Stearforth talked, largely about women he had seduced since leaving the university. As they were concluding the meal, he came around to the matter at hand and Matthew paid more attention.

"So how stands your learning of the confession?"

"Not well."

"But certainly you know the first page."

"Not so much."

"The first few sentences then? Can you repeat them for me now?"

Matthew did in fact remember the first few sentences, but in reciting them he deliberately confused the words, omitting a negative so it ruined the sense and stuttering over a phrase before shrugging in a semblance of utter helplessness.

"My God, man, you'll look more village idiot than murderer. Do you want to get out of this mess, or no?"

"Of course I do. Who would not move all the world to escape hanging?"

"You, evidently," Stearforth shot back. "You must do better. You go before the council in a few days. It is all arranged. You must have every word then. If not, it will be my neck as well as yours, and I assure you mine is of proper length already."

"I am doing my best," Matthew said, feebly, finishing the last piece of goose from his plate.

"Come, do you have the text about you?"

"It's upstairs."

"Marry, let us go then and practice. I'll be your tutor."

Upstairs, Stearforth took over his new calling with perverse enthusiasm. He made Matthew sit in a chair before him while Stearforth, standing, held the text of the confession, read a sentence or two aloud and then had Matthew repeat it word for word.

Matthew stumbled over the sentences; Stearforth became angry.

"Oh this is too much, Stock. The sentence is plain on its face."

"I am undone by your sitting there demanding this of me," Matthew replied.

"The council will do so," Stearforth said. "You must not only have your confession down pat. You must also be prepared to endure their questioning. They won't let one of their number stand accused without questioning you. There will be hell to pay. What, do you think to find salvation from this charge by faith alone? No, you must work. Learn your part. Prepare to be questioned."

Matthew said he would try to do better. Stearforth sighed heavily and handed him the papers. "Here, try it again. I'll leave you. When I come back, know the first five sentences. That will bring you up to the part where Cecil secures your services with a promise of twenty pounds and a house in Suffolk."

"Does he have such a house to give?" Matthew asked.

"Who knows? It will be thought he has even if he does not. Rumor has him landlord of every other house in England."

Stearforth shut the door behind him. Matthew decided he had provoked Stearforth enough. The man was beside himself with fear that Matthew would not perform. And why shouldn't he be? It was his neck too. His Grace would hold

Stearforth responsible if Matthew failed. So politic a gentleman as Stearforth was would understand that.

Matthew decided he might as well learn his text. If he scratched Stearforth more, he would bleed for sure. Matthew still had a few days until he was to be taken before the council. Between then and now he could contemplate his escape. But before he did that, he would discover the identity of His Grace.

The pain was so excruciating that Staunton momentarily lost consciousness. The dash of water in his face brought him to his senses again and he had time to cry out to his captors that he would talk after all before the man he had once been contemptuous of because he endured a menial job in Cecil's stable could twist the leather strap even tighter around his skull.

Pinkerton—that was the man's name. "You will say what you promised to say, or I shall twist again."

"Yes, yes, God, I'll talk."

His place of confinement was a room in the stable. They had set him down in fouled straw with his hands tied behind him and to a post. Around him was the smell of horses and leather and his own excrement, for his cleaning of himself had wanted thoroughness. Sir Robert had sent the three of them there because he didn't want his house polluted by torture, which he despised, he said, yet he would know to whom Staunton was conveying information or else.

The safety of the state depended on it.

Whose state? Staunton had thought while they were dragging him from the house, a gag in his mouth. Hers the state of England now was? Or his who was to come?

The second man, Chumley, one of the household servants, an ex-soldier whom Cecil employed more as bodyguard than butler, for Staunton had never yet seen the man do aught but lurk behind the master, went off to tell Cecil Staunton would talk. Pinkerton, a stout fellow with the knavish face of a highwayman, perched on a barrel top and watched his prisoner.

"Can you ease my wrists? They're bleeding," Staunton asked.

"They shall bleed more," Pinkerton said.

"Sir Robert won't be pleased if he comes only to find me dead."

"He won't find you dead. Peace, now, or I'll twist a few times more before he comes."

Staunton shut his eyes, remembering the agony of the tourniquet. He thought his head was going to explode. The pain had drained him of strength and will. What did it matter if he told? He would probably die anyway. Confession would at least reward him with a quick death. Then Pinkerton and Chumley or perhaps the both of them would slit his throat and his body would be found floating in the Thames. That's how it was done—where there was no body, there could be no murder. He had no strong loyalties to those who had promised him so much. A position in the new government—an undersecretary to some undersecretary. Enough to buy a new suit of clothes or a manor house where he could play country lord and have his way with the serving wenches, populating the neighborhood with his bastards. Perhaps he should have harkened to the voice of conventional wisdom that warned of such an ascent. But he couldn't stand the thought of ending up a mere cleric or worse, a schoolmaster drilling village brats in their Latin parsing.

Staunton heard Cecil's voice and turned his head to see the little hunchback strutting in with Chumley at his heels like a faithful hound. He realized suddenly how much he had always hated Cecil, quite without realizing it. Surely the man's physical deformity was a sign of some inward corruption. The very idea had helped Staunton justify his disloyalty. But now he felt he needed no justification. Pure hatred was enough. He tried to express it through his defiant glance, but Cecil refused to meet his eyes. He seemed to look everywhere in the stable but at the man he had ordered to be tortured, and his long aristocratic face was sad rather than triumphant.

"What has he to say?" Cecil asked, addressing the question to Pinkerton, who out of respect for his master was now standing at attention behind him. Staunton was so offended by Cecil's putting the question to another, as though he himself were absent, that he almost resolved to endure more torture than speak.

"Only that he is prepared to confess now, Your Honor," said Pinkerton.

"Then let him do so."

At last Cecil looked directly at Staunton. Staunton said nothing.

"Does he need more time with you alone?" Cecil asked.

"I'll speak," Staunton said, remembering the tourniquet that still bound his forehead.

"For whom do you spy?"

"My cousin."

"The house you were followed to."

"His house. I gave the copies to him."

"To what end?"

"Money. Surely you've found that too in my chamber."

"I mean what end were the papers to serve? They have no value in themselves."

"I don't know."

"Your cousin's name again?"

Staunton said the name.

"I've never heard of the man. What business does he have with me?"

"He works for another."

"Whom?"

"Some lord, someone important. He wouldn't tell me his name."

"He's lying, Your Honor," said Pinkerton from behind Cecil. "Surely a man knows for whom he works."

Cecil seemed to ignore the interruption. He kept studying Staunton's face; the intensity of his gaze made Staunton more fearful than the thought of another twist of the tourniquet.

"See if you can loosen his tongue, Pinkerton," Cecil said. He walked away into the shadows. Pinkerton moved forward to obey his master's order even before Staunton could tense his body for the agony to come. He screamed with the pain, but this time did not faint. He was blinded by tears and when he spoke it was more wail than words.

"For the life of my soul, I don't know, Sir Robert."

Staunton was vaguely aware of Pinkerton's hand at the strap and he screamed in anticipation of the pressure, but Cecil's command prevented it.

Cecil walked out of the shadows and looked down at Staunton again. "He probably doesn't know. To think that a man would sell his integrity to a master he was ignorant of. What if it is the devil you serve? How would you know it? Or would you even care as long as there were something in it for you in the short run? Unbind him. The very sight of him disgusts me."

Staunton breathed easier. Cecil's contemptuous words seemed almost to relieve his fear. Perhaps that would be the end of his punishment.

"Oh, one more thing," said Cecil. "What was it you told Matthew Stock in prison?"

Staunton thought about the question before replying. He had betrayed his cousin. Was there any point in concealing anything now? "I told him that you could do nothing for him. That you believed him to be guilty of the parson's murder. That he should pray to God for his soul."

"You lied to him then," Cecil said.

"Shall I kill the liar?" Pinkerton asked.

Cecil shook his head. "No, clean him up and bring him back into the house."

"If I had been the master, I would have twisted until your eyes popped out," Pinkerton said as soon as Cecil was gone.

Chumley untied him and helped him to his feet. His ordeal had left him almost too weak to stand. He wept silently with relief while Cecil's servants roughly brushed the foul straw from his doublet. Chumley said traitors deserved no dainty treatment and that the master was the soul of kindness in light of what Staunton deserved.

They brought him into one of the downstairs rooms which had been furnished as a waiting room for Cecil's many clients. Cecil was waiting there. Before him on a table was a silver goblet Cecil had recently received as a gift. Staunton had made his admiration of the article known to Cecil.

Cecil spoke sternly. "Chumley will gather your belongings from your room. From this day forward I don't want to see your face. You admired this goblet. It's yours. Consider it as severance pay, if you will. Or compensation for your torture, or even a bribe for your continued silence, what you will. But if you trouble me again with your treasons, or if you pass on to this cousin of yours another word of what passed in this house, it will be stolen, no gift. Pinkerton and Chumley will be my witnesses that you stole it. You will be arrested and tried for larceny and hanged. Your cousin will also be arrested. Don't ask on what charge, I'll find something and his imprisonment will not be sweet. It's as simple as that. Do you understand?"

Staunton said he did.

When Staunton was gone from the house, Cecil went upstairs to bed. It had been a very long day and the little man was weary, physically and otherwise. His health had not been good recently; he had already commenced his mourning for the queen, whose physicians daily prophesied her imminent death. And he missed his wife fiercely. The treachery of Staunton which he abhorred and the resort to torture, which he had no liking for either, deepened his melancholy.

Then there was Matthew Stock's situation. What must the poor man have thought when Staunton told him Cecil had repudiated him? And where was Joan Stock, who had been told to give him daily reports on her findings? He had his operatives out all over London in search of her, but there wasn't a trace.

Prepared for bed, he fell on his knees to pray. He prayed for his dead—his father, mother, wife. He prayed for his children, for his own soul. He prayed for his enemies and lastly, he prayed for Matthew Stock who was in prison and for Joan Stock, who seemed to have vanished from the earth.

15

THE sky was as dark as the sea. The ship seemed on the verge of foundering. The cabin had taken in water; water was sloshing on the deck, pummeling the leaded panes of the cabin's mullioned windows. From below timbers groaned under the strength of the tempest, and from everywhere Joan heard the hoarse cries of hapless men.

She clung to the braces of the bunk, too frightened to be sick, to think of Matthew, to think at all.

The cabin door swung open and shut freely. With every roll of the ship a torrent of water came down the hatch. She could hear it, a great gushing noise. She could not see out the stern windows. Then the men's voices grew louder and she heard the tone of anger, not just alarm.

She started as Morgan was dragged into the cabin with his arms held by two of the other men, the one-eyed mate and the man who had urinated onto the deck. They gave Morgan a shove and then slammed the door behind him.

"What's happened?" Joan shouted over the din of the storm. "Are we to sink or live?"

Morgan gave no answer. He picked himself up off the deck and stumbled toward his bunk, obviously in pain. He turned to look at her and she could see a savage cut above his right eye, and below the left his check was badly bruised. His eyes flashed angrily, but she understood his anger was not directed at her. He emitted a string of curses, calling his crew treacherous dogs and filthy base villains, every one.

"It's mutiny," he gasped. "They've taken over the ship. Turning it back. To England."

"Because of the storm?"

"Yes."

Joan was sympathetic with the captain's plight but not ungrateful to the mutineers. Nothing could please her more at the moment than the thought of returning to land. What puzzled her in the perilous circumstances was why Morgan should be so insistent in holding his course for France. How could the little vessel survive such a tempest?

As though reading her mind, he answered the question.

"It's safer to stay in open sea in such a storm than make for land again. They're cowards, all of them. Fearful of heavy weather and of a woman. They'll be the death of us all."

"They believe I've caused the storm?"

"Incredible, isn't it? Superstitious knaves."

She could feel the ship turning. Where before the ship was pitching violently as it headed into the seas, it now fell into the troughs between the waves, and she could hardly hold onto the bunk. The water on the cabin deck now sloshed upward to where she was. Whatever was not fixed to its place flew in every direction. Like a live creature, the ship shuddered and groaned. A sharp snapping sound came from above.

"That's the foremast going," shouted Morgan.

"Oh God help us!" Joan cried.

"Holding her into the wind was our only hope."

Morgan fell back onto his bunk and stared up into the ceiling of the cabin. Joan wondered if he was resolved to die or merely to wait out the storm. She knew there was nothing she herself could do. They and the ship were in God's hands now.

The next hour was hellish. The storm did not abate and yet the ship did not sink. Morgan, who said very little during this time but continued to stare moodily into the ceiling, at least let her know that the masts had been lost and the rudder earlier. Wind and current were now piloting the vessel.

"Are they likely to steer us to England?" she asked.

"Yes. If we are unlucky."

Joan shut her eyes and prayed, as earnestly as she ever had in her life.

Then as suddenly as the storm had arisen, it subsided. First the wind stopped its howling; somewhat later the seas calmed. She felt a resurgence of hope, but Morgan seemed more despairing than ever.

"The storm has ceased. Quiet at last. We're safe," Joan said.

Morgan laughed bitterly. "Would to God it were so. Your safety is a foolish dream."

She turned to look at him across the cabin, puzzled at his response. If the storm had run its course, were they not safe? The ship was still afloat. Would they not be rescued, perhaps by another vessel, or at least, be carried to land by a friendly current?

"They can't let me live," Morgan said in a voice without emotion. "They've seized the vessel, committed a mutiny. All shall hang. My testimony against them is their death warrant."

"You don't mean they'll kill you?"

"That's what I mean. And you too."

Morgan's words gave her a greater fear than the storm had done. But of course he was right. The men would understand that. The captain's death would be easily explained if the crew were put to the proof. He simply fell overboard in the tempest, or drowned in an effort to swim to shore. Her own disappearance would require no justification at all. There was no record of her presence on the ship. Her burial at sea would be the most obscure of deaths, without monument or epitaph. What the unknown engineer of these mysteries had forborne, nature had indirectly caused, in driving the crew to mutiny and by their crime to murder as a means of concealing it.

"Can we not reason with them for our lives?"

"Are beasts capable of reason?"

"Or secure the door against them?"

"They've secured it against our escape. With hammer and nail. Trust me, the mate will cheerfully feed me to the fishes. Feed the both of us," Morgan added.

Morgan seemed to have reconciled himself to fate; Joan was less inclined to give over the effort. She decided it was time to tell him who she was, explain why she had been sent to sea. What could she lose now? Perhaps his hate—if that was what was in store for her—would stir him from his lethargy, stimulate his mind to engage the problem of escape.

She decided to be direct.

"I know your wife," she said.

Morgan made no response. He lay staring up at the ceiling, his hands covering his chest as though he had been laid out for the grave. Then he rose on one arm and looked at her curiously.

"You know Elspeth? How?"

"My husband is Matthew Stock, the man accused of murdering Stephen Graham."

"My brother-in-law is dead—murdered!" he exclaimed in a way to satisfy Joan that this was the first news he had had of the event.

"You hadn't heard?"

"How could I? I've been at sea nearly a year. We weren't in England more than a day before we set sail again. I have had no news for months. I don't know whether the queen lives or whether her successor wears the crown. And you tell me my wife's brother has been murdered—and your husband is charged with the crime?"

Joan gave Morgan a shortened version of Matthew's story, explaining how Stearforth had come to Chelmsford and represented himself as Graham and lured Matthew and her to London.

Morgan was sitting up now and giving his full attention to her account. He had seemingly forgotten about the mutiny and Joan was gratified to see that he gave no sign of disbelieving what she had said.

"Why didn't you tell me this before?"

"I saw how close you and Stearforth were—and Motherwell; I suspected you were part of the conspiracy."

"Not I," Morgan said. "I despise the man."

"Then why did you so readily receive me and set sail when you had hardly drawn a breath of England's air?"

"Stearforth is secretary and general factotum to Lady Elyot, who owns the *Plover*. It was through her appointment I was made master of the vessel. When he told me I was to take you to sea I assumed the order came from her ladyship. What was I to do?"

"Stearforth has been dismissed from Lady Elyot's service," Joan said. "He now serves another, the man who gave orders to have your wife's brother murdered and my husband blamed. Stearforth anticipated your ignorance of these things. He took advantage of it."

"As he would do," said Morgan. "But tell me, how fares my wife and children? You've seen them all, then?"

"I saw them indeed—only a few days ago. Elspeth received me coolly at first, which was only natural given her belief I was a murderer's wife. But we talked and grew acquainted. She said she'd help me clear my husband's name, find a diary kept by her brother that might give a name to his enemies."

"And did she find the diary?"

"I found it myself, for when I returned the next day to receive it of her, she was colder than at first. I believe Stearforth had followed me to your house and spoken to Elspeth after I left. I suspect, too, that he threatened her and the children if any spoke kindly to me again."

"I will cut off the serpent's head when I see him again," Morgan said.

"You won't if we are fed to fishes," Joan reminded him. "Nor will Stephen Graham's death be avenged or my innocent husband freed."

"Who did you say Stearforth serves now?"

"I don't know," Joan said. "But I believe him to be a churchman."

Morgan looked incredulous. "What, a man of God a murderer and traitor?"

"Your brother-in-law was being considered for a bishopric. His outspokenness about Poole's resurrection—"

"Whose *what*?"

But of course Morgan hadn't heard about Poole either.

"Poole was a priest—a Jesuit. He died last year but swore before he would resurrect within the twelve month—or so his adherents claimed. Someone dug up his body. The Papists screamed miracle. Your brother-in-law denounced the fraud and so became a champion of the church, although the fraud might have been done to besmirch his reputation."

"If so, it had the opposite effect," Morgan said.

"And thereby put him in greater danger. Lord Bacon's party preferred another in his stead."

"As rector of St. Crispin's?"

"As bishop. I don't know what see. According to his diary, Ely was vacant, and one other soon to be."

"But would a man murder for a bishopric?"

Joan had pondered this same question. To her the church was her town parish; ecclesiastical authority her own parson. But she knew it was otherwise in the greater world. The lords spiritual of England did well for themselves. They lived in palaces and rode in coaches. Their voices were heard in the queen's own Privy Council, and their election to their princely offices were matters of considerable political significance. Joan might not know the bishop of Ely or London from Adam but the queen knew him and cared who he was and what he believed and so she had no doubt that even one of God's annointed might send another to a premature reward if moved by ambition or greed.

"He would—and perhaps even more gladly if he thought he could bring a great man down at the same time."

She was relieved that Morgan did not ask her who this great man might be. She was not prepared to allow her candor to take her that far. Morgan seemed preoccupied still with Stearforth's perfidy. Joan was more hopeful now. Perhaps a desire for revenge would do what mere self-interest could not—move Morgan to constructive action.

Joan went over to the window and looked out. Her heart leaped as she saw land in the distance, white cliffs rising from the blue-green sea. Without rudder or mast, the *Plover* was floating ashore, stern first.

Above her she could hear the sounds of men's voices. She listened carefully trying to hear the matter. It was the crew, arguing about what was to be done. A shrill voice rose above the rest to demand quick action. Morgan and the woman had to be disposed of, the voice said. The ship would be spotted from the coast. Salvagers would be scattering on the beach.

But some of the crew were hesitant. Joan heard another deeper voice raised in the captain's defense. Morgan was a fair captain, a decent man, the voice said. It was cold-blooded murder to throw him overboard.

She heard the shrill voice scream otherwise. If the captain was to be freed, they might as well hang themselves now, for it would be all over with them as soon as shore was reached and the captain had told all. There was a chorus of yeas to this reasoning, and Joan's heart sank. The deeper voice now fell silent; no voice was raised in her own defense. That she should be cast overboard seemed a matter of general agreement.

She turned to look at Morgan. He was sitting up in his bunk and by the look on his face she knew he had heard the voices too. And why not, with only a few inches of beam and board between their heads and the feet of the mutineers?

"What shall we do?" she asked.

Morgan got up and went to the window. "We're a furlong from land. Too far to swim and the ship's boat was crushed when the foremast fell. With this tide it will be less than an hour before the ship is on the beach. They may put down an anchor, but my guess is that this crew will be as eager as the rats to say farewell to the ship, damn them all to hell. Especially my mate. It was he you heard leading on in this mischief."

"And they'll kill us first?"

"Maybe not," said Morgan.

Morgan walked over and began pounding on the cabin door and yelling to be let out. He wanted to talk to Simkins, he said. Joan surmised Simkins was the one-eyed mate, the owner of the shrill voice.

Within a few moments, Joan heard the braces that had been used to make the cabin a cell removed and the door opened. Simkins and the cook came in. Simkins carried a sword, the cook a cleaver. Three or four others crowded around in the passageway, trying to see into the cabin.

Simkins flashed a look of contempt at Joan and then addressed Morgan.

"What do you want?" Simkins snarled. "If you intend to beg for mercy, you were better to forget it. It's too late for that now. Land's in sight."

"I've seen the land," Morgan said calmly. "I only wonder if you've thought wisely about what you do."

"Oh, we've thought wisely enough," replied Simkins. "We'd be at the bottom of the Channel had you had your way, Morgan—or at best at sea again for twelve month."

There was a harsh murmur of agreement from the other crewmen. The men's faces looked determined and unmistakably hostile.

"Well, then, perhaps you're right," said Morgan, in the same calm voice as before. "I can well understand your thinking. You're mutineers. I and this woman can testify against you. It's a dilemma, but one admitting to a simple solution."

Simkins and the others seemed taken aback by Morgan's concession, and yet Joan noticed no sign that Morgan's words were to be considered an invitation to begin the executions forthwith. Morgan had been successful to that extent. But then she realized that Morgan's oratory had not concluded. She could tell by his fixed expression, the look of a man completely in possession of himself. Had Morgan accepted his death like a condemned man on the gallows who blesses the executioner? Or did Morgan have a plan?

"You may do what you like with me but I hope you'll spare the woman for your own sakes."

"Her?" replied Simkins. "Why should we? She brought the storm upon us. She caused all this trouble."

"That may be true," said Morgan. "But I mean it's a shame to lose the reward."

"What reward?" asked the cook.

"Shut up," said Simkins, turning angrily to his companion. "Don't you see it's a trick? There's no reward. Why should there be?"

"Simkins is right, as usual," said Morgan casually, addressing himself to the cook and the other men. "I'm just making the reward up in my head. Just a trick to escape. But consider the circumstances in which this woman was brought on board. Simkins was there. So were you, Drury," he said, nodding to a thin man of about thirty standing in the passage. "Did you think her an ordinary passenger? See how she's dressed. Well enough to be a lady, don't you think? And don't you suppose whoever brings her to her husband safely after she's been abducted as she has been will be paid handsomely?"

Morgan got no answer to the question, not even from Simkins, who seemed, however, not as aggressive as before. Morgan continued. "That's what you'll lose, the reward for bringing her back. Of course, you'll trade the money for safety."

"By God, we will," said Simkins, asserting himself again.

"Although you could have them both—safety and the reward."

"You'd promise to shut up about the mutiny?" Simkins

asked, screwing his face into a mask of sarcasm. "Oh, yes, I'm sure you'd be as mum as a mouse, at least until we all got ashore and you let the world know what had happened."

"I'd be a fool to do so," said Morgan.

"What do you mean?" asked the cook.

"We've heard enough from him," interrupted Simkins. "I say let's throw them both overboard and look to ourselves. This talk of rewards is a mere device. There's no husband, and no reward."

"But how do you know there isn't?" protested the cook, turning from Simkins to Morgan again. "The woman was brought on board a prisoner. That was clear. And she's the age to have a husband and her clothes look as though he does well by himself. It might be true."

"It is true," Joan declared firmly, emboldened by Morgan's confidence. "I am a married woman with a husband who dotes on me. I was taken aboard this vessel against my will, and as God is my witness, my husband would give his fortune to have me home again."

"And who is your husband? Some greengrocer, I warrant," said Simkins with a mocking laugh.

"He's rich enough to make my safety worth your while," Joan said defiantly. "He's a servant of a certain high-placed gentleman I could mention. I was abducted because of some information I had that might be useful to this lord. Indeed, I think he might also be willing to reward anyone who might set me at liberty. And this lord I mention is one of the wealthiest men in England."

Simkins continued to look skeptical. He held firmly to his weapon but turned to search the faces of his followers, as though he expected them to share his disbelief. Joan thought, however, that the crew were wavering. The men in the doorway looked interested, and even the cook had lowered his cleaver to a less threatening position.

"A lot of good a reward will do hanged men," said Simkins.

"And who would testify that you are mutineers?" Morgan shot back. "This woman who would have great cause to love you for your service to her? Her husband who would likewise be grateful? This great lord, his patron, who would no doubt be doubly generous? You might retire from this profession of seaman for all the wealth you'd have."

"*You'd* tell," said Simkins accusingly.

"Oh yes, I'd tell," said Morgan with a laugh. "I'd tell and send myself to the gibbet."

"How's that?" asked the cook.

"What," said Morgan. "Accuse you of mutiny when I myself can be charged as abductor of this woman? It was I, after all, who brought her aboard my ship. The responsibility is mine, not yours. Believe me, I'm not so offended by the mutiny that I am prepared to hang myself to avenge you. My interests are in keeping silent, and in taking a share of the reward. You, Drury, were always a good man."

"You were a good master, Captain," said Drury, looking somewhat sadly in at the door. Joan recognized by his voice that Drury was the one who had spoken in defense of Morgan earlier.

"There now," said Morgan with easy assurance. "You'd have the reward, freedom from this ship, and a clean conscience."

"All that we'd enjoy without you," Simkins said. He had a smug look on his face.

"No you wouldn't," Joan said. "For without the captain's safety there'll be no reward, of that I assure you. If the captain's killed, I'll swear you abducted me, not he. Your reward will be the hangman's blessing. Let the captain and me go and no harm's done. Your fortune's made."

"This is a fool's game," Simkins said, his face contorted. "Seize them. Over the side with the both of them and be done with talk."

The other crewmen made no show to move. They looked at each other uncertainly.

"Not so fast, Simkins," Drury said. "Let's think the captain's offer through."

"We've thought it through," Simkins retorted, casting a menacing glance at Drury.

"I think Drury's right," said the cook, who had been silent for some time. "What's the point of putting our own necks in jeopardy? What's to gain? Now here's a fair offer from the captain and the lady, which, if they give their words and we ours, then a pact is made and all's well that ends so."

"I don't like it," said Simkins, turning on the cook and Drury, who had now come farther into the cabin and was standing by the cook.

"Do you promise, Captain, to lay no blame for mutiny at our feet?" asked Drury.

"With all my heart," Morgan said.

Drury turned to Joan. "And you, Mistress, do you promise not to say aught evil against us and to help us to a reward for your freedom."

"I do," Joan said.

"Well then," Drury said, "a pact is made and I am satisfied."

"And I am satisfied too," said the cook, turning to the men who were watching from the passage. There was a murmur of consent from them as well. But Simkins looked unyielding. He held the sword firmly in his grasp, pointing it at Morgan.

"What say you, Simkins?" Morgan asked. "You have no followers now that a pact is agreed upon. Will you join the pact or stand on your own—without clemency or reward? You can't have these without giving over your sword."

"I'll not give over my sword, or make a pact," Simkins said. He turned on his heels and pushed the cook and Drury aside as he went up the passageway. Morgan ran after. Joan followed.

On the main deck the ruin the storm had caused was more than evident in the clutter of fallen rigging and spars. Simkins had made his way to the afterdeck, a lone rebel now that the crew had been pacified, perhaps as much by the calmed sea as Morgan's compromise. He stood for a moment by the untended helm and then clambered over the rail. Rushing aft with the others, Joan heard the splash.

From the rail she could see Simkins in the water. He was already a dozen yards from the ship's side, swimming with powerful strokes toward the white cliffs in the distance. She watched with the other men for a moment in awe of his ability before being deafened by an explosion that seemed to go off not a foot from her ear.

She had not recovered from this before a second explosion occurred. She turned to look and saw Morgan standing against the rail, a heavy musket in his arms. The broad flaring muzzle still emitted a noxious vapor of gunpowder. She turned again to where Simkins had been but he was gone.

"Did you get him, Captain?" she heard Drury say from somewhere in the crowd of faces.

"God help me, I did," said Morgan.

Joan looked at Morgan. There was a broad grin of triumph on his face. "I hate a mutineer more than a rat," he said, noticing her look of surprise.

She turned toward land again, toward cliffs, searching the watery expanse that was now less tranquil with the approaching surf. Once, she thought she might have seen a head bobbing in the waters, but afterward there was nothing.

Morgan now gave orders that the anchor be set and the ship saved from going aground, but two crewmen returned presently to say that the anchor had been lost during the storm. "There's no help, then," said Morgan, "but to abandon the ship."

At this there was a general scurrying around the decks. Joan watched as at least a dozen men jumped overboard, while others clung to the railings and called after their brethren or threw spars in after them. The ship itself was beginning to pitch violently, even though the shore still seemed some distance. All around her now was a swirling of white water. The ship twisted, no longer heading in stern first but athwartships. A sudden jarring knocked her to the deck. The ship leaned onto its side and convulsed as though it had received a terrible wound, then righted itself but seemed lower in the water.

She heard men screaming—some cursed and others prayed. Someone pulled her to her feet and she saw it was Morgan. Only the two of them remained at the stern. What was left of the crew had congregated on the main deck and were looking toward the beach, which now lay about a furlong distant.

"We've hit the rocks," he yelled. "The ship's lost."

"Will we drown?"

"Not if I can help it, but we must wait until the last minute."

She saw that more men were leaping from the side. Most could not swim. She saw them bob in the water for a moment and then disappear under the waves. Meanwhile the forepart of the vessel began to sink lower into the water and at the same time slip over on its side so that she was at some effort to stand upright. Like Morgan, she gripped firmly to the helm. Above her the cloudless sky was in its repose in sharp contrast to the chaos on deck as the last of the crew gave themselves up to heaven and dove over the side.

"Wait here," said Morgan. He slipped down the deck and disappeared into the cabin below.

The ship gave another great jolt, but this time Joan was not knocked to her knees. She stood upright by the helm, as though she were piloting the *Plover* to its destruction. The forecastle, half-submerged before, rose up gracefully, while the stern began to slip under. Joan watched, frozen, as the ship twisted and leaned precariously, and water washed across the deck. She heard a loud cracking from below deck, and then with a more thunderous report the ship broke in half, the forecastle sinking again and then pulling away, while the after part of the vessel, nearly submerged, now rushed toward the cliffs.

Joan clung still to the helm, petrified. She could not remove her gaze from the white cliffs that seemed now to rise immediately before her. The broken vessel on which she rode twisted and then suddenly there was a loud scraping noise. She was flung so violently forward that she lost her grip, and the next thing she knew she was in the sea, flailing around in icy water and nearly blinded by salty spray. She could barely make out a few yards from her the carcass of the vessel, breaking into smaller pieces as it foundered in the turbulence.

At the same moment she was caught up in a powerful embrace. She looked up and saw it was Morgan. For a moment he was standing above her, his legs braced in the surf; the next he was in the water with her as both were seized by a huge wave and hurled toward the cliffs.

16

MATTHEW had a dream of Joan. He saw her in his mind as clear as day, standing in her kitchen in the big Chelmsford house that was also his shop. She wore her gown of pale green with the full slit sleeves. Her face shone with happiness, so much that it made his heart ache to see it. Their daughter Elizabeth was also there and his grandchild and namesake. It was some sort of family celebration, for all went to sit at the long trestle table, the surface of which could not be seen for all the plates, bowls, cups, and trenchers loaded with food of every sort.

Then Matthew looked up to see that a guest sat at his own place at the head of the table. It was His Grace, with his elbows firmly planted on the table. He was dressed again in that immense ruff collar, that fine cloth of one who wore his wealth. His Grace smiled and served himself. No one else ate.

A covered dish sat before His Grace. He lifted the cover and out crawled a serpent that began to wind itself across the table. Everyone but His Grace looked at the serpent fearfully, but he was calm. He smiled with his thin lips, smiled at Matthew.

A noise awoke Matthew, not the dream. It was not yet

dawn; the chamber was dark. He tried to remember Joan's face, her expression. But only the image of his captor remained.

He lay brooding for a while, disturbed by his vision, then got out of bed and dressed by the faint light of early morning. He looked out the window. They had given him a chamber in the back of the house where his view of the city was cut off, making it impossible for him to know exactly where he was. But the neighboring house was a fine one too, built in an older style, not the newer fashion of timber and plaster. If the front of the house was like the side he viewed, Matthew believed he could recognize it again.

When it grew light enough to read he fetched his confession. During the next hour he committed a good half of it to memory. Then Stearforth came. Buck was with him.

He told them of his progress.

"Very well," said Stearforth, with a skeptical glance at Buck. "We shall see. His Grace has asked to hear you recite this morning. I hope you will have the wisdom not to disappoint him."

"His Grace hates to be disappointed," Buck added.

Buck was very well dressed and acted cocky, like a new heir eager to show off before his old friends. It was hard for Matthew to associate this young dandy with the person with whom he had shared a prison cell. But of course Buck had never been a real prisoner.

"Shall I have breakfast first?" Matthew said.

"There will be time enough to eat after you've learned your part," Stearforth replied. "Give us a sample of what you know now."

Matthew could see in Stearforth's stony visage that his request was more a challenge than a mere invitation. He imagined Stearforth had been complaining to Buck about Matthew Stock's difficulties with the text. Had Stearforth realized that Matthew was merely buying time, or had he put him down as an idiot without the capacity of memory?

Matthew handed Stearforth the confession. Stearforth passed it to Buck.

Matthew recited, right up to the part where Cecil's name was first mentioned.

Afterwards, Stearforth looked surprised but pleased. Buck smiled agreeably. "That was well done, Stock," said Stearforth. "Wasn't it, Buck? You can't imagine the difficulty he had yesterday. But see what a good night's rest will do. It's as though he were a different man altogether."

"He is most perfect in his part," Buck agreed genially. "I cannot fault him for missing a single word."

"Now you must work upon your expression," Stearforth said. "You must stress the important words. Raise and drop your voice to strike the right tone. Creating belief is not a matter of merely saying certain things. You must say them with conviction."

Matthew noticed how easily this counsel flowed from Stearforth. Had he been a teacher that he knew so much about oratory? Or perhaps just a very practiced liar.

"Come, let's go get breakfast," Buck said.

Matthew accompanied his jailers downstairs. He never saw servants in the big house. He supposed there was an army of them, invisible somewhere behind the walls. Perhaps the idea was to keep him isolated. But didn't His Grace trust his own servants? Did he think he had some store of money about him to bribe one of them?

And to bribe them to what? To reveal to him the identity of His Grace? To tell him where his wife was kept? To send a message to Cecil?

They ate in the same chamber as before. The table was set with a rasher of bacon, boiled eggs in a bowl, bread and cheese, a pitcher of milk. Buck and Stearforth fell to eating at once, almost seeming to forget his presence. Matthew helped himself to a boiled egg and some cheese. His dream of feasting in his own house had left him without appetite. He thought about escape and its problems.

There was Joan, captive. His own escape might well mean her death. Stearforth had implied as much and the very fact he was allowed in his own chamber suggested not so much that they trusted him as that they knew he would not risk his wife's safety. He was as much a prisoner in the great house as he had been in Marshalsea.

But between escape and resignation to his lot there was a middle thing—a message to Cecil. Matthew had not believed Staunton's discouraging words when he heard them, although sometimes since he had had terrible fears that he might have been truly abandoned by his patron. In his better moods he had faith still in Cecil, who might, as far as Matthew knew, be ignorant of his fate and Joan's.

The question was how to get word out of the house.

Breakfast done, Stearforth led him into an adjacent room into which he had not come before. It was a kind of salon or music room, longer than it was broad with a magnificently ornate ceiling depicting clouds and angels, as in a church. Dark portraits adorned the walls, a succession of faces and forms. At one end was a pair of virginals of highly polished wood. All around were elaborately carved chairs and the vague odor of incense.

"What happens now?" he asked Stearforth.

"We wait," said Stearforth.

He and Buck sat down and pointed to a vacant chair where Matthew was to sit.

A few minutes passed in silence, then Buck got up and walked over to the virginals. He began to play, badly Matthew thought, who did not play himself but had a very good ear for music and was somewhat gratified to find Buck so lacking in skill.

The sound of voices at the end of the room now attracted Matthew's attention. Buck stopped playing and rose from his seat. Two men entered, His Grace and a second gentleman, wizened and stooped and who by his clothes and grave bearing was no mean personage of the kingdom.

The grave gentleman took a seat at the other end of the room while His Grace approached.

"Good morning, Master Stock. I trust you slept well and that such rest as you had has invigorated your memory and your consciousness of your crimes."

Matthew gave a low bow of assent while Buck and

187

Stearforth took turns assuring their master that Matthew truly had made progress.

"The proof's in the pudding, then," said His Grace with a tolerant smile. He sat down heavily in front of Matthew and crossed his legs to reveal silk hose and shoes with silver buckles. He nodded toward Matthew. Matthew knew the nod was a command to perform.

His nervousness at his captor's sudden appearance and the silent observance of the grave gentleman at the other end of the room caused him almost to forget the opening lines, but after a moment's hesitation he came out with them.

"I appear before this honorable body with fear and trembling as one who has defied man's laws and God's."

Matthew paused and looked at the grave gentleman who was a silent witness to these proceedings. In the poor light Matthew could make out the contours of the man's face, which was somewhat shriveled with lines so strongly scored about the eyes and mouth that Matthew could discern them even at the distance he was from him. The man's beard was white and cut in the French fashion to a sharp point, and he plucked at it thoughtfully as though he were somewhat unnerved himself. Matthew could not tell whether this unidentified personage was superior to His Grace or an inferior, who as a consequence of Matthew's success or failure would then be given instructions concerning him.

"I confess I took the life of Stephen Graham, rector of St. Crispin's Church. I slit his throat with a knife with my own initial carved in the haft and the worthy sexton of the church as a witness."

"And why did you do it?" His Grace interrupted suddenly. "Be prepared for interruptions such as this one and don't let them cause you to lose your place so that you forget something important."

"To silence his railings against the true faith."

"The Bishop of Rome, His Holiness," His Grace prompted with a kind of enthusiasm.

"Yes," Matthew continued, "and his calumnies against Christopher Poole, a martyr of the true faith."

"Excellent, Stock. You make a better Papist than half of those who worship at St. Peter's. Now tell us again how you killed Graham."

"I gained admission to the church on some pretext."

"What pretext?"

"That he had sent for me."

"To what purpose?"

"To inquire into the truth of Poole's disappearance—that is, the disappearance of his body."

"And—?"

"We conversed on this point. I asked him to show me the church monuments, where Poole's grave was, or had been, and then the belfry. I asked to see the bells. We were quite alone there, or so I thought, ignorant of the sexton's presence. I came at Graham from behind, drawing my knife across his throat before he could cry out."

The old man at the end of the room suddenly spoke. "Who bid you do this wicked deed?"

Matthew looked straight at the man and said, "Sir Robert Cecil, whom I have served on more than one occasion and whom all the world knows as Her Majesty's principal secretary."

"And why, why?" said the old gentleman.

"Because he would please the Infanta of Spain, whom he would have succeed Her Majesty when God pleases to call her hence."

The old gentleman rose from his chair and came forward. He spoke to His Grace.

"Who will believe that Cecil has turned Papist, or favors Spain when he has been so zealous a suitor to James?"

His Grace answered, "No one need believe anything regarding Cecil's faith, since some question whether he has any at all. His political acumen is another matter. That he corresponds regularly with the Scots king is no state secret, except perhaps from the queen. Why should he not be thought to have dealt with the Spanish claimant?"

"This is an enterprise fraught with risks," said the old gentleman, shaking his head.

"What enterprise worth its salt is not so?" His Grace said. "But our friend Stock here will stir up such a cloud of doubt regarding Cecil that King James will rather have one of our people as his minister than one besmirched beyond redemption, linked to murderers, Papists, and pious frauds. Trust me, this is only the beginning."

"How much did Sir Robert give you to murder Stephen Graham?" His Grace asked Matthew abruptly.

"Twenty pounds," Matthew said.

"A paltry sum," said the old man.

"All the more credible," His Grace answered. "Murderers are always poorly paid. What else?"

"A house in Suffolk—a manor, with one hundred acres attached."

"Ah, yes," said His Grace, "a more substantial reward. Land does not so readily slip through a man's fingers."

"Well, it shall be as God disposes," murmured the old gentleman. He gave Matthew a long look and then returned to his chair.

His Grace told Buck and Stearforth that they had done well, shook Matthew's hand firmly, and said, "Master Stock has evidently learned not only testimony but where his advantage lies. Look after him well. If he wants anything within reason, provide it to him."

He left the room, taking the old gentleman with him.

"I have learned my part, done what was required of me," Matthew said to Stearforth when they were alone again. "When shall I see my wife?"

"You will see her soon enough. Tomorrow, after your appearance before the council," said Stearforth.

"Can I not know where she is, that she is safe?"

"Oh, she is safe, Master Stock. You can trust me on that point. Indeed, she's out of harm's way. Where no London constable can apprehend her. We've taken very good care of your wife, haven't we, Master Buck?"

Buck agreed and said they had taken good care indeed of

Mistress Stock and that Matthew should be more grateful than otherwise, for had they not taken care of her she would be languishing even now in the same prison he had been held in and charged as an accomplice.

The three men walked toward the door and into the passage. As they walked, Matthew noticed a bundle of letters sitting on a long narrow table next to the wall. He caught a fleeting glance at the letter on top and saw that it was addressed to a person in London. He surmised that these were His Grace's letters, waiting for some servant to carry them to their destinations.

"Come, Master Stock," Stearforth said. "Your performance was able, but far from perfect. You must practice the rest of the day, prepare yourself for the council."

Stearforth did not leave Matthew in his chamber. He propped himself up in the corner with a book, a faithful if somewhat preoccupied guardian.

Matthew paced up and down restlessly, worrying about Joan and his ordeal to come at the same time. Then he remembered the letters he had seen on the table in the passageway and said, "Were I to write a letter to my wife, would you see that it is delivered?"

"You'll see her soon—perhaps tomorrow afternoon."

"It would please me to write her. Your employer said you were to gratify me. Any reasonable request, he said. It's a small thing I ask. What effort will it cost you?"

"Oh, well, I suppose there'd be no harm in it," Stearforth said. "Now that you've proven yourself a little more cooperative."

"I'll need paper and pen."

Stearforth laid down his book. "I'll see what I can find."

It seemed an hour before Stearforth returned, during which time Matthew considered what he would write to Joan. He knew the letter would be read by Stearforth—even by His Grace. It would be unthinkable that they would allow an uncensored letter to leave the house. Stearforth would pounce upon the text no sooner than it was indited. Matthew would have to choose his words carefully.

Stearforth returned with paper, pen, and ink. He handed them to Matthew and Matthew sat himself at a little desk in the corner. Stearforth was reading his book again, but Matthew felt he was still being watched.

Out of some surprising magnanimity Stearforth had brought him three sheets of paper. Matthew took the first, dipped the quill in the ink, and began to write. He had already thought of some words—an assurance of his well being, a testament of his love. Innocent words that would not arouse the suspicions of his captors. But as he wrote, he regretted he could not use some secret language to communicate his true condition, some furtive code revealing the fullness of his heart. Then it occurred to him to exchange the names of their household cook and their daughter, Betty and Elizabeth. Joan would know the letter was truly his own, but that the confusion was a signal of distress.

If she received the letter at all.

It would do more good to get a message to Cecil. But he knew there would be no bribe he could offer Stearforth to match the value of his service to His Grace.

He finished his letter, blotted the ink, and read over the text. It was brief and simple. He turned to look at Stearforth. The man was still absorbed in his book, his legs propped up on a stool in front of the chair he sat in.

Matthew looked down at the two clean sheets remaining. He recopied the first letter quickly and then even more quickly wrote upon one of the remaining sheets.

This new letter was not to Cecil, but Matthew knew that it would get to him. He wrote:

Stock is held a close prisoner in my house. His wife we have as credit for his faithfulness. He confesses before the council tomorrow that Cecil is the only true begetter of Poole's resurrection and Graham's murder. Your presence at the council meeting is urgently sought for whatever help you can give.

Matthew would have signed his captor's name had he known what it was. He folded the letter and put the name of Michael Hickes on the front, trying to imitate the penmanship of the letters he had seen in the passage. Hickes was Cecil's former secretary and good friend, a man of unquestionable loyalty and integrity. Hickes would get the message to Cecil if anyone would.

He tore up the first letter he had written to Joan, trusting that Stearforth would not recall the precise number of sheets he had given to him, or if he did, think Matthew had made two false starts rather than one.

The sound of ripping paper made Stearforth look up.

"Second thoughts?" he asked.

"Yes. I badly worded the first."

"My ambition in life is to be able to employ one to do all my writing for me," Stearforth said. He continued his reading.

Matthew folded the letter to Hickes and slipped it inside his jerkin. Then he folded the letter to Joan.

"Have you any wax?"

"I'll take care of the sealing," Stearforth said, rising from his chair and coming over to take the letter. He did not examine it in Matthew's presence, but carried it out.

As soon as he was gone, Matthew removed the letter to Hickes and read it over again. How he wished he could provide some clue to his whereabouts or to his captor's identity. He regretted not having wax to seal the letter, but then perhaps he who was to deliver it would think the lack of a seal a mere oversight. And if the deliverer stooped to read the letter, he might reasonably concluded Hickes was another of the conspirators.

Stearforth returned promptly and resumed reading, without commenting on the letter. Matthew thought it better to say nothing himself.

By late morning, Buck came to relieve Stearforth. "I have read the letter you wrote to your wife," he said.

"I regret the hospitality afforded me did not extend to a little privacy," Matthew said.

"Bless us, Master Stock, I regret the invasion of your privacy, but on the other hand we can't have everything in life. Be grateful a means has been found to your salvation. Isn't it enough that you have been spared the rope, your children from ignominy?"

Matthew said he supposed it was.

Within the hour Buck was escorting him downstairs. It was time to eat again. Matthew walked slightly behind his companion. When they came to the passageway he noticed that the bundle of letters that had been on the side table before had been removed, and a new group left in their place.

He slipped the letter to Hickes in with the others, not on the top where it might be noticed and the differences in handwriting observed, but towards the bottom. If God blessed him, the deliverer would take no notice of the missing seal or the alien hand.

"We did not find her, Your Honor, but we did discover where she had been."

Cecil could not remember the names of the men before him. They were young men, neatly dressed; they looked very much alike, each in his early twenties—half Cecil's age, mere children to one of his experience. The new breed of courtier, not like his or his father's generation, men of probity who served one master. They were all recently down from the university, the young men, eager for a place in Cecil's household, not caring much as to what the place was but only that there was one. Every place was a beginning, at least, and in their circumstances the opportunity of working for so important a person as Cecil was sufficient. Therefore they had not asked to know why Cecil was so interested in learning how a murderer imprisoned in Marshalsea fared, or the whereabouts of a Chelmsford clothier's wife. They had only done his bidding and inquired at every inn in the city and in the suburbs too.

"There is no prisoner named Stock in the Marshalsea."

"What?"

"There's no record of him. We spoke to the master of the

prison and to the chief warder. Neither would say there was a man named Stock there."

"He's been moved, then. What of Joan Stock?"

"A woman answering her description lay at the Rose for two nights, then according to the host, departed with her husband."

"What makes you think it was Joan Stock?"

"He mentioned she had gone off without her belongings, had left all of a sudden. We thought this suspicious."

"Had she settled with the host?"

"Her bill was paid by another man."

"Her husband?"

"No, sir, another. He did not give his name or his relation. The host assumed he was a servant of the husband."

"What name did the woman give?"

"*Gray*, sir."

"That might be Joan. She was a fugitive. Of course she would give a false name."

"There was another thing, sir."

"Which was?"

"We talked to a boy who works at the inn. He said he was paid a sixpence by two men to lead them to the woman. He said she was taken by force, because she would not return to her husband."

"Did he say where she was taken?"

"No, sir. Only that she was."

"Did he describe the men who took her?"

"One was young, tall, well favored. Well spoken. The other was an old man, stout, evil featured. The boy said he had a big knife at his belt."

"But he couldn't say where they took her?"

"No, sir."

Cecil told them to keep looking.

"But where shall we look, sir?" the tall one asked.

"Just look, will you?" Cecil answered. The day was starting badly. His rheumatism was killing him. Joan Stock seemed beyond retrieving and perhaps her husband too.

* * *

In the afternoon Matthew was left alone for about an hour. He used the time to inspect the windows, having discovered immediately that he had been locked in. He also searched desk drawers and cabinets, thinking he could find a clue to His Grace's identity, perhaps an initialed garment or bookplate. There was nothing.

When Buck returned Matthew was surprised to see that he was not alone. His Grace was with him, as was Stearforth.

"I understand you have written a letter, Master Stock?" His Grace said.

"Yes, sir, to my wife. Master Stearforth said he would deliver it to her."

"I don't mean the letter to your wife. I mean your letter to Master Hickes."

He held out the letter.

Matthew didn't know what to say.

"Did you think my servant so unobservant as to overlook an unsealed letter addressed to Master Hickes, who all the world knows is snug in Cecil's pocket? I must admit the letter is artful, as was your plan. Had the letter been delivered, I'm sure Hickes would have carried it straightway to him for whom it was really destined. As is, it has only cleared up some doubts of my own—doubts about your honesty."

"There's nothing amiss in my honesty," Matthew said, deciding further duplicity was futile. "I am a prisoner here. I'm being forced to comply with your wishes for my wife's sake."

Stearforth stepped forward and slapped Matthew hard in the face. Matthew reeled from the blow; tears came to his eyes.

"Easy, Stearforth," said His Grace. "I think such measures can wait. We still have his wife, and if he wants to see her again he will cooperate. But since he's proven himself a ready penman, we'll put his demonstrated talents to use."

Matthew noticed now that Buck was carrying paper and pen. He handed these to Matthew.

"You will write out the confession you have been at pains to memorize. Then it will be witnessed."

"You mean I won't have to stand before the council?"

"Oh, yes, we still have that planned for you. But the writing is a kind of security for us, you see. I underestimated you, Stock, and I am heartily sorry for it. But, believe me, I won't make the same mistake again. And if you should be so unwise as to try another effort to communicate beyond these walls—or to escape—then we will use your signed confession and you and your wife will be taken care of in such a manner as not to hurt our cause. Do you understand?"

His Grace turned to Stearforth and Buck and said, "You will not leave Stock alone again. Imagine that your very lives depend upon it. Your imagination will not fall short of reality."

17

*S*o weary was she from her struggle with the sea that she sprawled face downward on the wet stones for a long time. She was half-conscious; the surf pounded in her head, filling her mind with strange images.

It was a while before she remembered Morgan, who had helped her landward, supporting her by his strong right arm and determination that the sea should not have them. When she did remember she sat up and looked about for him.

Above her the cliffs were naked but not so white as seen from the sea at a distance. The stones at her feet were shiny wet. Unsteadily, she turned to look at the sea. The stern quarter of the *Plover* was being battered by the waves about twenty feet off shore, where it had been fixed on a large rock. Around her, the shingle was strewn with wreckage and the twisted forms of drowned men.

Alarmed that Morgan might too be dead, she picked herself up and began searching among the bodies, dreading what she might find. Joan had never seen a field of battle, but she imagined it must be like the scene before her, except the bodies were not wounded with swords or arrows. They lay, rather, unbloodied as if asleep, as if at any moment they would wake from their exhaustion and congratulate themselves on their salvation. But the men were not asleep; they would not wake in this life.

Some of the faces she recognized. Faces she had seen of men working on the deck to raise the sail and, later, to save the ship from the storm. Some of the dead had been in the mutinous gathering in Morgan's cabin. They were no threat to her now. God had blessed her: He had stretched down His great hand and snatched her from the deep, as He had done the old prophet Jonah. For this she was profoundly grateful. But she also felt guilt and confusion. Why she, and not the others? Was she really more deserving than they? Or was it all happenstance? Joan could not believe that sad philosophy. "God in heaven be thanked," she said aloud once, and then she said it again, softer, in a reverential whisper, as though He to whom she spoke were beside her.

She almost stumbled over a piece of wreckage that upon closer view proved no wreckage at all, but another body. It was the ship's cook. His huge frame was bent over a rock. His eyes were wide open and staring at the stones with that intense interest the dead take in the last thing they look upon.

A little farther on she found the man Morgan had called Drury, the one who had spoken in Morgan's defense, had been first persuaded that freeing the captain and the woman was a good plan, of profit to them all. Some profit it had proved to them. Morgan had said the ship would survive the open seas but not the vengeful land. He had been right. The rebellious crew had turned the ship around to their own destruction and found disaster where they sought safety.

Drury's head was bloody from being battered on the rocks. His arms and legs were scraped and torn, and she turned away quickly to say a prayer for his soul.

She was so appalled by this scene of desolation and death that when presently she turned her gaze from the stony shingle to the near distance and saw a company of living souls approaching her they seemed dead men made alive again.

She almost cried with joy when she saw Morgan among

them. His clothes were torn and he was limping badly, using a piece of the wreckage for a staff to lean on as he navigated amidst the wreckage. As he drew nearer she could see a large gash in his forehead.

She ran toward these living men, but Morgan called out before she could speak.

"Mistress Stock! Thank God you've been saved too. At least we passengers have survived if the captain and his brave crew have not."

Morgan's words puzzled her. She was about to ask for an explanation when she caught a look of warning in his eye and then took a closer look at his companions. There were about a dozen of them, coarse-featured men as filthy as beggars. Some of them carried staves and picks and they were eyeing the carnage about them with cold eyes. They stared at her curiously as though she were to be a part of the prize they sought and she was afraid. She realized these were the scavengers Morgan had spoken of. If Morgan had some compelling reason to disguise his identity as a captain, then Joan would not dispute it, trusting he had good reason for the deception.

Morgan turned and said a few words to him who apparently was the leader of this band and then approached her and spoke loudly with the obvious intention of being overheard. "These good men say there's a town not five leagues hence where there's a good inn for travelers. Though we have no money we'll make our way there now. Perhaps the host will be charitable to stranded wayfarers. There's no more that can be done for ship or men. What's left of our brave bird is theirs by rights, since no other party lives to claim her."

Morgan drew her away before she could reply to this. They walked as fast as Morgan could with his bad leg. He said in a lower voice, "I didn't dare let on I was captain. They would have killed me then and there for the salvage, and I'm not sure now but that they suspect the truth. We'll lay at no inn five miles hence, but under open sky if we must."

"Did any other of the men survive?" she asked, wondering still that only the two of them had been saved.

"Only one," Morgan said grimly. "The scavengers said they saw him run off as they came down from the cliff. He wore an eye patch, they said."

"Simkins."

"The cursed dog. I thought I had him with the musket. Would he have died in the sea rather than the others, among whom were several true men. His survival is a bad omen for he has as much reason to hate me now as I him."

They came to a place where there was a steep and narrow path up the cliff. Here Morgan stopped to catch his breath. He was obviously in considerable pain. The hose on his left leg was soaked with blood. They turned to look down the beach. The salvagers were picking over the ruin of the ship which they had managed to bring ashore with their ropes. They were tearing the hulk apart, dismembering it the way ants did the corpse of a wasp or fly.

"Damned villains," Morgan spat out. "Like carrion birds they feed off the worthier dead. Yet they shall not feed on our carcasses. Come, Mistress Stock, we'll make our way to London where your husband lies, and I to my wife—and revenge upon the devil Stearforth who has betrayed us both."

"But how shall we travel without money? My purse was lost in the sea."

"And so was mine, or so I declared to the scavengers, and yet do you remember when I returned to my cabin just before the ship broke up? It was to get the wherewithall to get us home again."

With some difficulty, Morgan bent over and reached inside his boot. He showed Joan what he had hidden there, three gold angels. It was the money Stearforth had paid Morgan for her abduction. "There's enough and more for London," he said smiling.

Joan had to help Morgan up the path because of his bad leg. She asked him if they couldn't rest a while, but he said no. The scavengers could not be trusted, he said. "Now their heads are full of treasure, since I told them the ship had just come from the Indies and was laden with Spanish booty. When they find out the crew was poor and the ship empty of cargo they'll be in a mind for mischief. We don't want to be around then."

Atop the cliff, they rested again, then walked for an hour or more across a high plain carpeted with brown stubby grass. All the while Morgan seemed in a great agony but encouraged her with reports of how much farther it was to the town and how important it was that they get to London as quickly as possible, as if she needed to be reminded of that.

In late afternoon they came to a road that ran next to a newly ploughed field and shortly thereafter, they saw at the edge of a copse a cottage of clay and wattles where the field's owner dwelt. Morgan admitted he was not able to proceed farther, and Joan said she was in like condition, for her legs were undone by the walking and she was so hungry that if she saw anything alive she would eat it whether it be cooked or no.

"We'll put the farmer's hospitality to the proof, then," Morgan said.

When they were within calling distance, Morgan halloed the cottage and almost immediately a man came out. He was tall and rawboned. He had a weather-beaten face and was dressed like the farmers in Joan's neighborhood in a buff-colored smock, loose-fitting britches, and a wide-brimmed hat. But in answering Morgan's greeting Joan heard a lilt and thickness of speech unfamiliar to her.

"We're shipwrecked travelers," Morgan explained.

"Pity that. Many they be," said the man, whose long, leathery face was covered with an unkempt beard, but whose expression was kindly. A woman's face appeared in the doorway. This Joan took to be the farmer's wife, for she was about his years. She was as rawboned as her husband and her hair was scraggly, but she had a cheerful look, and had she been crabbed and hostile, the sight of another woman would have been welcome to Joan after her sojourn in the ship.

The wife said something to her husband, which Joan interpreted to mean, "Are they hungry?" for the woman rubbed her hand on her aproned stomach and a wonderful smell came from the house.

"Oh, we haven't eaten in days," Joan said.

The farmer looked at her uncomprehendingly. Joan nodded her head vigorously and smiled. The farmer's wife smiled back and the farmer beckoned them to come in.

The habitation of these folk was more hovel than house. The floor was strewn with old rushes and here and there it was bare enough for Joan to see the earth beneath. There was a single room, and in the middle of it was a fire going and above nothing but a hole in the roof for a chimney. There was hardly a stick of furniture but for several mats placed near one wall, and on these nestled the couple's young children, two girls and a boy, although it was difficult to determine the sex of any since they were all dressed alike and their hair was all unshorn and tangled.

They were invited to sit down in the straw, while the wife went to stir the pot that cooked upon the fire and the farmer looked on without saying anything. The children, who seemed more wary of strangers than their parents, stared on in silence.

Joan was too weary to do much more than eat, which she did heartily when presently the farmer's wife poured some of the pot's contents into a bowl and handed it to her. She was given no spoon, so Joan merely raised the bowl to her lips. Even before she tasted she could inhale the deliciousness of the broth, which is what she had been served. There was no meat within. She detected carrots and leeks and a hint of herbs. The flavor was wonderful after her long fast and the firmness of the ground beneath her was also a delight. She could not remember when she had enjoyed a meal so much, or company, although there was silence all the while they ate and the children on the mat kept staring as though she were some alien creature with two heads.

After the broth, the farmer's wife served some little slices of cheese on a plate. The cheese was hard and sharp as a razor and to Joan's sensitive palate almost inedible and yet she gnawed upon it until it was all gone. Morgan, she noticed, did the like. He had not spoken a word since entering the farmer's house except to say to her that he felt much better than before. But she thought he looked worried, despite his brave talk along the way about reaching Canterbury by the next morning and London the day after.

After this humble supper, the farmer said, "Will ye twa have yon' bed?" and pointed to the wider of the mats, which was next to the smaller where the farmer's children were curled up together asleep.

Before Joan could explain that she and Morgan were not married to each other, Morgan declined the offer. He said that the barn would do well enough, and when the farmer did not seem to understand, he said it again, but in another way, and pointed out of doors. This the farmer seemed to make sense of and yet his face showed some doubt as to why a couple would prefer to sleep outside rather than on a perfectly comfortable bed. Joan thanked the farmer and his wife and followed Morgan outside.

It was nearly dark and the air was cold. She looked up into the heavens and saw, for the want of moon and stars, that it was covered with clouds. She wondered if there would be another storm.

Morgan had walked off into some bushes for a moment but presently returned, and Joan noticed he seemed to limp less than before.

"There's a cowshed down in that copse. We can sleep there tonight. Before dawn we'll be on our way. I know this road and this country. We can't be a score of miles from Canterbury and from there it is no more than three score to London. We'll ride the way. You can ride, can't you?"

"Well enough," Joan said, thinking Morgan's estimate of their travel time was overly sanguine, but as desirous as he of coming to London as soon as possible.

The place he led her to was somewhat less than what she

would call a shed. It had been constructed of rough-hewn timber and built into a hollow out of the wind. The rear of the structure was solid earth. Inside, the farmer's single cow stood in her stall, radiating dependable animal heat and Joan, a country woman, was well used to the strong scent of animal ordure. Morgan removed his jerkin and gave it to her. "Here," he said. "You may need this."

Joan was glad that they had come to the shed before it was completely dark, for the little light of day let her see only enough of the interior to find her way to a pile of straw. Here she laid down the captain's jerkin and then herself upon it, so tired she was asleep before she could inquire where Morgan was to make his own bed.

Perhaps it was the cold that woke her, perhaps the rustling noise outside the shed. Inside it was pitch black. She was vaguely aware of soft snoring nearby. That would be Morgan. As her eyes grew accustomed to the darkness she could see his form. He was sitting up in the corner, his head resting on his arms and knees, forbearing the straw that would have conferred too great an intimacy to their sleeping together.

She heard a crackling sound, for all the world like footfalls. The feet of man, though, not animal. Was it the farmer or his wife? She had no idea of the hour, how long she had been asleep. Was it time for the cow to be milked, then?

She could dimly make out the cow in her stall; the beast made no stirring or lowing as cattle do for want of milking. Joan moved, slowly and with difficulty since her body was stiff, toward Morgan and shook him by the arm until he snorted once, and then awoke abruptly, seizing her hand in a powerful grip as though she were an enemy.

"What?" he said in a voice much too loud.

She hushed him. "Listen."

She was still holding his hand and his grip had not relaxed.

The noise came again. Whoever it was was making his

way around the shed, looking, she supposed, for the door. But surely he could see that now, now that the clouds had cleared and there was something of a moon to give light.

Then it occurred to her that whoever it was was not seeking to know how to get in but how otherwise she might escape. Her heart beat at such a furious pace she drew her hand away to hold it to her breast to still it.

She heard a sound, wood falling against iron. She knew what it was, the bar being placed across the shed door, locking them in. Morgan knew too. He was on his feet in an instant, throwing his weight against the door with a wordless fury.

She smelled smoke. Looking up, she saw that the thin frame that supported the thatch was on fire, burning at such speed that glowing fragments were falling down all around her, starting smaller fires. Morgan was now beating on the door, cursing and screaming to be let out. Joan stamped out the little fires with her feet. Above Morgan's roaring she could hear maniacal laughter—like that of the Bedlamites she had mimicked to get Cecil's attention. No, this was not the farmer's work. She thought rather of the scavengers. And yet it hardly seemed possible they would carry their vengeance so far.

There were too many fires now for her to put out and too much smoke. She could hardly see Morgan, only hear his angry protest. He would not give up at the door. The flames had descended to the side wall, consuming the timbers with terrific speed. Then she realized Morgan was beating on the sturdiest part of the structure, the door. The walls were of more flimsy stuff, timbers with mud to fill the chinks. She seized the piece of spar that Morgan had used as a staff, and began to whack away at the burning wall nearest to her. Her poking and the heat of the flames caused the wall to give way easily. Part of the roof collapsed. She called over her shoulder to Morgan and leaped over the ruin, falling on the cool grass beside the shed. She scrambled to her feet, whispering a prayer of thanks for her miraculous escape and at the same moment saw Morgan, his clothing aflame, make the same desperate leap, a second before the entire shed collapsed in a blazing inferno.

Morgan rolled over and over on the grass, until the flames were extinguished, then lay on his back gulping great mouthfuls of air and his chest heaving with such force that she thought his heart would break.

The air was filled with smoke and burning cinders. She heard the farmer's voice and his wife's and younger voices, of their children. She knew the farmer was lamenting his burned shed, and worse, his dead cow. She scurried over to Morgan. He was alive, just exhausted, as was she.

"Who did this?" she gasped.

"It was Simkins," he said weakly. "I recognized his cackling. I'll kill the bastard, so help me God."

"How is your back? Are you burned?"

"I don't think so. I'll need a new shirt, I think."

Morgan laughed a little, and she knew he was all right, but still his expression was contorted in anger.

The farmer and his wife came over; the woman looked horror-struck. It wasn't clear to Joan what impressed her most—the fire that had destroyed the shed and cow or the fact that she and Morgan had managed to escape. Her husband was angry. He pointed his finger at Morgan, then at the shed, and then back again, all the time sputtering in his rude dialect. Yet it was clear to Joan that he was blaming them both for the fire, and none of Morgan's efforts to tell him otherwise were doing any good. The farmer had evidently seen no one but them. The shed was sound before they occupied it; now it was destroyed. It all seemed to be a simple matter of cause and effect. Or so Joan was able to decipher of the farmer's logic.

Morgan, frustrated by the failure of his efforts to explain, reached into his boot and withdrew one of the gold coins he had shown Joan earlier. "Here," he said. "Buy yourself a new cow. That should buy a small herd. With what's left over you can build a new shed too. But do yourself a favor. Make it with two doors, will you?"

It wasn't clear to Joan that the farmer understood this

counsel but he did understand the coin, which she believed was doubtless a greater sum than he had ever had in his life, and there was nothing more said about the dead cow or the burned barn.

"If it was Simkins, where is he now?" Joan asked, after they were out of sight of the farm and on their way again.

"If we're in luck, he thinks we burned in the fire. If he does, he's in for a surprise when next we meet, believe me."

"I hope he's not lurking in the darkness," Joan said.

In Canterbury, Morgan used the second of the angels to buy a hearty breakfast, new clothes for them both, and a good sword and knife, which he said he would need when he caught up with Stearforth or Simkins. Not far from the cathedral they found a shrewd hostler who said he would give them the use of his best gelding and mare for the ride to London, providing they would leave the horses with his brother, a butcher, who lived in Eastcheap, near the parish church of St. Andrew's. Morgan haggled a half hour with the hostler over these terms, much to Joan's annoyance, for she was eager to continue their journey. But the hostler would not give an inch. "If you will not have my horses, you may have the road, although it's a long walk to London," he said.

Later, the terms reluctantly agreed to by Morgan, he complained to Joan that they might have bought both beasts outright for the charge, but Joan reminded him of the need for haste. Her husband was in peril; Morgan's wife hardly less.

There was no time to lose in haggling over horses.

Morgan agreed. By mid-morning they were on the road to London, riding as hard as Joan had ever rode. Joan did not know this flat, verdant country of Kent, but Morgan knew it well, and he seemed as comfortable on horseback as he had in walking the decks of his ship. They stopped three times in the next eight hours, to rest themselves and their beasts, and each time Joan begrudged the time, although she well understood that exhausting the horses would serve no purpose. They spent that night in a village inn, with separate rooms and a good meal. They were on their way again several hours before dawn, galloping through the darkness.

As she rode, she could think of little else but Matthew; a terrible dread settled upon her. It was a fair, dry day for the ride, but her mood was so dark it might have been dismal midnight. When at dusk the great city came into her view, she almost cried with joy. Now, she felt, the miracle of her salvation was nearly perfect; she had been saved from the tumultuous sea, the burning shed. God knew what other perils might stand between her and her husband, and yet she felt ready for them. If God had carried her thus far, would He not carry her farther?

Morgan wanted to go at once to see his wife, saying the Eastcheap butcher might wait until morning for his horses, and Joan made no objection. She was eager to see Elspeth herself, thinking that the young wife might provide a clue as to Stearforth's whereabouts.

Arriving at the cottage, she stood discreetly back as husband, wife, and children embraced each other, mixing tears with laughter. Elspeth expressed alarm at her husband's face, which still bore witness to his crew's treachery, and she would not be satisfied until she had bathed his wounded leg twice over. She had not heard of the wreck of the *Plover*, but as she declared, a sailor's return is always a miracle to be thankful for, especially when his household is threatened by enemies.

That story came out a little later, while Elspeth stirred the pot and her little daughter set out plates for her father and the family's guest.

"Stearforth threatened me and the children if I was to say so much as a good morning to you," Elspeth said to Joan. "For a while he or another man lurked in yonder field, watching the cottage. Once Stearforth came to the door. The very day you came for the first time. He must have followed you."

"He was watching from the field," Joan said. "I thought he was a cowherd, for so he was dressed. But it was Stearforth."

"I'll kill the man, I swear it," Morgan said.

Elspeth rushed to her husband's side and put her arm around him. "Oh please don't talk so. Let the law take its course. Let God avenge."

"The law has failed in this case," Morgan said bitterly. "As for God, He is not above letting mere mortals be his instruments. I could cite you cases aplenty."

Elspeth said she hadn't seen Stearforth or the other man for several days.

"That's because he believes I am out of the country—in France or on board your husband's ship," Joan said.

"If word comes back concerning the loss of my ship, he'll believe you were lost at sea," Morgan said, eating ravenously, while his children gathered around his legs.

Joan told Elspeth about the discovery of her brother's diary and about what was written there about the bishopric.

"Yes, my brother mentioned that. He said he had no ambition to be a bishop, but that he would not decline the appointment if it came. He said it would be God's call, although the queen was His mouthpiece. Stephen was a humble man," Elspeth said. "No ranting Puritan or would-be Catholic, but of the middle ground. But now I have heard another has been chosen in his place. A good and worthy man, I hear, whom the queen was thinking upon as well before Stephen's murder."

"What is his name, this new bishop?" Joan asked.

Elspeth said she could not remember. Her brother had mentioned the name once or twice, but she had not paid that much attention. There had been no need, then.

"Well," said Joan, "many names are mentioned in the diary. Knights, bishops, great persons. Most mean nothing to me, but no doubt Sir Robert knows them all."

"Where is the diary now?" Morgan asked.

"At the Rose—where I lay before Stearforth and

Motherwell abducted me. I hid it well, if the two of them did not find it afterward."

"There's a good chance it remains where you left it," Morgan said, between mouthfuls.

"Then that's where I must go and afterwards to Cecil House."

"But you must be weary unto death after such a mad ride," said Elspeth.

"And so I am," Joan said. "But not unto death, at least not yet. This matter cannot wait."

Morgan offered to escort her to the inn and then to Cecil House. Joan was reluctant to take the good husband from his wife, but then she thought of Elspeth's warning about the dangers of London at night and accepted the offer.

Within the hour she was mounted on horseback again, her nether parts so aflame with sores she could hardly sit.

18

SIMKINS had his joy of the fire he had set and would have lingered to watch the burning shed until the screams of the doomed occupants had ceased, had not the farmer and his wife come to see what the turmoil was. Wanting no witnesses to his arson or to its mortal consequences, Simkins skulked off into the night. By late afternoon of the next day he was walking through the streets of Canterbury as proud as you please. By nightfall he was in Maidstone, where he snatched a purse from a local burgher to finance his immediate expenses, and then parlayed his new status as shipwrecked mariner into a free ride to London in a merchant's wagon, satisfied he had given his former captain and the Stock woman their comeuppence. Simkins was also interested in capitalizing further on what he knew. After the incident in St. Crispin's churchyard, Stearforth had told him to stay out of London, but with the shipwreck, Simkins believed the case was altered. Besides, he was now destitute and desperate. He was confident that Stearforth who had helped him before, would help him again, glad to receive intelligence as to the treason and subsequent lamentable deaths of Edmund Morgan and the female passenger who had cursed the ship.

From his last employment, Simkins knew exactly where Stearforth was to be found. He went to the house in the Strand, and having the practical wisdom not to march up to it directly, he waited until a servant came out, confronted him, and begged him to carry a message to Stearforth to the effect that a certain old acquaintance from his days at St. Crispin's waited without with important news. Simkins was not altogether sure that he had not worded his message too cryptically, but he knew Stearforth well enough to know that the man was nothing if not curious.

He waited about an hour in the street outside the house and was about ready to despair when the same servant came out again. The servant said Master Stearforth would meet him at a tavern in Milk Street about nine o'clock and he was to go there directly to await him.

Stearforth came somewhat later than promised, so much so that Simkins had begun to wonder what he should do if Stearforth did not come at all.

Noisy and rather down on the social scale, the tavern was not one of Stearforth's regular haunts. Simkins could tell that by the look of uncertainty on Stearforth's face as he came in the door and by the fact that no one greeted the young man familiarly. When Stearforth spotted Simkins standing by the bar, he frowned and waved him to a vacant table in the corner.

Stearforth looked around him nervously and spoke in an urgent whisper. "What the devil are you doing here? Where's the ship?"

"Wrecked in Dover. She'll not sail again."

"My God. And the Stock woman?"

"Dead."

Stearforth breathed a sigh of relief. "Well, I am glad of that. What of Morgan and the rest of the crew?"

"The crew's all drowned, but I thought you ought to know about Morgan."

"What about him?"

"Once at sea, he betrayed you, made friends with the woman. They planned to return to London."

Simkins fleshed out the details, not mentioning, however, his own efforts to put the ship around.

"I tried to stop him, knowing well your orders. He threatened to have me hanged as a mutineer, but I vaulted the rail, swam for shore with musket balls flying above my head. I gave him quittance, though, later."

"I thought you said Morgan went down with his ship?"

"He escaped. The woman too. But I followed the both of them and knowing their return was contrary to your orders, I thought best to roast them both while they dreamed, or niggled in the straw—I know not which nor could care less."

"You set fire to them!" Stearforth looked disbelieving.

"They were asleep in a shed. I shut them in, then set a flame. It was all over in a minute or so, such a volley of oaths and pleas from Morgan you can't imagine."

"And from the woman?"

"What you would expect—shrieks and appeals."

"You're sure they're both dead?"

"As dead as Adam and his brethren. No one could have survived such an inferno."

Stearforth sighed again, drumming his fingers on the table. He stared into the middle distance. Simkins saw he was thinking the matter through, and he hoped Stearforth was not unmindful of what Simkins might deserve for his service.

"This is a turn I didn't expect," Stearforth said, "but I don't see how it works to our hurt. The ship's no loss of mine, nor its crew, nor Morgan. The point of the voyage was to get the woman out of the way."

"Oh, I'd say she's well out of the way now," Simkins said.

"Yes," Stearforth said. "Yes, she is out of the way now." Stearforth smiled for the first time during their conversation and Simkins felt more at ease. He liked his present drinking companion no more than he liked Morgan, but he did have an unerring instinct as to where his advantage lay and at the moment everything depended upon Stearforth's good graces.

Obviously in a better mood, Stearforth ordered another round of drinks and also some cheese and bread.

"You must be hungry after your ordeal and journey."

Simkins said he was, by God, as hungry as a dozen men. "I have no employment now that the *Plover*'s sunk and gone."

Simkins was annoyed that it took a moment before Stearforth got the point.

Stearforth said, "Yes, ill luck, the ship sinking the way it did. But I'm always happy to help a man who's down on his luck."

Stearforth reached into his purse and pulled out a palmful of coins.

It wasn't much, Simkins thought, quickly taking the measure of his companion's generosity. "What I need, Master Stearforth, is employment, not charity. I'm a whole man, despite the lost eye, and you've used me to good purposes before."

"And will again. You did the right thing reporting this," Stearforth said. "But keep it to yourself. Just we two will know of it, understand?"

"Oh, I understand perfectly, Master Stearforth."

"I'll have some work for you. Come back with me to the house."

"Is it work of the kind I did before? In the churchyard, I mean?" For all his desperation, Simkins didn't like mucking around with the dead. He didn't mind making an enemy of a dead man, but once dead, he preferred to be done with the matter.

"Hush," Stearforth said, with a look of warning to suggest that even in the obstreperous tavern their conversation might be overheard. "Say nothing about that. But as a matter of fact, I shall be needing your help along those lines. I've some unfinished business with that body you dug up, a second grave so to speak, and your help in the project will save me the trouble of explaining myself to some new assistant. Do you get my drift, Simkins?"

Simkins said he did but in fact wasn't sure he understood. Stearforth must have caught the confusion in his eye.

"I mean," the younger man said, "that your help is worth that of two men. So you should receive double wages for your pains."

These were words Simkins did understand. Feeling much better now, he finished his ale. Stearforth ordered another, and then Stearforth filled him in on the details.

Morgan accompanied Joan into the Rose. The innkeeper was upstairs and had to be sent for. When he came down he looked at Joan as though she were a ghost.

"God save you, Mistress Gray. You've come back," he said. Then he turned to look at Morgan. "And this I take it is your worthy husband."

"A worthy friend, rather," Joan said, not inclined to clarify her identity or Morgan's. "I left something of value in my chamber when I departed so abruptly."

"But your husband and his companion removed it all," the innkeeper said looking confused.

"Not all," Joan interrupted impatiently. "As I say, he forgot something important and I wish to retrieve it."

The innkeeper sent one of the chambermaids to look for the boy, Jack, but there was no Jack to be found. He said he would show her up himself and she should look to her heart's content.

In the chamber, Joan went at once to the hearth and probed the recess where she had concealed the diary, but her fingers felt only cold brick. She turned to Morgan. "It's gone."

"Could Stearforth have found it?" he said.

"Perhaps." She turned to the innkeeper who was standing patiently at the door. "Have you had guests in the chamber since I was here?"

"A merchant tailor from Lincoln," the innkeeper said. "A

man and his wife from Bath. No others. None mentioned finding a thing that wasn't theirs."

"Why should they?" Morgan said. "Many who find things of value prudently keep their mouths shut."

"Why should they even look?" Joan added. "The hiding place is not so that one would stumble upon it by accident. The diary was searched out. If not by Stearforth and Motherwell, then by whom?"

"Perhaps they returned since our sailing, found the diary, and therefore could not brag of its discovery," Morgan said.

Joan acknowledged that this was a possibility but in her heart she knew it was otherwise. Stearforth had asked about the diary but had seemed persuaded after all that she had taken nothing from the rectory. Besides, she was not sure he had time to return to the Rose before shipping her off on the *Plover*.

"Is there a maid who cleans these rooms?" she asked, not content to abandon her search.

"There is," the innkeeper said. "But she's been sick abed these three days."

"Then who cleaned them in her absence?" Joan said.

"Jack, the boy."

Joan exchanged glances with Morgan. On their way to the Rose she had explained young Jack's part in her abduction, and her own uncertainty as to the depth of his complicity. Was he an innocent victim of Stearforth, or had Stearforth found some flaw in his character? Jack had a fresh, disarming expression, a guileless countenance. But that didn't make him a saint, and in truth she thought his superficial appearance would make him an excellent cutpurse.

"Where's this Jack?" Morgan asked the innkeeper.

"Why, that's what I would know," the innkeeper said, seeming to understand that his servant was under suspicion and not eager to be blamed for any wrongdoing Jack might have done. "He's never been accused of theft, at least before, if that's your meaning. Yet I'm not against your questioning him. A boy can as easily turn bad as good. That's been my experience."

The innkeeper nodded judiciously and smiled, as though anticipating congratulations all around for these sentiments.

"Where does he sleep?" Joan asked.

"In the stable. He sleeps in the loft. But this time of night he should still be here. If guests have luggage it falls to him to lug it and he lugs it back down again."

Joan asked if she could see where Jack slept. There was a reward to be had if she found what she had lost, she said. This seemed to be a satisfactory inducement for the innkeeper, who offered to lead the way.

The Rose was an inn of medium size, as London inns went. Surrounding its central courtyard were three stories and twenty or so chambers and smaller rooms, and of course its guests often had horses that needed to be stabled and fed. No inn was fully adequate that did not have a stable, often, as in the case of the Rose, beneath the chambers themselves. Thus the guests could ride into the yard, dismount, and hie themselves to bed not a dozen feet above the beasts that brought them.

At the Rose the stable had stalls for twenty or thirty horses although at the present time only half were occupied. The hostler had his own quarters there and when the innkeeper told him what was needed, he obtained a lantern and led the way to the rear of the stable where there was a ladder leading to the loft. The hostler was a sinewy, long-faced man, somewhat resembling the beasts he cared for, with stringy dark hair that hung to his shoulders like a horse's mane. The loft was full of hay except at one end where it had been cleared away and there was a mattress lying and also a small battered chest with a broken latch. Without seeking anyone's permission, Morgan went at once to inspect the chest, while Joan held the lantern above him.

"There's nothing here but old moth-eaten clothes," Morgan said with a heavy note of discouragement.

"Not even a knife or some other bauble?" Joan asked.

"Two shirts, a pair of patched hose," Morgan said. "Yes, a belt and two caps."

"A paltry store of possessions."

The innkeeper said Jack was an orphan. The man had employed him for charity's sake, but the truth was that the boy was lazy and the innkeeper was thinking of sending him off.

"A paltry store even for a lazy orphan," Joan said, sensing that there was some clue here, even in the absence of any object that might have been called one. She knelt beside Morgan and searched carefully through the clothes. They were even as Morgan had said. There was nothing suspicious here.

Then she said, as though thinking aloud, "Boys always have baubles—things they pick up, small change, a broken knife, a piece of glass. It's their nature. Such penury as this chest reveals is unnatural."

"We aren't even sure the boy found the diary," Morgan said. He stood and looked at her doubtfully. All the riding, climbing, and kneeling she had asked of him were taking their toll on a man who had been grievously injured only two days before and had spent most of the day on horseback. She knew she owed it to him to forgo her search, to allow him to go home to his wife and children. But she could not give up, not as long as Matthew lay in prison under sentence of murder.

At that moment Joan became aware of someone approaching from the other end of the loft. She looked up and saw it was Jack. He looked startled, but made no move to flee.

"Oh, there you are, boy. Where have you been?" demanded the innkeeper.

"On an errand—for one of the guests," Jack said. He looked at Joan and his jaw fell slack.

"You remember me, do you?" Joan said.

"You're the woman whose husband came to fetch you home again."

"I left something behind in my chamber. A book. It has no value to any other than myself."

"I found no book," Jack said with the same innocent expression he had used just before Stearforth and Motherwell had burst into her room.

But she was not to be taken in this time. She went up to him and looked him in the eye. There was a way to deal with dishonest servants and Joan, like any good housewife, knew what it was. One didn't back down until the accused had furnished evidence of innocence, and to Joan's mind Jack was far from having done that.

"I don't believe you."

"I swear to heaven, mistress," Jack said, his face coloring a little. His eyes darted from her face to Morgan's and then back again. "I never found any book that I can recall."

"Did you look for one?" Morgan said.

"No, why should I? I can't read."

"Yet you know a book when you see it," Morgan said.

"Yes, sir."

Joan heard the boy's voice tremble. She could see by the rise and fall of his chest that he was breathing deeply to control his fear, and that he was more fearful of Morgan than of her.

"I'd be willing to pay generously for its return," Joan said.

Jack looked at the innkeeper, at Morgan, and then back at Joan. Joan caught in his hesitation a glimpse of the truth. Now she knew she was right. The boy was considering his choices. Money was to be had for the book but would it be enough to make up for the loss of his employment? Surely, the stern innkeeper would want no confessed thief and liar in his employ. Jack would be lucky to escape a beating, and he couldn't be sure he'd get the reward offered for the book.

"Where do you keep your treasures?" Joan asked.

"My treasures?"

"Things you find, baubles. You're a boy. You must find things. All boys do. I'm not accusing you of stealing. But

220

if someone finds a lost article in the street, he might keep it. What's the proverb—finders keepers? Your chest contains naught but clothes."

"What's wrong with that?" Jack asked, his tone suddenly insolent.

"I think you've hidden the book, along with your own treasures," Joan said.

"I don't know what you speak of, mistress," Jack said.

Joan thought he had the same guilty look he had when he had betrayed her before. "I think you do. My guess is that you search the chambers when guests have left, looking for what they may have left behind. And more, I think, you know every chink and crevice in that chamber and have found things concealed there before that were not yours."

"I'm honest, Master Terrance," Jack said, looking to the innkeeper. "Must I hear this?"

"You will listen for the nonce," the innkeeper said. "Go on, mistress, ask him these questions, or I begin myself to smell a greater fault in him than ever I smelled before."

Joan looked around the cavernous loft. The light radiating from the hostler's lantern left much of it in shadows. Morgan must have read her mind. He said, "Will you show us where you hid the diary, or must we tear every board from its place? If we find you lied it will go very bad with you."

Morgan underscored his threat by going directly to Jack and seizing him by the collar.

"Don't hurt me, masters," he wailed. "You may have the book."

"Where is it?" Morgan demanded.

"I'll show you, just let me go, will you?"

Morgan released him but kept close by. "Show us, you young thief."

"I'm not a thief," Jack protested. "I only found the book after. I thought to sell it at some bookstall, but hadn't time to take it."

Jack's hiding place was not far from his bed. He knelt

down by the mattress as though he were about to pray but pried up a loose board in the floor instead. Morgan pushed him aside and reached down.

It was just such a collection as Joan had imagined although somewhat more extensive, consisting of coins, a small mirror with the glass cracked, a string of beads, and a leather-bound book Joan recognized as Graham's diary.

"That's it," she said, drawing closer to see. "Thank God he had not time to sell it or we might have spent our lives searching the bookstalls."

Morgan handed the diary to Joan, and at the same moment she heard the sound of running. She looked up in time to see Jack vanishing into the darkness.

"Stop him," Morgan cried to the innkeeper, who also seemed to have been taken by surprise at Jack's sudden escape.

The host hurried after him, but so corpulent a man could not be expected to overtake a boy fleeing for his life.

"It's all well he's gone," Joan said, clutching the diary to her breast. "We have what we wanted. The boy has a larcenous spirit. If he escapes the rope today, he will meet it tomorrow or the day after. Come, it's late. This has been the longest day of my life, and I have yet to show this diary to Sir Robert."

Cecil House was so dark as to seem uninhabited, but Joan managed to raise a serving man with her pounding and needed only to mention her name before she and Morgan were let in. Despite the lateness of the hour and his anxiety about meeting the queen's principal secretary, Joan insisted that he accompany her. She wanted Cecil to meet her rescuer.

They were shown into the same downstairs parlor where she had spoken to Cecil before but had to wait nearly a half an hour before Cecil appeared. He was garbed in a dressing gown of silk and his eyes were heavy with sleep, but seeing Joan he went directly to her, grasped her by both hands, and said, "Thanks be to God for your deliverance. When we heard you were taken, we supposed the worst."

Joan introduced Morgan as one without whom she would have experienced just such a fate as Cecil supposed, and then lost no time in filling Cecil in on what had happened since her abduction. Cecil listened without comment except for an occasional remark of wonder or anger. At the conclusion of her narrative, she showed him Stephen Graham's diary, and more particularly the page she had noted.

He read leisurely, perhaps, Joan thought, twice over, then turned to the pages preceding and still later to those following before saying anything. During these few minutes, Joan began to have her first doubts as to the significance of her find. She exchanged glances with Morgan. Since entering the great house, he had seemed overwhelmed by its splendor and its owner's name. He had bowed awkwardly when Cecil had thanked him for his services and said they should not be forgotten. Now he seemed as concerned as Joan, or perhaps that was only her imagination.

"We may have motive here," Cecil said, stroking his beard thoughtfully. "That my undoing is the ultimate aim of this mischief is already established. The question has been *who*. Now here this good man writes of his nomination as bishop. And true, the queen was considering his candidacy."

"Elspeth Morgan said a new bishop had been chosen but did not remember his name," Joan said.

"Peter Wilks. Dr. Wilks is dean of Windsor and has been offered the bishopric of Worcester, although doubtless he would prefer London or Durham. The family is well connected. They were supporters of Lord Essex before his fall, but escaped guilt in that foolish lord's rebellion. Bitter enemies of mine, I might add, because of my opposition to Peter's brother as attorney general ten years past."

"Could this conspirator be the brother, then?"

"Sir Thomas Wilks? Possibly. Old grievances such as his die hard. The Wilkses are an ambitious breed. Even the clergymen among them have the temperament of wolves."

"But the queen appointed another, not you," Joan said.

Cecil smiled pleasantly and laughed a little. "The governing of England is more complicated than you suppose, Joan. It's true the queen appoints in both Church and in state, yet her counselors have her ear. For that reason I spend much of my time answering the pleas of those who would crawl into some niche in the order of things—God's or man's. So therefore while the queen's decisions are entirely her own, she harkens to me—and to others. And for what patronage we supply we are both blessed or cursed by our clients, depending upon their success. Had Wilks been appointed attorney general rather than Sir Thomas Egerton, whom I favored, he would have declared himself in my everlasting debt. Instead, I earned his hatred. The Essex matter did not make matters better between us."

"Was Stephen Graham murdered then only because he was in the way of a bishopric, which another cleric wanted for himself? Are you traduced and my husband imprisoned for this?" Joan exclaimed, feeling outrage swell within her.

"Oh, Joan, I could tell you tales that would curdle your blood and make your faith pale. These bishoprics are not empty dignities. They mean money—and power. You take the see of Worcester. It remained vacant for years, it being so poor that no one would take it. Durham is the fatter calf by far, and London a pregnant sow with enough meat on her bones to feed a hundred ambitious men. The deviousness of an ambitious dean or archdeacon or even eloquent preacher is not to be underestimated. They will plead and bribe and threaten and keep a foot in every camp to secure their success. Believe me I have seen it done."

"In such a world how is my poor husband to fare then?" Joan asked.

Her question caused a change in Cecil's countenance. Where he spoke confidently before of politics, he now seemed hesitant and sad, as though he were harboring a secret grief.

"What has happened to Matthew?" she said, almost fearing his answer.

Cecil frowned, hesitated a moment, then said, "Matthew has been taken from the Marshalsea. I have not been able to determine where. The officials of the prison profess to be in darkness as to his whereabouts. The last of my men to speak to him has been proved a traitor, who gave him to believe I had forsaken him. I have men searching the city but so far they have found nothing."

The word turned her to stone. She felt struck at the heart and as dead as Poole. She could hardly bring herself to ask, "You don't think they've killed him?"

"Surely not," Cecil said. "They need him alive to testify against me."

She thought for a while, her fear not subsiding. Then she asked, "This traitor you mentioned, he who misrepresented you. Did he work for your enemy? Surely, if you found him out he could tell you who gave him orders."

Cecil shook his head sadly. "He didn't know himself. A cousin put him up to it, paying him but not mentioning the name of him who would ultimately benefit. I am having the cousin's house watched. As yet nothing has been observed but ordinary comings and goings."

"This cousin has no connection with Sir Thomas Wilks?"

"None that has been observed."

"Or with any other of your enemies?"

"I have not enough men to watch such a multitude," Cecil said. "There's a meeting of the Privy Council on Friday. It's possible that charges will be laid against me then. They're keeping Matthew out of sight until the last moment. Surprise is better than a troop. This is a sort of war without drum or cannon but also mortal."

"Then you don't think he's in danger in the meantime?" she said.

"No, but I am. Yet this diary you've brought is a great help. We know that this Stearforth and Motherwell, the sexton, are instruments. It is not improbable that Sir Thomas Wilks is the father of this plot. This diary is valuable, but no conclusive proof. Yet it points true like the needle of a compass."

"What can I do now? I must do something," Joan said.

"Both of you can help. You both know this Stearforth and Motherwell too. It's likely that they are still up to their necks in this plot. We do not know where Stearforth lies, but the sexton lives at the church. Go there under some guise and watch for Motherwell. I understand St. Crispin's remains the resort of pilgrims wanting to see the empty tomb. You may use the crowd to your own advantage. Besides the conspirators think you're in France—or dead. They won't be watching for you now. See where the sexton goes and with whom. He may lead us to Stearforth and Stearforth to Matthew. Chances are they plan to have him confess to the murder and name me as the promoter. Matthew himself may be brought before the council."

"Matthew would never confess to what he never did."

"He might—if your death were the alternative. Remember, as far as he knows you are still a prisoner. I could not blame Matthew if he succumbed to such a threat. A wife must come before a friend in such dealings."

"But should he confess under such a threat, what of you? I'm thinking of the council. And would not Matthew be hanged anyway?"

"Let's not talk of hanging," Cecil said, rising to signal they had had enough of talk. "As for the council, I welcome the discovery of these conspirators and their devious stratagems. Let them show their faces, declare themselves openly, I shall speak the truth—and shame the devil. You were their prisoner before who are now free. That's an advance for our side. If we can find Matthew and make him aware that your life is no longer threatened, we may undermine the plot entirely. I'm of the same mind as you, Joan. Matthew would never confess to a crime he did not commit without a threat of violence against you."

Cecil summoned the servant who had brought them into the house and ordered him to provide chambers for Joan and Morgan. "Tonight you will be my guests," Cecil said. "Sleep. The climax to these proceedings is yet to come. Tomorrow make your pilgrimage to St. Crispin's."

Cecil returned to his bed, but not to sleep. He had slept fitfully before Joan's unexpected arrival. He knew his own ways: now he would lie awake in the darkness, his mind as busy as in the daylight, his body as stiff and immobile as an effigy on a tomb.

He had spoken to Joan bravely about confronting his accusers. But the truth was that he was afraid. The historical moment was not propitious for such confrontations, not when so much hung in the balance. Not with James Stewart watching hawklike from his impoverished northern kingdom, listening for the second the queen's heart should stop and he should swoop down upon the throne and riches of England. And whom should he choose for his counselors? Cecil had taken infinite pains to ingratiate himself with the monarch to come, as he had spent all his energy to please the monarch that was. He had corresponded in secret, advised, pledged, knowing at the same time the little Scotsman was a cunning fellow, politically astute and no more trusting of Cecil than Cecil would be of him. Politics made friendship difficult. Royal service made mutual trust impossible. But it was the world Robert Cecil had chosen. What else was a little hunchback to do? He had been devious enough for the church, but too passionate. Politics was in his blood, as it had been in his father's.

Yet all his effort could be lost in a few minutes by the charges that he had ordered the murder of a churchman, promoted the martyrdom of a saint, offered his support to the royal claims of the Infanta.

On the face of it, the charges were absurd. But by such charges, good men and true had exposed their necks to the executioner's ax. Would he share the fate of Essex?

Cecil rolled to his side. He thought of his dead wife, and felt a loneliness so profound that he groaned as though his heart had been seized with a physical pain.

19

*S*TEARFORTH shook Matthew roughly, as he might have shaken a nodding apprentice. What hour must it be, Matthew wondered, sensing it was not yet dawn. He had dreamed of being in prison again, dreamed of his cellmate who had been marched off to hang. The dream had been so real it still clung to him, confusing him about where he was and with whom.

Stearforth's voice came again, commanding him to awake. Matthew remembered where he was. Buck was also in the room, standing by the door, watching. Buck had become more sober since his days as Matthew's counselor in the Marshalsea. His witty manner had been replaced with a sullen melancholy. Matthew had noticed a friction between him and Stearforth, as though they were competing with each other for the attention of His Grace. That's the way it was: in the pursuit of favor there could be no equals. Matthew wanted none such tricks of the courtier's trade.

"Where are we going?" His tongue was still thick from sleep, and his own voice sounded strange.

"Never mind. You'll see soon enough. Get dressed," Stearforth said. "Don't give us any trouble—not if you want to see that wife of yours again."

Matthew rose, put on his clothes, while the two men watched. Before his attempt to send a letter to Cecil through Michael Hickes they had regarded him with grudging respect, as a recruit to the plot in which he was the essential element. Since then, he had been treated as a traitor.

When Matthew finished dressing, Stearforth said, "This morning you will show certain officers where you laid the bones of Christopher Poole."

"Where I—?"

"You will go where I tell you to go and will say nothing. You have confessed to the murder. We have that in your own writing. Now you will seal your confession by producing the bones you dug up to further your Jesuitical plot."

"But I have no idea where—"

Stearforth cut him off. "This you will do because you love your wife. If you say anything to contradict your confession she will be killed. Is that plainspoken enough?"

"It's plain," Matthew said.

Downstairs were more men. Matthew recognized Sir Thomas Bendlowes, the magistrate who had ordered him to prison. There were also two sheriff's men. One manacled and blindfolded him.

Then he was made to sit alone in an unheated anteroom for what seemed several hours while he could hear the mumble of voices from an adjacent chamber.

Finally, they came for him again. He was led outside and placed upon a horse. The little company rode in silence through the streets for about a quarter of an hour before the blindfold was removed and Matthew could see that they were near St. Paul's. It was now about seven o'clock, he judged. The streets were full of people, walking, riding. The little company rode slowly. He felt he was in some sort of ceremonial procession, and his manacles caught the attention of passersby, who looked up and then away again. The transporting of prisoners was not that uncommon a sight in London, and the authorities delighted in making their transport highly visible, both to humiliate the prisoner and to deter other malefactors.

When they came to St. Crispin's Matthew noticed that the number of pilgrims who had come to the new shrine had increased from his first visit. They had formed a long line along the street in front of the church, pressing themselves against the iron railing that separated the churchyard from the street, as though even a glance at the sacred precincts would work a miracle. Where before the crowd seemed made up by the idly curious, these seemed more believing. They were not boisterous but stood in reverential quiet, looking through the iron gates, trying to glimpse the place where Poole's body had lain before its resurrection.

The company stopped in front of the church where Matthew was helped down by one of the officers and led into the church through a side door and from there into the nave. Hopwood and Motherwell were there to greet them, along with another man he had never seen before. This man was small but sinewy, with sharp hawklike features. He had a patch over his left eye; the right, slightly enlarged, stared boldly at Matthew as though the two men had met before. Matthew was sure they had not. He would not have forgotten that face, that eye.

Hopwood profusely welcomed the others, as though their coming to the church was a personal honor. He seemed to ignore Matthew's presence deliberately, and Matthew wondered if the young cleric was in on the plot and might feel guilty for his complicity. Hopwood said he had something to do about the church and excused himself. Buck and the officer remained at the rear of the nave while Stearforth escorted Matthew forward.

"Now he'll show us where he hid the body," he said, clinching Matthew's arm to signal that he was not to respond to this.

They passed up the church aisle and toward a door where the stairs to the belfry were. Matthew thought he was to be taken to the place of the murder again but before the stairs they turned and went out of the building into a parcel of the churchyard out of sight of the pilgrims. The burial plots edged up against the church itself and there was only a narrow walkway between the crosses and other monuments. They followed a stone path to the other side of the building until Matthew could see the street again and the faces of the pilgrims peering through the fence and then he saw a low structure ahead of him that he surmised to be a mausoleum, but it turned out to be the charnel house.

This gloomy structure was a half-cellar whose roof was only five or six feet above ground. It was situated in the far corner of the roughly rectangular churchyard at the farthest distance from the church itself. Above the door was a frieze ornately decorated with images of skulls and crossed bones and other emblems of frail mortality. Motherwell, who had been following with Harking hurried ahead to unlock the door.

Matthew was led down a half dozen steps into a long, low-ceilinged room. A putrid odor assaulted his nostrils and made him draw back, but Stearforth pushed him onward. The odor was noticed and commented on by the other men as well and Bendlowes remarked that if those within were not dead when they were brought there they should be dead by now by the very stench.

Behind Matthew, Bendlowes asked if a lantern or torch might be needed, but Motherwell assured them their eyes would adjust soon and they would see as much as they desired.

The charnel house consisted of a single, long crypt with a slightly arched ceiling. There was a long central aisle on each side of which shelves had been built. These were ladden with a disorder of gray and yellowed bones, lying every which way, with skulls thrown against shanks, feet and hands, so that one wishing to reconstruct a body from its bony frame would have been at a loss to know where to begin. The odor of death being as strong as it was, Bendlowes and Harking put handkerchiefs to their noses. The one-eyed man had turned deathly pale. Only Motherwell seemed unaffected by the stench, and he seemed to take a perverse delight in his immunity, moving vigorously about the chamber as though he were a busy host, anxious for his guests' comfort. Manacled still, Matthew could do nothing but endure in silence, but he prayed that his stay in this habitation of bones would be short for he felt such a stirring in his stomach that he thought at any moment he would retch.

"I hope to God this won't take long. Stearforth," Bendlowes said.

"Only so long as needful for you to witness where the body lay after it was taken up," Stearforth said, stopping at the very end of the room before one of the shelves. "We'll handle the rest. Then you gentlemen can go to breakfast."

"If we have stomach for it," said Harking. "I'd as leave take your word that Stock showed you the place."

"Oh, no," said Stearforth. "It's imperative that everything be done in good order. You and Master Bendlowes shall bear witness that Stock showed you the place himself, that you saw the body removed to the coffin. Most important, that the body is indeed Christopher Poole's."

"I don't know that I would recognize him—not as he is now," the magistrate said.

"Never mind," Stearforth said. "You'll recognize him, never fear. Who else could it be, but Poole? Unless, of course, you give credence to the story of his resurrection."

"I certainly do not," said Harking firmly, looking as though the very idea he should believe was more repugnant to him than the stench of decay.

Matthew noticed that against a wall an open coffin had been stood on end, as though its occupant had just been discarded in the rubble of bones. The wood was new, raw, still smelling of the tree. Matthew felt that something portentous was about to happen, and that he was at the center of it. He glanced around him and saw that the other men were rather pale looking. Even Motherwell seemed more subdued. There were a great number of bones in the chamber. He imagined what a gathering there would be at the resurrection, when these departed spirits should collect their mortal parts. A man could be trampled to death in the rush.

"This is where he hid the body," Stearforth said, pointing

to a shelf so heaped with yellowed bones that Matthew wondered that the wood frame could support the burden. "He showed us yesterday. We left it where it lay so that you could see for yourself."

"Well, let's be done with this business quickly," Bendlowes said, his voice muffled by his handkerchief.

Stearforth nodded to Motherwell, who took a rusty shaft that was propped against the wall and began to dislodge a mass of skulls and other bones to uncover a cerecloth draped figure beneath. He untied the cord that covered the body.

Everyone now drew near to see the face, even Matthew, whose curiosity was more powerful than his revulsion. Matthew had seen many a corpse in his time and a few well ripened in decay, but Poole's body was remarkably preserved for one a whole year dead. As for the face itself, it was a scholar's face, or perhaps a saint's—ascetic, strong featured, almost handsome. Matthew could understand why Poole's flock might have readily believed in his prophesy. The eye sockets were sunken deeply, figuring forth the skull beneath the thin layer of flesh. The prominent forehead of the man was slightly mottled, but the flesh of the hollow cheeks and the well-shaped lips were as white and smooth as alabaster. He might have been as young as thirty for the smoothness of his face. The torture and starvation that had taken his life were not reflected in the untroubled countenance, and only the odor of the body refuted the belief that Poole had died yesterday, quietly in his sleep with a conscience as untroubled as a child's.

"Look, sirs," Stearforth said, in a witty tone that seemed more forced than usual, "and tell me if this isn't our resurrected saint himself. But if in the resurrection we all stink so, who could wish for the company of the saints?"

No one smiled or offered a retort. Bendlowes made the sign of the cross and turned his head away. "Yes, that's Poole all right. Now let's get out of here."

But Stearforth insisted that Harking agree on the identification.

"It is Poole, as God is my judge," Harking said.

Stearforth smiled slightly, looking relieved. "Master Buck remains in the church with documents affirming the same, which if you gentlemen will be pleased to go in, they can be signed."

Bendlowes and Harking started for the door immediately. Matthew was led out by Stearforth while Motherwell and the one-eyed man stayed behind. Matthew could not imagine the next step in these devious proceedings; he was too relieved to have this step over and done. It was a hideous thing to disturb a corpse, even if he was a Papist. Almost as hideous as blaming an innocent man for the disturbance.

The pilgrims, many mothers with small children, were forbidden entrance to the churchyard, but someone had tied a red cloth to the fence rail directly opposite where Poole's grave was thought to be, and it was to this spot that the pilgrims waited to come to stare, cross themselves, and then give way to others. Joan, dressed in her old woman's disguise as before, and Morgan, who had shaved his beard and declared no one would recognize him without it, waited an hour to reach the coveted position only to find there was little to see beyond the headstones. Poole's grave, she had been told, had only been honored with a simple cross as a monument and could barely be distinguished from the score of other crosses and oblong markers in the general vicinity. The earth had been filled in, by order of the authorities, not wishing to further what they considered a fraudulent claim. There was some discussion among the pilgrims as to which stone was the priest's.

Joan was waiting for their third pass of the morning, hoping for a view of Motherwell, when Morgan drew Joan's attention from the churchyard to the little band of horsemen approaching from the lower end of the street. "I think that's Stearforth in the lead."

Joan turned to look. "God bless us, that's Matthew behind him. See, he's in manacles."

They left the line of pilgrims and crossed the street for

a better view of the procession, Joan trying to restrain her urge to cry out and identify herself. How she longed to speak to Matthew, to touch him. Never in their married life had they been separated for such a stretch. How long had it been, a mere week? A month? It had seemed like a thousand years. But she dared not do what she was so powerfully inclined to do. Matthew was a close prisoner. The officers looked around them with watchful eyes. They would apprehend her if she left her place, showed too much curiosity, flung herself at them.

But why was Matthew being brought to the church? She asked this of Morgan as they watched from their vantage point at the opposite side of the street.

"I don't know," he said, keeping his eyes fixed on Stearforth. "Perhaps to bring the accused man back to the scene of his crime."

The mounted band tied the horses to a rail beside the church porch and went inside.

"We've got to get inside the church," she said. "I must know what's happening."

"We'd be thrown out on our ears," Morgan reminded her. They had seen two of the pilgrims attempt an entrance to the main door of the church earlier that day but with no success. It was as though St. Crispin's was under siege with the newly appointed rector determined to repel all invaders.

"There must be another entrance to the churchyard." Joan said.

"If there were, the pilgrims would have found it and the parson made it secure."

Joan caught a glimpse of some figures through the fence and thought she recognized Matthew among them. She crossed the street quickly. Matthew and the officers were away from the pilgrims now, farther along the street to the other side of the church building. Here, too, there were graves, but having not had the distinction of a resurrection, no one was paying attention to them.

"Look," she said, grabbing Morgan's hand and drawing

him to the pickets and straining her eyes to see. "That's Matthew, and Stearforth. And Motherwell too."

"And my erstwhile first mate, if my eyes do not fail me," Morgan said.

It was Morgan's turn to drag her. They moved quickly along the fence to a side lane that ran alongside the church. As they went, Joan caught glimpses of Matthew and the other men.

"They're going to the charnel house," she exclaimed, more puzzled than ever. "That's not where the murder was done. It was in the belfry."

Matthew and the others disappeared from view just as they rounded the next corner. Joan and Morgan found themselves in a narrow alley with the churchyard on one side and a wall of shabby tenements on the other. About fifty yards ahead the fence abutted against the charnel house and then continued on the far side.

Morgan cautioned her to go stilly as they moved up to the wall. He was able to stand on his tiptoe and look inside the horizontal slits that ventilated the building, but to Joan he did not seem so much to be seeing as listening. He made another gesture of silence and she was forced to wait, although she was beside herself with curiosity and fear for her husband. Had they brought Matthew to that awful place to murder him as someone had murdered Stephen Graham?

Morgan listened at the slit for some time, then turned to Joan.

"They found the dead man's body," he whispered excitedly.

"Which?"

"Poole's—the martyr's."

"Have they hurt my husband?"

Morgan shook his head. "They're leaving now, all but Motherwell and Simkins. Your husband went with them. They claim he was showing them where he had hidden Poole's body beneath the bones."

"Treacherous liars," she said too loudly.

Morgan reminded her of the need for silence. "We need

to follow them—to see where Matthew is being taken now. He's being returned—returned to wherever he was before. You follow. You're less likely to be recognized. Even without my beard Stearforth may recognize me. I have a little business to settle here in the churchyard."

"But there's two of them," she said, fearful of what manner of business Morgan intended to settle.

"I have surprise on my side," he said. "That's as good as another pair of hands."

In the charnel house Motherwell told Simkins he had a desperate need to make water and out of respect he would not do it on holy ground. Simkins gave his companion a skeptical, sidelong glance. "I suppose your desperate bladder means I must play undertaker to this moldering tub of Papistical guts."

Motherwell smiled. "Well, sir, that *is* what Master Stearforth is paying you for, isn't it? Marry, sir, a laborer is worth his hire, as I think you once said yourself on the occasion of our planting Poole's corpse here the first time."

"What is it to be done with him?"

"Pull him out from his second grave that he may have a third and rest in peace at last," said Motherwell over his shoulder. "The coffin's against the wall and ready. When the martyr's snug, nail it shut. I'll be back and we'll load it in the cart together."

Simkins cursed when Motherwell was gone. He might have expected to be left with the dirty work himself, knowing Motherwell for the knavish villain he was. Fate had dealt him a hard blow. He hadn't deserved it, to his own way of thinking. He realized that he had fallen very low since his recent days as first mate of the *Plover*. His need for money had driven him to take orders from the likes of Motherwell. It had driven him to a charnel house, which he regarded with a kind of sick dread, and now he must lay hands upon a rotting corpse. Thanks be to God the corpse was dressed so he need not touch the wormy flesh itself.

He walked to the open door of the building, took a deep

breath of the purer air, and then returned to finish the work assigned him. He grabbed the staff and began to push away the bones under which Poole's body had been buried. The rattle of bones and his intense concentration on the labor at hand caused him not to notice that he was no longer alone.

When out of the corner of his eye he saw someone in the doorway he thought it was Motherwell come back. But Motherwell was shorter and stouter than his visitor. Still, there was something familiar about the man—the way he stood, his powerful upper body, and his eyes. And in the way he said nothing, but just stood there watching him from the doorway, as though he were waiting for Simkins to speak first.

And then Simkins saw through the absence of beard.

"Morgan!" Simkins gasped. He backed to the far wall confused and fearful. He stood next to the coffin, holding the staff out in front of him to ward off what he had taken to be a ghost.

"In the flesh, Simkins."

"But I thought—"

"I warrant you did, but you see now the case is otherwise."

"I'm not alone here," Simkins said, his voice shaking a little. "The sexton will return presently."

"No fear. Our business will be concluded by then," Morgan said, who was now standing so close to Simkins that Simkins could feel his breath in his face and knew surely that this was no ghost confronting him.

Motherwell had to go to the privy at the other end of the churchyard to relieve himself, which he did with no little pain in his nether organ. He knew he must have some disorder there for so much pain to be caused, but had no faith in medicine and so endured it and the stink of the privy for a little while, hoping that when he returned Simkins would have Poole's body put in the coffin and the both of them could go somewhere for a drink. Motherwell didn't like

Simkins, but he preferred not to drink alone and such mischief as all this has always stimulated his thirst.

When he returned to the charnel house he found the coffin on the floor and the lid nailed shut, but Simkins gone. Motherwell cursed. "I suppose he thinks I'm to lug this mess to the cart myself," he mumbled aloud.

He walked out to the churchyard and looked around, thinking Simkins might have come up out of the charnel house for a breath of air, but there was no living thing among the stones and so he went back down and did the work himself. Motherwell was past fifty years, but he had hefted many a coffin in his time, although usually to the churchyard rather than away from it. The idea amused him a little and made him forget his resentment of Simkins, who having fled before his work was fully done, should not now be paid in full. Since Motherwell had been commissioned to be paymaster in that regard, he felt fully justified in keeping the money Stearforth had given him for himself.

Joan was hard put to keep up with the riders, who rode as fast through the streets as their narrowness and human congestion would allow, with one of the officers riding in the forefront and crying out "Make way, queen's business." Speed was more difficult for her. No one was willing to accommodate a lone woman on foot; of the horses it was different; people had a healthy fear of being trampled, if not prevailed upon to give way to lawful authority.

Near St. Paul's, the crowd became so great that Joan lost them entirely, although she kept going west for some time in hopes of spotting them again. The trouble was that in that part of the City there were considerable numbers on horseback and at a distance she could not tell one from the other. The streets went in all directions. Matthew and his captors might have taken any one of them, indeed might be at their destination now, the horses stabled and Matthew concealed again. She wept with frustration and grief.

There was nothing to be done but to return to Cecil House and report. This she did, but since Cecil was out for the afternoon at Richmond Palace where the queen lay, she had to wait until nearly supper for him to return.

Meanwhile, Morgan came back. Joan was relieved to see that he was all right.

"Did you conclude your business?" she asked, hoping that he would spare her the details.

"I did."

"With the two of them?"

"Only with Simkins," he said grimly. "He will lead no more mutinies, set no more fires. You need not be afraid of him."

Morgan said he wanted to go home, see his wife, kiss his children, fondle his cat. He had had enough, he said, of the sea and the conspiracies. He wanted peace.

Joan could not deny him his wish. "Go," she said, "with my blessings. You've done all you need to do—and more. God bless you, Edmund Morgan."

"When you tell Sir Robert of what we saw at the churchyard, say nothing about Simkins. I mean, say he was there and what he was doing, but not that I—"

"Trust me," Joan said. "I'll say nothing beyond what they said and did."

Around seven o'clock Joan had the chance to keep her promise. Seeing how weary Cecil was from his ride and distraught, she assumed, over the queen's condition, she did not at once begin her report but asked how Her Majesty fared.

"The City puts on its mourning garments. The theaters are ordered closed. Her Majesty sits upon her cushions, staring ahead. She will take no medicine but spiritual."

"May God make her suffering short," Joan said.

"Amen," said Cecil. "And now to your matter, Joan, for we must look to the living, even as we grieve for the queen."

Her report seemed to rouse Cecil from his melancholy. He listened carefully, seated at his desk as though he were prepared to write down her words as she spoke them. She told Cecil about the events at St. Crispin's, describing the men and what Morgan had overheard in the charnel house.

"Only Stearforth and Motherwell did I recognize. Morgan said Simkins was there—the mutinous first mate who tried to burn us alive in the Kentish barn."

"They uncovered Poole's corpse, did they?" Cecil asked.

"Morgan stood on tiptoe staring in the little slit in the wall. I didn't see anything, but I take his word as gospel."

"It stands to reason, then," Cecil said. "Why disinter the body and go to the trouble of transporting it to the outskirts of the city when they can conceal it in the charnel house? Who would think of looking for it there in so obvious a place? Who would want to sift through dead men's bones?"

"They say Matthew dug Poole up and then concealed the body."

Cecil nodded. "That, too, fits the scheme. Matthew is forced to confess to the murder and to the Papist plot, which is verified in his showing these other officers where Poole's body was hid. What more is needful, but that the dead man rise up in fact, his own witness of bones, and declare Matthew and me murderers and traitors both?"

"What will happen to Matthew?"

"I pray to God nothing but his exoneration from these falsehoods, Joan. At least I know the full scope of their intent. You have done well, you and your captain. Like naughty boys with rocks, the plotters will cast them and they may wound, but they will not surprise, and that snatches from them much of their advantage. My only curiosity is who in the Privy Council will speak on their behalf. Tomorrow, we shall see. For now, go rest. You deserve it as much as I. It will turn out as God disposes."

20

MATTHEW did not sleep all that night, but thought of how he should face the ordeal to come. The prospect of his execution might have been easier, in which case he might have prayed for his soul's salvation and then been done. What else was there to do in such an extremity, given that every man owed God one death at least? He would die, but it would be an honest death; his conscience would be clear if his name wasn't. But to be dragged before such an august assembly and to have his confession thrust under his nose, to be forced to lie under solemn oath and say, yes, these things I did, may God forgive me. These were heavier matters. Such a lie, violating God's canon against false witness, would surely kill the immortal part of him.

His religion offered no assurance that his desire to protect Joan's life would acquit him of that sin. He should then owe God two deaths—one of the body and one of the soul. Two graves should be his, one in some earthly plot and the other in hell, where his soul would writhe in torment.

Yet he had no doubt in the world that he would lie, all the same, whether it condemned his high-born friend or whether the lie cost him a place in heaven. Joan's life must not be sacrificed.

Stearforth and Buck came for him in the morning. They gave him no breakfast, but caused him to dress hurriedly, manacled him and marched him to the stable where he mounted and was led by an even larger troop of officers and officials of the court toward the west, toward the great rambling palace and that noble chamber from which England was ruled, where the queen's counselors deliberated on the affairs of state.

The journey was not long, and it passed as a dream. They had not blindfolded him, and his face was so set on events to come that he had not taken the trouble to take in the outward appearance of his place of confinement or noted landmarks, or which church steeple thrust up where, or where the broad river lay. Rain fell in a steady drizzle, and by the time they reached Westminster Matthew was soaked and chilled to the bone.

At the jumble of buildings that was Whitehall, his escort was reduced by half. Stearforth and Buck stuck by him, as much overawed by the place and circumstances as he; they were joined by Sir Thomas Bendlowes and Master Harking, the latter having a load of documents beneath his arm, so that he looked all the world like a harried clerk. There were also several other gentlemen whose identity was not made known to him, but who were addressed with such respect by Bendlowes and Harking that Matthew was certain these must be persons of high place in the government. They talked in urgent whispers for a while and then he was led through a succession of rooms and up several flights of stairs and down corridors of increasing width and splendor with guards in shining breastplates and fierce halberds lining the walls, and candles blazing in huge candelabra even though it was broad day.

From a distant room, glimpsed briefly as he was led by in a quick march, he could hear the strains of pleasant music, but the harmonies disappeared in the clack of guards' boots on the marble floors. Finally, he was brought into a sort of anteroom hung all about with ornate tapestries and portraits and with fine chairs to sit upon. There was a fire going in the hearth, tended by three young servants; the other men drew close to it to warm their hands, but they made Matthew stand in the corner where he shivered for his damp cloak and the chilliness of the room and felt anticipation gnaw within him. He asked if he might draw near to the fire to dry his clothes, but Bendlowes said to keep well back from the fire—that he not throw himself in for very fear of what was to follow.

They had told him he would be taken before the council at nine o'clock. The appointed hour came and went, and it was nearly an hour after before someone came into the room to say that their lordships had been caught up in some more urgent business, and they must be patient.

During this time, Matthew was forced to stand while the others occupied stools or chairs or walked to and fro. There was almost no talking and such as there was concerned the most trivial of matters, so that Matthew thought the men might have been congregating at a tavern rather than assembled to address the most powerful lords in the kingdom.

All this while he thought of how he should conduct himself and arrived at no solution to his dilemma. He sent up a prayer to heaven for an answer. Perhaps the heavens were as perplexed as he.

It was a little past noon before the same gentleman returned to say that the council was now ready. Stearforth walked over to Matthew and whispered:

"Buck and I will be going in with you. Remember, you must agree to whatever you wrote in your confession which their lordships will have already read. Recant a word and I swear to you your denial will not refute the power of the written document and will be a sentence of present death to your wife. It will also infuriate the lords of the council."

"Will His Grace be there to accuse me?" Matthew asked, thinking that at last he should know the chief conspirator's name and rank.

"Don't be foolish," Stearforth said. "But greater than he will be there; fear *them*, Master Stock, if you fear anyone at all."

Stearforth took him by one arm, Buck by the other and they left the waiting room, went down a long passage, and entered a very wide door that was held open by two tall guards with pikes.

Inside a spacious and ornately decorated chamber about a dozen or more men were assembled about an oblong table covered with maps and other papers. The men were dressed like princes with chains of office about their necks and a king's ransom of lace ruff, fur facing, satin doublets of green and gold, and white. At least one seemed a prelate by his dress, and several wore daggers at their belts with silver or jeweled pommels. While some were middle-aged most were old men with drawn faces as though the very weight of their garments, chains, and jewels were as much a burden as their office. A large fire roared in a fireplace, but seemed to do little to remove the chill that pervaded the palace and left the council chamber as frigid as the anteroom. Matthew had heard that the queen had moved deliberately to Richmond to escape the cold, making the journey in a downpour. He could understand why. This royal palace was not friendly to the thin blood of the aged.

Matthew stared at the faces that stared at him, looking for Cecil and almost hoping that he would be absent, perhaps with the queen at Richmond. The faces looking back were unfamiliar faces and they were unfriendly. They glared, more than stared, with a mixture of hostility and contempt. He felt like some outlandish creature just arrived from America.

Stearforth and Buck who had entered on either side of him, forced him to kneel and then stepped back against the wall as though touching him somehow contaminated them. At the same time, Matthew glimpsed Cecil at the end of the room.

It was a wonder to Matthew that he had not spotted Cecil at once, given his desire during the past week to communicate with him. But the little hunchback had been partially concealed behind a taller lord, and only now did he emerge into Matthew's full view, an isolated figure even in the company of his peers.

Cecil's strained expression confirmed Stearforth's remark that the council would have heard Matthew's confession prior to his being led into the chamber. He saw that his case had already been judged, although he had been assured that his appearance would not be a trial but a mere interview to determine what further action might be taken.

The first to speak was not Cecil but a wizzened old man with a tuft of white hair at his chin. Despite his years, the old man stood very erect and spoke with a loud voice used to command. Suddenly, Matthew realized he knew who this personage was. The old lord had been pointed out to him once as he rode by in a procession of other dignitaries of the court. The old lord was Henry Howard, the great Earl of Northampton, Lord Admiral of England, and he who commanded the fleet that destroyed the Armada, but one who, Cecil had once noted, was not unfriendly to Spain or to Catholics, although he changed the outward form of his own religion according to the season. Matthew felt humbled. His patron Cecil might be the most powerful man in England, but the Lord Admiral was a legend whose family had enjoyed ducal dignity when royal Elizabeth's had been Welsh yeomen.

The earl took several steps in Matthew's direction and regarded him sternly. Between his thumb and bejeweled forefinger he held a piece of paper. Matthew recognized his confession.

"Matthew Stock?"

"He is, your lordship," Stearforth and Buck said in unison.

"Herein, Matthew Stock, you have confessed yourself to fraud and murder—the one in exhuming the body of Christopher Poole. The other in taking the life of Stephen Graham, late rector of St. Crispin's. How say you to these charges?"

Matthew was cold; the kneeling position was hard on his joints; his teeth chattered and his mind clouded with fear.

He knew not how to answer. He could hardly bring himself to face this intimidating nobleman, nor could he look at Cecil. He did not answer the charge.

"I take by your silence that you give consent to the charge," said the earl. No one else in the room spoke.

"You have also identified Master Secretary Cecil as he who put you up to these crimes, saying here that he did so that Papistry should thrive in the kingdom and the princess of Spain should succeed to the throne. These are serious accusations. Do you affirm them?"

Matthew shuddered at the words. Somehow in the mouth of the old earl the accusations seemed all the more repugnant. He felt as though they were really true, these calumnies, and that he must appear to the nobles present as the most abject of traitors, not worthy to breathe another breath. He felt an irrational shame, the worst he had ever felt and something within him wanted to confirm the false confession if only to put an end to his mental and physical suffering. But he did not speak, and the silence in the room became even heavier.

The earl repeated the charge, then said, "Again, your silence along with your hand to this confession confirms its contents." The old man sounded weary. Matthew looked up into his face. It was not as hostile as before. But it was a politician's face, not easily read.

"May I put a question to the prisoner?" asked another lord, a younger man with a breastplate visible between the folds of a green velvet cloak.

"Put the question," said the old earl.

"This confession. Did you write it?"

"I did, my lord."

"Well," said the second lord. "We have now shown that the prisoner is capable of speech, if there was any doubt before."

"And confirmed that his silence is not without significance, since he can say yea or nay at will," said a third gentleman.

Matthew looked up at Cecil, who during all this time had

247

not spoken but continued to look at Matthew. There was no fear in his face. He seemed extraordinarily calm.

"We have other evidence against the prisoner and against Sir Robert," said Bendlowes from behind Matthew. "The weapon by which the murder was done, with the accused's initial carved in its haft. That's damning enough, but also the testimony of one eyewitness to the murder—the sexton of the church. The new rector, Master Hopwood, will also testify of the accused's presence at the church. Lastly, we have the body of Christopher Poole, which this fellow disinterred at Sir Robert's instructions so that a miracle might seem to have occurred."

"Where was the body found?" asked the earl.

"In the charnel house, your lordship. Beneath a pile of bones. Stock showed Master Harking and me where the body was concealed. There can be no doubt who it was. I knew the man when he lived. I knew the face as well as my own."

Then Cecil broke his silence and asked if he could question the accused. All heads turned toward him.

"The evidence is powerful, Sir Robert," said the earl. "I think it would do little good to his case or to yours."

"Surely the custom is that the accused may face his accuser," Cecil said. "At least, it has always been so, unless English law is to be turned upon its head. I don't need to remind Your Lordships that I am accused of murder and also treason. To foment rebellion among Her Majesty's Catholic subjects could be hardly considered a lesser offence."

"Speak then," the earl said. He stood aside and Cecil walked toward Matthew, stopping about a foot away.

"To the charge that you have served me and Her Majesty in the past I make no denial, Master Stock. Your efforts were applauded by this very assembly when your quick wit saved Her Majesty's life from a brazen assassin at Smithfield, two summers ago. There was no talk of murder or treason then, but of courage beyond duty and of yeoman service to your queen."

"I did what any of Her Majesty's subjects would have done," Matthew said.

"Oh, I think far more," Cecil said. "You had good opportunity then to keep silent and let the crazed wretch accomplish his purpose. The queen would have been slain and those purposes now attributed to you might have been advanced considerably, but you spoke out."

"It was my wife who cried out, sir," Matthew said.

"Your wife? Yes, it was Joan Stock, if memory serves. I'm coming to her presently," Cecil said, with an expression that hinted to Matthew that he should make no further interruptions.

"My point, Master Stock, is that this new role imputed to you of traitor and murderer fits very incongruously with your previous service. Such incongruity might well make a reasonable man suspect that these charges are a transparent effort to undo me by incriminating you."

"We have the man's signed confession, Sir Robert," said the earl, who seemed to Matthew not unhappy to find Cecil accused. "And he has confirmed that it was his hand that wrote it, denying it not, whereby I think we can take the whole story to be true."

"I only ask Your Lordships' indulgence for a few more questions of the accused man," Cecil said. "If proof be as certain as the Lord Admiral declares, surely he won't begrudge me a little more time. Who knows, I may dig my own grave more deeply, which I suspect would please more than one of you present."

"I have no objection to further questions of the accused," said the young lord who had spoken earlier. "Although I find Sir Robert's implication that some among us are his enemies as offensive as it is untrue."

"Master Stock," Cecil said, ignoring the lord's comment, "I understand that your wife, Joan, has been accused as an accomplice. Where is she now?"

Matthew saw by Cecil's expression that this was one of the questions Cecil did intend for him to answer, and he spoke honestly. "I don't know where she is."

"Strange for a husband not to know where his wife is. You don't know in truth," Cecil said, "or are you concealing her whereabouts?"

Cecil had altered the tone of his voice; it was not sympathetic as before, but ironic and accusatory. It was a tone Matthew had heard him use with unruly servants and with prisoners. He looked into Cecil's face; it seemed a stranger's countenance, hard and unyielding. It was suddenly as though Cecil had changed roles; where he was Matthew's defender before, he was now his prosecutor.

"As I hope for my soul's salvation, Sir Robert, I have no idea where my wife is."

"Is she alive?"

"God knows, Sir Robert."

"Isn't it true, Master Stock, that your wife is being kept a close prisoner so that you will affirm this tissue of lies? Has her life not been threatened?"

Matthew suddenly felt hope; so Cecil had learned after all how things stood with him, with Joan. Hope, opened like a flower within him. But if he said yes to Cecil's question he would be putting Joan at risk. If he said no, it would be the first falsehood that had slipped from his mouth. If he said nothing, his silence would be construed as consent.

"No, sir, I have no certain knowledge that she is being held a prisoner."

"No certain knowledge," said Cecil, mimicking Matthew's accent. "But were you not told by these gentlemen who have brought you here that you will see your wife again only if you testify against me? Were you not forced to write this ... so-called confession?" Cecil paused and held the document by the ends of his fingers as if it were a dead mouse he had snatched from the pudding. "Was the knife not stolen from your house in Chelmsford a week before Stephen Graham's murder?"

Matthew's confusion grew; his knees now ached mercilessly and while his body had warmed, his flesh felt clammy. Matthew wanted to answer yes to these questions, but he was still afraid. Stearforth stood behind him, noting every syllable and intonation. It would be his word against Stearforth's, an uneven contest.

"Still he makes no answer, Sir Robert," said the earl. "But methinks he is more confused by the multitude of your questions than affirming by his silence."

Cecil ignored this theory and said, "What then, Master Stock, if you were told your wife is in the adjoining room, safe in my custody? Were I to bring her in, would you still refuse to speak?"

Matthew had no time to answer before Cecil himself strode across the room, opened a door, and Joan entered. She curtsied to the lords, then looked at Matthew and smiled reassuringly.

All this was done so suddenly that Matthew could hardly believe what he saw. Was he dreaming now, as before, when he walked and talked with Joan familiarly, or was this she in the flesh, safe from the hands of Stearforth and His Grace?

She greeted him with a soft, timorous voice. He could see she was as intimidated as he was by these awesome lords from whom the queen herself sought counsel. He spoke her name, breathing it out with a sigh of relief. He could say no more but continued to look on her, smiling despite his determination that he should not and remembering that these proceedings had mortal consequences.

Cecil swept his eyes over the other gentlemen at table. "This, my lords, is Joan Stock, wife of the accused. She was carried against her will toward France, escaping only when the ship that carried her foundered and the whole crew lost save the captain." He paused and turned to face Joan again. "Mistress Stock, can you point out him in the room who was responsible for your abduction?"

Joan pointed to Stearforth and said, "That's the man, Sir Robert, he standing in the corner. Humphrey Stearforth."

"And can you tell us why Master Stearforth spirited you from England when by rights he should have surrendered you to the authorities in London?"

"I cannot, Sir Robert, save the mischief proceeded from him alone. I sought out the truth from the dead man's sister; he threatened her and her family should she speak to me again. He sent me off to France to keep me from these inquiries that might have cleared my husband's name."

"It is no wonder, Sir Robert," interrupted the earl, "that the wife should defend the husband by accusing his captor. Her word cannot be considered credible evidence."

"This poor man's extorted confession has been used as evidence, when it is most obvious that the man was forced to it," Cecil replied, raising his voice. He turned to Matthew again. "What say you now, Master Stock? Your wife is safe here, no more a ploy in this conspiracy. What say you now?"

Matthew's heart raced; he tried to keep his voice steady, not wanting to sound a liar or coward. "I say I was never hired by you to dig any grave, murder any man, nor did I undertake these acts of my own accord. I was falsely accused, my knife was stolen from my house. I was summoned to London under false pretenses by Stearforth, who claimed to be Stephen Graham."

"And the confession, what of it?"

"Forced to write it—told that my wife would be killed if I did not or denied the confession's validity afterward."

From the back of the room, Stearforth and Buck were both denouncing these statements as boldfaced lies, while there was a confused murmur of voices at the table as the lords discussed how this charge should be construed.

The earl called for silence. He said, "These mutual recriminations accomplish nothing. As I have said. It is no novelty for the accused to accuse the accuser. How can we know this woman was truly prisoner and the confession extorted when he who affirms it is no neutral witness but a party to the charges? A warrant exists for this woman as an accomplice of her husband. Sir Thomas Bendlowes? You said there is further evidence that no recantation of the accused man will impugn."

"There is, sir," Bendlowes said.

Anxious to learn what this new evidence was, Matthew turned his head slightly to see out of the corner of his eye, the door he had entered earlier open and Poole's coffin born in by two of the palace guards. Following it was Motherwell. He had been fitted out in a new suit of clothes for the occasion and his beard had been trimmed so that one who did not know the truth of his profession or character would have supposed he was an honest merchant of the town. His craggy face wore a solemn expression. He looked once at Matthew and Matthew caught a glint of malicious triumph in his eye.

"This is Master Motherwell, my lords," Bendlowes said. "Sexton of St. Crispin's. It was he who saw to Christopher Poole's burial and also was eyewitness to Matthew Stock's murder of Stephen Graham."

The earl asked Motherwell if all Bendlowes had said was true, and Motherwell said it was as true as Christ's word.

"I presume the body of the Papist is in this coffin?" said the earl.

"It is, my lord," said Bendlowes. "I was present when Matthew Stock confessed to where he had concealed it. In the charnel house it was, beneath the bones of worthier men."

"I never confessed, sir," said Matthew, unable to let this lie pass and no longer fearing for Joan's safety. "I was taken there by Stearforth and Buck. I knew no more where the body lay than any other honest man here."

"The proof is before you, my lords," said Bendlowes. "If the council will suffer the coffin to be opened."

"Open it," said the earl. "We shall see for ourselves."

Motherwell drew his knife and pried open the coffin lid. There was a general movement in the room toward the coffin; even Matthew was bidden to rise from his knees and allowed to look.

Motherwell removed the lid and set it against the coffin, then looking in, he let out a guttural noise of surprise that seemed otherwise to render him dumb. He looked once at

Stearforth and then turned quickly to the lords, his expression confused and fearful.

"This isn't Poole," Bendlowes said.

The body in the coffin had been treated with no great reverence by whoever had disposed of him. It lay on its side with the knees thrust up towards the chest and the arms pinned behind. He was dressed in ordinary clothing rather than burial weeds and wore a patch of dark cloth over his left eye. The neck of the dead man was terribly bruised as though the windpipe had been crushed. The tip of his tongue lay upon his lower lip.

"This is no seasoned corpse," said the earl. "But fresh. The man has been strangled. Sir Thomas, what manner of trick is this?"

"My lord, I know not what to say. This is not Christopher Poole, but one whom Master Motherwell secured to aid him in removing Poole's body."

Everyone turned to Motherwell. The earl said, "What say you, Master Motherwell? You swore you saw to the burial yourself, but this is some other body."

"Simkins, sir. Simkins was his name," Motherwell said in a voice hardly above a whisper. "He's been murdered."

"We can see that," said the earl.

"Stock murdered him, sir, then hid Poole's bones again," Motherwell said.

Bendlowes said, "My lord, the prisoner left the charnel house with us. Motherwell and this Simkins remained behind together. Stock couldn't have killed Simkins."

Cecil asked now if he could speak again. The earl seemed hesitant; he was staring at Bendlowes, then at Motherwell with deep interest. He nodded in agreement.

Cecil said, "Master Motherwell, Sir Thomas has caught you in a blatant falsehood with his testimony, unless you intend to give him the lie."

Motherwell looked confused by Cecil's challenge; he gaped stupidly and beads of sweat broke out on his forehead.

"Or perhaps you can offer a theory explaining how a man can be in two places at once?"

"It is not unlikely that Stock has other accomplices in this mischief, one of which revenged himself on Simkins," Stearforth offered in an unsteady voice.

"That's true, Sir Robert," Motherwell said. "There was a time I left Simkins alone to put Poole's body in the coffin. When I returned, Simkins was gone. I thought he'd done his work and gone home. The coffin was closed. I had no reason to open it again."

"This seems not improbable, Sir Robert," said the earl.

"Perhaps," Cecil said. "But it is also possible that Master Sexton, being left alone with a man whom he owed money, had a falling out over the wages."

"If so, he would hardly have concealed the body in a coffin he knew was to be opened," said the earl. "Look, the sexton seemed as surprised to view the corpse as anyone here. I suspect some trickery here, but not Master Motherwell's."

"You may be right," said Cecil, nodding politely in the earl's direction. "On the other hand, what say you to the readiness with which our good sexton makes a lie? First he affirmed that the body was Poole's, then discovering it was not, lays the blame most confidently on a man he knows full well was in custody of Sir Thomas when this new murder must have occurred. Sirs, I accuse Motherwell not of murdering this poor fellow in the box, but of being a habitual liar. I have read the report of his previous testimony. According to him, his prodigious bladder accounts for his presence in the belfry, where he happens to see Matthew Stock murder Stephen Graham. Then this same demanding bladder takes him from the work of laying Poole's body to rest in its coffin so some mysterious intruder can wreak vengeance on Simkins. No, my lords of the council, I say not that Motherwell strangled his fellow worker, but that he is so practiced a liar that lies fall from his lips like rotten fruit, riddled with worms. If he so much as farts, it was done by yonder dog, whom he presently kicks for the impugned offense. Would such a miserable fellow not as readily blame another for his own murders, yea, and swear falsely whatever he was paid to?"

Cecil swung around and addressed Matthew.

"While you were being imprisoned by these persons—Stearforth—did he not say who had really killed Stephen Graham?"

Matthew had the feeling he was to answer yes to this question, but before he could think of a reply, Cecil fired another question.

"And isn't it true that he named Motherwell as the murderer?"

"I never said so much," Stearforth protested, and then looked abashed, as though he realized how he had forgotten his inferior place in the room. Cecil ignored this breach of etiquette and continued in the same strident vein as before.

"How much did you say, then?"

"I said nothing at all. Why should I? Stock's guilty. All the evidence is for it."

"It is not, Master Stearforth," Cecil said. "A man's character must be worth something. Stock has acted honestly in the queen's affairs. He's no Papist, and most certainly not a murderer. One must be half asleep not to see through these shifts. But look at our sexton's face. There, my lords, is a face of a conniving villain if ever one was born. See, Stearforth, despite your resolute denials Master Motherwell understands that you betrayed him. And why should you not? What's he to you?" Cecil marched over to Stearforth and looked up at him accusingly. "You sweat, sir. Is the fire too hot? Is your choler risen? Or do you fear for your own life that you would fob off your own crimes on Motherwell?"

"Oh, he shall not do that," said Motherwell, visibly trembling himself now and looking around him wildly. "If he told Stock 'twas I that cut the rector's throat he's a damnable liar, for I never did such a thing. And if I did, then 'twas Stearforth that bade me do it."

Cecil approached Motherwell, who had fallen on his knees before him and let his head drop as though already he accepted his fate. The room fell so silent that for a few moments Matthew could hear the faggots crack with their burning.

"It was you, Master Sexton, who exhumed Poole's body in the first place," Cecil said. "Did you do it of your own device—because you are a Papist sympathizer, a traitor who would see our beloved queen followed by the Infanta? Or was it out of some perverse desire for infamy?"

"Not I, sir," said Motherwell, his head bent so far forward that only his white hair showed. "Truth is, I have little religion at all and hate Papists as I hate the plague. I am true to Her Majesty, Sir Robert, and would not think of harming a hair of her blessed head."

"Her Majesty is poorly blessed in such subjects as you, Master Motherwell, who give the church of God a bad name by your very association. Did you have help in exhuming the body of Poole?"

"Simkins helped me, your honor. He that lies in the coffin. But I never killed him, and we were paid to do the work by Master Stearforth."

"He lies, Sir Robert," Stearforth cried, pointing at Motherwell. "*He* murdered Stephen Graham. I had nothing to do with that either. He's lying now to save his own poxy skin."

"And you're telling the truth to save yours?" Cecil said, turning slowly. "Let me suggest that it is your turn to play the liar. You hired our sexton to dig up a dead man's grave that he might become a wonder to the credulous. Then you went to Chelmsford where you pretended to be Stephen Graham and urged Matthew Stock to follow you to London, which, he doing, you then contrived to murder Graham with the knife you stole from Stock's kitchen."

Stearforth's face was as white as that of Simkins in his coffin, although he was sweating hard. He sank to his knees as Motherwell had done. "I never killed anyone, I swear it before God. It *was* Motherwell who killed Graham."

"And Motherwell says it was you," Cecil replied, suddenly calm. He turned from both men and faced the other Privy Counselors. "My lords, this tedious matter has kept us long enough from our work. Whether Master Stearforth committed the murder as Master Motherwell declares, or Master Motherwell did it as Master Stearforth affirms, it is now clear that Matthew Stock and his wife have been falsely accused and implicated in a plot to bring me into disgrace. The ultimate contriver of these plots we shall discern in due course. But now I beg you to excuse Matthew Stock and his good wife, who have done no wrong in this business, but have borne the brunt of the plotters' evil designs."

"So be it," said the earl coming slowly forward. "Guards, take Stearforth and Motherwell to the Tower. As for you Master Stock, Sir Robert has played his part of advocate well and cleared you of blame."

"And himself," said another lord at the table.

Matthew watched while Stearforth and Motherwell were led out by the tall guards who had stood sentry at the door. Then he turned to Joan. Her eyes were filled with tears and she was smiling the way she did when she was keeping some secret from him and wanted him to know of it.

21

In the antechamber, Cecil satisfied their curiosity about the true begetter of the Poole conspiracy. Cecil's spies had done their work, retracing Matthew's journey from the place of his concealment to the palace by querying bystanders who had watched and remembered the manacled prisoner on horseback and the troop of guards.

"It wasn't *his* house," Cecil said, "but a relative's. I know the family well. A suborned servant confirmed what I suspected in the first place."

"Then this person will be exposed, brought to account for his crime," Matthew said, and wanted to know the name that had been forbidden him.

"No, Matthew," Cecil said. "It's better you do not know. Let him think he has escaped. You'll be safer that way. You'll pose no threat. Let him worry about Stearforth's blabbing tongue. It's sufficient that I know his name and he knows I know. Such mutual recognition will pluck out his sting, believe me. Your safety lies in innocence."

"In ignorance, rather," Joan said.

"I'll not distinguish between them," Cecil said. "The important thing is that the gentleman's plan failed."

"He won't be punished then. If not, there's no justice," Joan said.

"There's justice," Cecil said. "But its workings are less simple than we suppose. God deals craftily with evil men. For a little season He turns his face away, seemingly indifferent to their mischief. And so they thrive, swell with pride, engineer a hundred plots, but when the end shall come we shall see and be seen. Every sin will be known and accounted for."

Still Matthew was unsatisfied. His resentment at his imprisonment by His Grace would not be appeased. His mind was filled with it and he only half heard Cecil tell him to go home to Chelmsford, enjoy their lives and be at peace. And then he felt Joan touch his arm.

"Come, Matthew, we must leave Sir Robert to his business. It's time to go home."

She led him off, and looking at her, smiling as she was and happy after her own ordeal, he forgot about Cecil and the nameless plotter who had caused them so much grief, and thought that Poole's rising from the dead was not half the miracle she was.